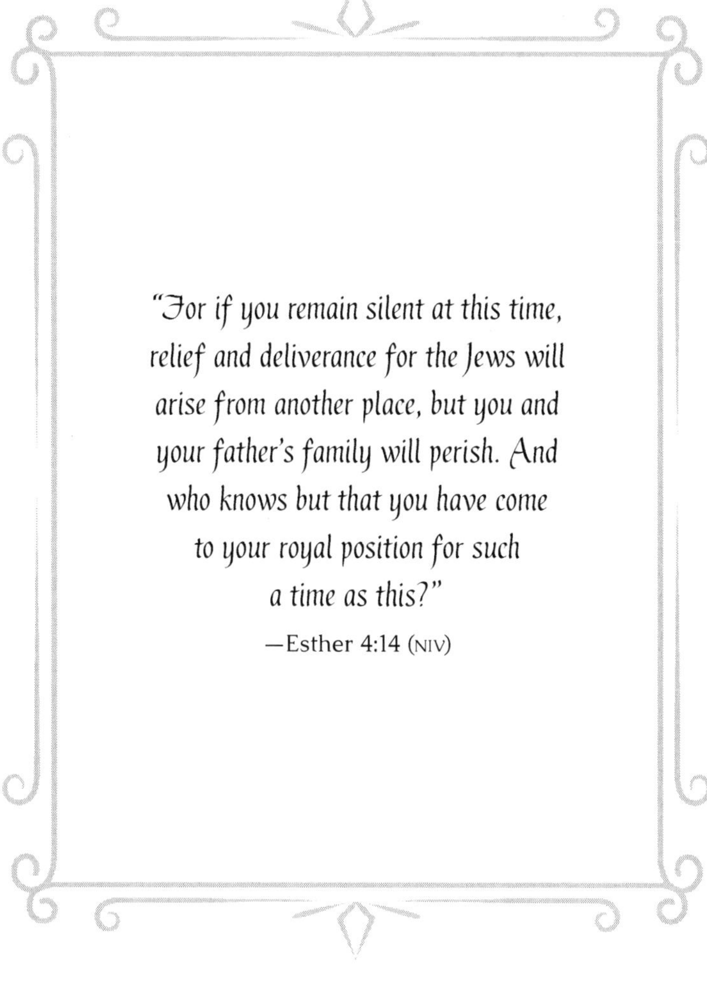

"For if you remain silent at this time,
relief and deliverance for the Jews will
arise from another place, but you and
your father's family will perish. And
who knows but that you have come
to your royal position for such
a time as this?"

—Esther 4:14 (NIV)

Extraordinary Women of the Bible

HIGHLY FAVORED: MARY'S STORY

SINS AS SCARLET: RAHAB'S STORY

A HARVEST OF GRACE: RUTH AND NAOMI'S STORY

AT HIS FEET: MARY MAGDALENE'S STORY

TENDER MERCIES: ELIZABETH'S STORY

WOMAN OF REDEMPTION: BATHSHEBA'S STORY

JEWEL OF PERSIA: ESTHER'S STORY

Extraordinary Women OF THE BIBLE

JEWEL OF PERSIA

ESTHER'S STORY

Tricia Goyer

Published by Guideposts
100 Reserve Road, Suite E200
Danbury, CT 06810
Guideposts.org

Cover and interior design by Müllerhaus
Cover illustration by Brian Call represented by Illustration Online LLC.
Typeset by Aptara, Inc.

ISBN 978-1-961441-70-5 (hardcover)
ISBN 978-1-961441-71-2 (softcover)
ISBN 978-1-961125-61-2 (epub)

Printed and bound in the United States of America

Extraordinary Women of the Bible

JEWEL OF PERSIA

ESTHER'S STORY

DEDICATION

For my daughters, God's jewels. May you always know
Yahweh is only a whispered prayer away.

ACKNOWLEDGMENTS

I am thankful for the wonderful team at Guideposts, who are great to work with, and for my agent, Janet Grant. I'm blessed to be part of such an amazing team. I appreciate my amazing husband, John, and my friend Deb Sadler, who were always willing to listen as I shared all the interesting things I learned about Esther's time in the Persian Empire. I'm thankful for my children, who understand long writing days and who celebrate with me when I finish each book. I'm thankful for my assistant, Christen Krumm, who keeps all the plates spinning when I dive deep into a book. Also, I must thank my author friends who join me on writing sprints and spur me on during long writing days, especially Jenn Pierce, Kelly Underwood, Lisa Phillips, and Kate Angelo. Thanks for encouraging me.

Cast of
CHARACTERS

Aafreen • Esther's handmaiden

Anahita • one of the young women taken to Xerxes's court with Esther, not friendly with Esther

Hadassah/Esther/Dido • Jewish orphan, storyteller, and wife of King Xerxes

Haman • descendant of Agag, enemy of the Jews, official in Xerxes court

Hathak • one of the king's eunuchs assigned to attend Esther

Hegai • the king's eunuch in charge of the harem

Hormoz • official also present with Haman on the night of the queen's banquet

Jabez and Mara • Nazanin's parents

King Xerxes • great king of the Persians and the Medes

Leila • one of the young women taken to Xerxes's court, and Esther's friend

Mordecai • Esther's older cousin who raised her and becomes the king's vizier

Nader • Persian storyteller and friend of Mordecai

Nazanin • Esther's friend who was one of Vashti's maids

Queen Vashti • the former queen

Sarai • elderly neighbor of Mordecai and Esther

Shaashgaz • the king's eunuch in charge of the concubines

Soraya • one of the young women taken to the palace with Esther

Tawana • Esther's handmaiden

"Also, seek the peace and prosperity of the city to which
I have carried you into exile. Pray to the Lord for it,
because if it prospers, you too will prosper."

Jeremiah 29:7 (NIV)

PROLOGUE

Hadassah didn't know if her cries or the men's laughter had woken her from her sleep. She stretched her hand, searching the mat, and then she remembered. *Abba* was gone.

Day by day, he had grown sicker. Her cousin, Mordecai—nearly eighteen years old—had done his best to care for Hadassah's ill father and her ill mother before that. He even found a physician to bring medicine. But nothing helped.

Hadassah pulled her knees to her chest and wrapped her arms around them. Then she tucked her body deeper under her blanket. She tried to hold back her weeping, but it was no use. Tears flowed like a fountain from her eyes.

The door opened. A face peeked in through the doorway. Mordecai's wide, kind eyes looked down on her, reminding her she wasn't alone.

"Esther," he whispered.

It took her a moment to remember that was her name. That is what her cousin said he would call her now. It was safer that way. *Safer?* Hadassah rubbed her brow, wishing she could understand.

Mordecai entered the room and knelt beside her bed. "Don't cry, little one—my heart breaks. If you'd like, you can come and meet my friend. Nader tells the best stories. Would you like to hear one?"

Hadassah sat up, nodded, and rubbed her eyes. She stretched her arms upward. Mordecai lifted her as if she were as light as a feather and pulled her into his arms. He carried her with sure steps into their living space, where an oil lamp blazed.

A large, round man sat high on a cushion. Nadar's stomach was so round it appeared as if he hid a melon under his vest. His skin was dark, and his white beard reached his lap as he sat.

"Well, there she is, the little deer," Nadar said as Hadassah floated in on Mordecai's arm. The man's laughter shook his whole frame.

Mordecai lowered himself onto his cushion, sitting Hadassah on his lap. Her cousin felt warm and safe. She snuggled deep into his arms. Mordecai's beard was scratchy as she tucked her head under his chin, but Hadassah didn't mind. It reminded her of Abba's arms, his itchy beard.

Nadar lifted his thick white brows and wagged a finger in her direction. "I've never been known to be quiet. But I can be entertaining. Would you like to hear a story, little one? Your cousin always asks me to tell him a tale or legend whenever I visit."

Hadassah stuck her thumb into her mouth and nodded.

"A long time ago, in the country of Sistan, which is eight hundred miles from our great city of Susa," Nadar began, "there lived a king named Azadbakht, who had a vizier named Sipehsalar. A wise, kind vizier who always had his king's best interest in mind." Nadar winked.

"Sipehsalar had a daughter who was the most beautiful young woman in the kingdom. She had jet-black hair that smelled like all the spices of Arabia."

Mordecai stroked Hadassah's hair as Nadar said that part, and she couldn't help but smile.

"Sipehsalar loved his daughter to the point that he could never spend more than an hour without her," Nadar continued. "But one day, Sipehsalar had to go to the countryside to check on the kingdom. He hoped he wouldn't be away for very long.

"The journey took longer than he wanted, and Sipehsalar was distraught to be away from his daughter for so long. He sent messengers to bring his daughter to him. The messengers hurried back to the capital city. They prepared the young woman to take her to her father."

As he continued, Nadar's happy face darkened, and Hadassah guessed there would be trouble. Her eyes fluttered closed, and then she quickly opened them again. She wanted to hear the story. She needed to know the fate of the beautiful young woman.

"On the way out to the countryside to meet her father, the travelers met up with King Azadbakht. The king was returning to town after a day's hunt when he saw the palanquin. At that moment, a wind blew the curtain of the covered litter, and King Azadbakht witnessed the beautiful young lady sitting inside. Immediately, he fell in love. The king no longer thought of returning from the hunt.

"With authority, he spoke to his messengers, 'Travel to Sipehsalar and give him this news. Tell him that I want to take his daughter as my wife.'

"'Oh, great king,' the messenger said, "let us first take this daughter to her father. Later we will tell him about your request after their most joyful reunion.'

"'No!' The king's anger burned. 'No, I will take this young woman to my palace. Instead, you tell Sipehsalar about my desire.'

"Sipehsalar's daughter was taken into the women's quarters of the palace, where she received a great honor. The king summoned all his top officials to the palace in the morning. 'I desire to marry the daughter of the vizier, Sipehsalar. Please tell me your thoughts on the matter.'

"All the advisers and judges said, 'King, it is a perfect match, and preparations for the wedding should be made at once.'

"The king dictated a letter announcing his marriage. He had his messengers take it to every corner of his kingdom. And to Sipehsalar, the king wrote a personal letter, saying how honored he felt to have Sipehsalar's daughter as his bride, hoping that Sipehsalar would bless the union."

Hadassah yawned. Her eyes fluttered closed, but she pushed them open again, trying to focus on Nadar's face.

"When Sipehsalar received the letter, he was in tears. But instead of tears of joy, his tears were a mix of sorrow and anger. He only wished the king would have allowed him to see his daughter once more before whisking her away. But Sipehsalar was also a man of wisdom. He wrote to the king and told him of the gladness of having a splendid son-in-law and that he hoped the union would be a happy one."

Hadassah's eyes closed again. In her mind, she saw the princess standing before the king. Nadar's words continued, but they faded as a new sound filled her mind. Mordecai's heartbeat pounded in her ear as she drifted back to sleep in his arms.

CHAPTER ONE

483 BC

The sound of music carried on the wind as it did every evening. Living just beyond the King's Gate, Esther had seen the honorable men of the city—and visiting nobles—journeying from the citadel of Susa to the palace as the afternoon sun bathed brick buildings in its warm light. Only later, when the palace was aglow with the light of a thousand lanterns, did singing and chanting mix with melodies and rhythms of the harp, lute, and zither. Never once had Esther dreamed she might raise her voice with them, until today.

Built on a high, rocky outcropping, massive walls—reinforced with towers—surrounded the capital city. Inside the citadel, family homes were nestled among palaces, temples, and administrative buildings, as well as gardens and expansive green spaces—man-made oases in the desert climate. The citadel was the center of the city's political, religious, and cultural life. More importantly, the great king of the Medes and the Persians had chosen this place, among the Zagreb Mountains, as his home.

King Xerxes had been the king for three years, and he'd already put down several rebellions in his empire. Now, with the provinces of Babylon and Egypt back under Xerxes's thumb, the days of celebration turned into weeks, and weeks into months. Had there ever been a time over the last six months when music didn't play? Esther wasn't sure if she could even fall asleep without the rhythmic sounds. Not that sleep was on her mind now.

Pacing back and forth inside their dwelling, Esther hugged her arms tightly to her chest and pressed her lips into a smile. Her simple trip to the market this morning had been like any other. Yet when she arrived home and saw the messenger waiting, the ordinary day had become so much more. She paused and glanced out the window, sure she would burst if she didn't tell someone her news: *Esther, storyteller to Queen Vashti.*

Esther drew in a breath and slowly released it. Would Mordecai approve? Even though her cousin didn't always have kind words about the warrior-king, Xerxes, Mordecai believed good things about Queen Vashti. Two decades ago—before Esther had even been born—Mordecai's father had worked as a court official in Babylon and had known the princess, made queen.

Surely Mordecai will not deny me the opportunity to be the queen's companion. At least until he finds the right man for me to marry.

To have her stories matter, especially to a queen, would make all the difference. Esther had burdened her older cousin for too long. In his care for her, Mordecai had denied himself the opportunity to marry and have a family. Her appointment would no doubt free up her cousin to follow his dreams too.

Looking out the doorway, Esther scanned the busy street. A brightly dressed river of people walked toward the King's Gate.

Very few walked toward the houses beyond the river where she'd lived with Mordecai for the last ten years. Her cousin was nowhere to be seen.

Esther turned and pick up a bowl of rising dough and then hurried toward the inner courtyard to bake the evening bread. She stepped in tempo to the music notes that carried on the warm evening air. A shiver of excitement traveled up her arms.

Esther paused and closed her eyes. Her stomach rumbled at the aroma of roasted meat wafting down the hill from the expansive citadel. In addition to weaving a tale for Queen Vashti, Esther hoped for a taste of the feast and a glimpse of the king. Perhaps he wasn't the temperamental, brusque ruler her cousin believed him to be.

Her heartbeat quickened as she thought of thirty-five-year-old Xerxes. Mordecai claimed that the One true God put every ruler on a throne. What type of man did God choose for such a role? Indeed, a man of strength and confidence. *Just the kind of man I'd like to marry someday.* A man brave enough to make the journey to Jerusalem, not as a king but as a faithful pilgrim. She and Mordecai had many conversations about such, and she hoped someday that her cousin would choose a man who also wished to travel to the Holy City and start a new life there.

Esther's father had been such a man who'd dreamed of returning to Jerusalem and seeing the rebuilt temple with his own eyes. Her mother had told her as much. If only her parents had risked the journey when she was a small child instead of waiting until she was older for the trip. Would they have lived happily there together? Or would illness still have taken both of her parents too soon?

Of course, the man she married would have to walk in the way of the Lord and believe in Yahweh's true ways. She had no doubt Mordecai would see that it would be so. Also, this new job with Queen Vashti could give her the funds to make that possible. Then Esther simply had to wait and pray for the man God had chosen to journey with her.

Tears pricked her eyes as she thought of her parents, and Esther blinked them away. Mordecai would be home soon. She didn't want him to believe her to be ungrateful for the home he'd provided. Perhaps she was just getting wrapped up in her imagination again. Who was she to consider being a storyteller to the queen or even dream of leaving their simple life in Susa? Still, hope stirred inside her. She did have the invitation to meet Vashti tonight.

Esther opened her eyes and rounded the corner, pausing briefly when she noticed her older neighbor in the shared courtyard ahead. *Faithful Sarai. So she gets to be the one to listen to my news first.* Esther rushed to help the thin, hunched woman. She circled her arm around Sarai, gently easing her to a cushion on the ground.

"Sarai, I must tell you my news! I have received an invitation from the queen. It was delivered by one of the queen's eunuchs just today." Esther had been so startled to open the door and see the man in his white linen robe and shaved head. She'd seen eunuchs in the marketplace and traveling with royal caravans, but she'd never spoken to one. Yet the man had been kind as he'd delivered good news.

"The queen requested me to enter the palace through the King's Gate," Esther continued. "She's giving a banquet today. My friend Nazanin is now one of Vashti's handmaidens, and she told the queen about me—about my stories."

Tossing her silky black hair over her shoulder, Esther straightened her frame. She would not tell Sarai about becoming the queen's official storyteller. Not yet. "I hope that my cousin will allow me to go. Many of my friends have married at fifteen, yet Mordecai still sees me as a child."

Sarai's almond-shaped, dark eyes grew round. She brushed a strand of gray hair from her face. "Dear Esther, you have grown into a beautiful woman—sprouted up before my eyes. No one would see you as a child. And I imagine even the queen would enjoy hearing of legends of old rather than talk only of war."

Esther bit her lip and nodded as she prepared coals for baking the bread. "I overheard Mordecai talking with his friends. They say the king's recent banquets have been a war council."

"King Xerxes is trying to finish what his father, Darius, started." Sarai shook her head. "This is the problem with the Persians. They take war too much to heart."

Like Esther and Mordecai, Sarai was one of the Jews in their neighborhood. Yet they were the minority compared to other nationalities. The Medes and the Persians had taken over the world, and people from all nations resided in Susa. The Persians had even conquered the Babylonians—the ones who'd destroyed the Holy City of Jerusalem and had taken the Jews into captivity. That was how Esther's family ended up in

Susa. Her grandparents had served the Babylonian kings. Then, after the Persian victory, they and their son were taken to Susa to serve the new king. But for Esther, Susa was all she'd ever known. Still, that didn't keep her heart from longing for Jerusalem.

"Let's hope it's just talking." Esther fingered the coarse fabric of her dress. She imagined herself seated before the queen and her handmaidens, just as she often sat before her cousin and his friends. She wanted nothing more than to weave a tale to capture their imaginations. To see their gazes on her and know that, for a moment, a powerful queen could become enraptured with her words. She'd seen this repeatedly happen as men's and women's faces fixed on hers as she spoke. Their brows lifted in reaction to the danger and drama woven with syllables and sound slipping from her lips.

"Yahweh has given you a gift," her *imma* had told Esther as she lay on her deathbed. Although her body had failed, Imma had smiled when young Esther told a made-up story.

But what good is my gift if I only entertain my cousin's friends or the travelers who stay in our home for a night or two?

Sarai waved her hand as if shooing her away. "Begone with you, girl. You have a banquet to attend. You must take in every detail and return to tell me. Though I long to join you, my body will not carry me thus far. Mordecai was here not two hours ago. He has not heard of Nazanin's request for you to weave a tale for the queen, but he did hear about the queen's banquet. All the women of the kingdom are invited. It took some convincing, but your cousin told me he'd allow you to go." Sarai sighed. "If I were younger and did not fall asleep as soon as the sun falls, I would be there too."

Esther smiled. Was it just her imagination, or did the music rise higher and the laughter sound stronger than usual tonight? "Sarai, now who's the storyteller? I had hoped…. But my cousin would never allow it. What you say cannot be true."

"Never?" A twinkle lit Sarai's eyes. "Your cousin already obtained a gown! Have you been to your sleeping quarters yet?"

"No. I must make…dinner." Esther didn't know why her words sounded so uncertain when she'd been bold only moments before. She had cooked dinner for Mordecai for the last decade. Why would things be different tonight? Indeed Sarai was wrong. Yet why did hope light her heart?

Again, Sarai dismissed her with a wave of her hand as if she were the queen herself. "I can bake your bread along with mine. I will throw a few more lentils into my pot to feed your cousin. I will have no problem feeding one more. Now, go. Look in your room." Sarai's eyes twinkled. "I guess the gown was made for such a time as this."

CHAPTER TWO

Esther blinked slowly at Sarai's words. This had to be a dream. She'd gazed upon the palace gates every day, yet never before today had she considered entering them.

After giving Sarai her bread bowl and a quick hug, Esther hurried to her room. Her steps hesitated inside the door, and she rubbed her eyes, disbelieving—a gown. Sarai was right. A beautiful dress lay across her sleeping mat. Esther's hands flew to her lips. *Truly, I will attend the queen's banquet tonight.*

Bending down, she reached for the gown made of soft linen. It was white with gold thread woven along the hem, and a gold-colored belt. A band of the gold cord was also included to braid into her hair.

Her fingertips brushed the gown, but her knees trembled at the thought of picking it up. Where had Mordecai obtained such a garment? From the time she was a child, Mordecai had allowed her to wear only the plainest clothes, even though not a day passed that Esther didn't wish for something beautiful to wear. She'd seen every fashion from the kingdom's 127 provinces with the steady stream of visitors across the bridge. Yet she'd never been one of the fashionable ones.

Out of all the places Esther could have lived in Susa, she and her cousin lived just beyond the bridge that led to the

King's Gate. While Susa's walls stretched farther than she could see, Esther lived close enough to walk across the roadway to the door set into the palace walls where Mordecai's office was located. Wherever she went—from their home to the market or to visit friends—her cousin could practically watch her every step from his work. After the death of Esther's parents, Mordecai had been extra cautious. Most likely because he knew Yahweh's ways were the opposite of the luxury that they witnessed daily going into the palace and returning from it. Although Esther and Mordecai lived in this world, they were not of it. Her cousin often reminded her of that.

Yahweh's ways were different from those of every other people, conquered or not. Esther saw this clearly from the worship of people around her. Unlike the Babylonians, who had conquered Jerusalem and demanded the Jews worship their graven images, the Persians let each people worship their own way. Throughout the city, different sects had set up their own places of worship.

Cyrus the Great, who'd liberated the Jews from the Babylonians, had even allowed some Jewish people to return to Jerusalem. Yet most Jews remained scattered over the Persian empire, either because they didn't have the means to return or they'd become too comfortable in their lifestyle. Or, like her and Mordecai, they were waiting for the right time when Yahweh would open the doors to make their return possible. Until then, they worshiped in their way, as Yahweh desired, keeping the Shabbat and taking that day to rest. Their worship was quiet, private, and not on bold display like others who lived along the road near the King's Gate.

Esther and Mordecai had only four rooms to themselves—a central living area and three small sleeping rooms. One for her, one for Mordecai, and one for guests from throughout the Persian empire. In contrast, the palace was room after room, as far as one can see. And tonight, she'd get a glimpse inside.

Sucking in a deep breath, Esther dared to lift the gown to her frame and press it against her. She swished its fabric from side to side, still in awe of what was to come.

The opening and closing of their front door caused Esther's fingers to tremble. She hurried to the front living area, the gown still pressed against her. Mordecai stood there with a wrapped package in his hand. He panted to catch his breath and wiped the sweat from his brow. He had rushed to get here, but why? *Has he come to stop me? To tell me he's changed his mind?*

Ignoring the package, Esther looked at her cousin's face. The worry lines across his forehead deepened. His thick curly hair looked disheveled as if he'd been running his fingers through it, as he always did when he was anxious.

Esther puckered her lips and swallowed the worries that knotted in her throat. "Is it true, Cousin? Tonight will I be allowed to attend the queen's banquet?" She held her breath as she waited for his answer.

Mordecai's eyebrows lifted. "Do you not hold a gown in your grasp?" His tone was light and playful, as if he was trying to ignore the worries the tight lines on his face displayed.

Esther rubbed the fabric between her fingers. "Yes, but how can such a thing be? Where did you get it?"

"Maybe from the one who told you the gown was in your room?"

"Sarai?" Esther folded the gown across one arm, ensuring the hem did not touch the ground. She glanced to the doorway that led to where the older woman baked Mordecai's bread, and then Esther looked back to her cousin. "But where would Sarai come by such a garment?"

Mordecai wiped his brow again with the sleeve of his robe and then settled onto the cushion by the doorway, releasing a heavy breath as he sat. "Twelve or thirteen years ago, Sarai cared for a granddaughter. It was before you came. The little wealth Sarai's husband had accumulated over his lifetime went to the young woman."

"And what happened to her?"

"The same sickness took this granddaughter that took your mother. The disease came upon her, and she was gone by the week's end." He nodded his chin at the gown. "Sarai got rid of most of the young woman's things but not all. She believes I have sheltered you. She claims you must have a chance to feast with our queen while you have the opportunity. There are reports that even now, Xerxes's army is preparing their march to Greece."

Esther considered telling her cousin of the eunuch's visit and her friend Nazanin's request for her to weave a tale for the queen. Yet, for the moment, Mordecai agreed to tonight. Esther didn't want to press the matter and give him a reason not to allow her to attend.

Instead, she focused on the rumors of war. "A march to Greece? Will Shahanshah not be satisfied until he controls the whole world?" The name for King Xerxes that she heard daily slipped from her lips.

Her cousin's head snapped back as if her whisper of that name landed a physical blow upon his cheek. "Shahanshah? Do you dare to call him that? There is only one King of Kings, Esther, and it is not Xerxes, no matter how great he seems." He glanced out the window toward the palace. "Seventy-two stone columns within his front palace courtyard and walls hundreds of feet long, but what King Xerxes has on earth pales in comparison to our God."

Esther nodded. "Yes, but sometimes you must admit it's hard to believe our king is only human when his power and glory seem untouchable." She shrank back even as she said those words. Yes, they'd been in her thoughts. Still, she couldn't believe she dared to speak them, especially tonight when one word from her cousin could keep her home instead of allowing her to weave her tales at the knee of Queen Vashti.

Mordecai scoffed. "I see a man who surrounds himself with evidence of his spoils because he fears the war to come."

"Who wouldn't be afraid of the Greeks, especially after his father's great loss?" She looked out the window toward the king's palace. It stood in all its grandeur like a towering citadel on the other side of the river.

Mordecai stroked his beard and cocked one eyebrow. "Child, you speak as if you're part of the war council yourself."

Esther jutted out her chin. "How could I not know? Nearly every night, our home is filled with a guest or two. They are from all over the kingdom. Are their voices not heard from every corner of our rooms?"

"God has given you extraordinary wisdom. You are no usual child. So you know then that when Xerxes gives lavish parties it is to gain the favor of rulers and men. He honors the leaders of each province, and soon an army rises from each province, coming together for our king's next conquest. Yet, no matter how large the number of fighting men, they are only as strong as their leader."

Esther listened, knowing her cousin would not dismiss her to get dressed until she understood the type of environment she was walking into.

"I have many friends who work close to Xerxes, and there is much purpose for the rivers of wine that flow into boasting mouths. Fruit from the vine causes the weak to claim strength. Xerxes may be great, but he is also a mere man. Demons from the battlefield chase him, even here."

"You speak such words of a king?" Esther feigned surprise.

"I speak such words of a man who God, our King, has allowed the ability to rule for a season. And no matter the nobility of those who gather around Xerxes's throne, we must remember who we are as we stand among them. We are a chosen people. And Yahweh is the true King." Mordecai placed a hand over his heart, palm pressed and fingers splayed.

Esther nodded, and a soft stirring within spoke truth to her heart. "Greatness depends more on who one is rather than on what one has," she repeated the words she'd heard a hundred times if she'd heard them ten.

"We are a chosen people," he repeated.

Esther cast him the sad smile she always did, yet this time a stirring in her heart told her that his words were closer to the truth than she'd ever believed.

From when she was young, Esther had been told the Jews were Yahweh's people, but being poor—without the power to make any difference in the world—she felt anything but chosen. These were mere words. She saw the contrast. And tonight, she'd witness the power and glory up close.

"Xerxes's party continues. Will you not go too, Cousin?" she dared to ask.

"This is the seventh night of the king's feast, Esther. With each day, the men drink more. They will be bringing in the dancing girls and concubines."

Heat rose to Esther's cheeks.

"This is why you must stay with the women. I am still determining if you will be exposed to things you ought not to see. But I cannot let my fear hold you back. I trust you will be safe. And this may be your only opportunity for many years, if not forever."

Forever? "Cousin, what do you know?"

"Since I work at the King's Gate, I know the soldiers. I see things.…" He cast her a knowing smile. "I will not ruin your evening. Within days, you will see."

"I don't have to wait until tomorrow, Cousin. In the marketplace, I heard thousands of soldiers, even the king's elite, already gathered in the city."

"The Immortals," Mordecai mumbled under his breath.

"Excuse me?"

"That's what the Greeks call our elite troops because their number never varies. It's always ten thousand strong. When one falls, another takes his place. And you will be able to tell the ones who are in closest attendance to the king. They have golden apples for spear butts."

Esther's eyes widened. "How many are they?" She wasn't sure she'd heard correctly.

"Ten thousand." Mordecai crossed his arms over his chest. "And the cavalry is of equal number. There are also soldiers from every province, you will see. Then this week's festivities prove what you've heard is correct. The king will be leading his troops to Greece soon."

"To fulfill a promise made to his father, yes." She'd heard of that promise. Everyone had. "A countless number of soldiers will leave mothers and wives—which is why the queen honors them tonight."

Mordecai nodded and tapped his temple. "Yes, you understand. And remember, Hadassah, who you are even as you walk among them and sit in the queen's shadow."

Hadassah. Tears sprang to her eyes, hearing her given name. Yes, she was Hadassah, the Jewish girl. She was also Esther, her Persian name—the one her cousin had given her when she became his ward. While she never truly understood why he had changed her name, she trusted him. Her new name was Esther, yet she often referred to herself by the name of the Phoenician princess, Dido, meaning "wanderer," when she told her stories to visitors. Yet no matter what name Esther went by, she always knew what she longed for.

She'd lived in the great city of Susa her entire life, but her heart belonged to the distant land of Jerusalem, the promised land given to them by God. Yes, it was still mostly rubble, and it paled to the excellent kingdom built by their ancestors David and Solomon, but in her heart, it was home.

She offered her cousin a knowing smile. "I will remember who I am, Cousin."

His eyes studied her, and he must have seen the truth of her words.

Then, remembering the package in his hand, he opened it. A gasp escaped Esther's lips as he revealed a pair of fine slippers. "The final touch. Now go dress."

As she dressed, Esther focused on Mordecai's stories of their people's captivity from Jerusalem. "Look around at the men and women, our fellow Jews," Mordecai had declared from when she was a child on his knee. "They are our people. Jerusalem is our home."

And if I become a storyteller to the queen, I can earn the money we need to make it our true home, she thought as she braided the golden cord through her hair.

It was strange to long for a home she'd never been to, especially when Mordecai questioned if they'd return in their lifetime. She, of course, believed differently. Hoped differently. Tonight could make the difference.

Once dressed in the gown with her hair braided, Esther placed the golden slippers on the ground before her. A smile filled her face as she slipped her feet into them and hurried to show her cousin.

The appreciation in his gaze told her he approved. He smiled, pinched the brim of his nose, and lowered his head, holding back tears. "If only your mother could see you this day," he muttered. "Such a beauty you have become."

"Of course, you have to say that, Cousin." She stepped forward and placed a soft kiss on his cheek. "And thank you for letting me go."

Again she considered telling him of the eunuch's visit, but the words stayed on the tip of her tongue. No use getting him worked up about something that might lead nowhere.

Until this day of her first banquet, she'd heeded Mordecai's advice not to walk in the way of the rich, seeking pleasure and entertainment without concern for God's ways. Before today she'd watched from the window—an exile from a distant land. A stranger to the life of wealth and pleasure just beyond her door.

How could her God find pleasure in a girl such as she—a wanderer of heart? And if she did become a storyteller to the queen, would she be caught up in the opulence? Or would her heart still long for Jerusalem? For home? Esther prayed it would be so.

CHAPTER THREE

Esther walked past the marketplace, seeing that most vendors had shut down for the night. Merchants' booths sat empty, and only a few beggars milled around, looking for scattered items left behind. She moved past the stalls toward the offices where Mordecai worked. This time of evening, there were no scribes or tax collectors. There were no import or export officials.

She'd visited Mordecai at his work often enough, but tonight for the first time, she continued past the offices and storehouses that ringed the base of the royal fortress, through the entrance of the King's Bridge.

With quickened steps, she crossed the bridge over the river and walked through the King's Gate. Tiles lined the walls in the design of the king's guardsmen. Their mosaic forms were prepared for battle, and the artwork was exquisite. She longed to reach out and run her fingers along the beautiful tile work, but she refrained and continued with the flow of women.

Across the bridge, she paused at the foot of the wide staircase that led up to the king's palace. Other women, each dressed in their finest, stepped past her, with excited chatter spilling from their mouths. She searched the crowd, hoping for a familiar face but seeing none. *I can do this. I am no longer a*

child. I am a guest. More than that, I am requested by the queen.
She stroked her braid and then took a breath for courage as
she started on again.

With slow steps, Esther climbed the stairs and then approached the entrance to the palace courtyard. How many people
had she seen coming and going from the palace in her lifetime?
Thousands. And now, she was one of them—in her stunning
white and gold dress. Those who walked alongside her looked as
lovely and colorful as the landscapes in the king's garden.

She paused and sucked in a quick breath. The courtyard
was beautifully decorated with white cotton curtains and blue
tapestries, fastened with white linen cords and purple ribbons
to silver rings embedded in marble pillars.

As the sea of women flowed around her, someone bumped
into her. Esther jumped and turned, expecting a scolding. "I
am so sorry."

A tall Egyptian woman with dark skin and white teeth
smiled at her. She was young too, no older than Esther.

"Do not apologize. I did not see you stop because I was
gawking also." The young woman swept her hand toward the
display ahead. "It is not as if we see this every day of our lives."
Then she moved on.

"You're right," Esther whispered, knowing the young woman
was too far ahead to hear.

Esther followed the others through the enclosed garden, taking in the opulence. Beneath the white and blue fabric, couches
of gold and silver sat on a mosaic pavement of porphyry, marble,
mother-of-pearl, and other costly stones.

Stewards carried wine in vessels and poured them into ornate goblets, each different from the others, handing the goblets to the women as they entered. Esther waved her hand, passing up the drink as she continued. She needed her wits about her to share a story with the queen. In the distance, men's laughter rose and fell. Were there truly dancing girls entertaining those men? She shook her head, not wanting her thoughts to linger there.

The stream of women continued through the first court-yard and then into the second one. Esther's gaze lifted, and she locked eyes with a face she recognized. The young woman was standing by the open doorway, scanning the faces of the women—looking for her. *Nazanin.*

Spotting her, Nazanin's eyes widened, and she hurried toward Esther, arms outstretched. She wore a sheath of fine linen, and a veil was fastened to her light brown hair with silver clips. Her bright eyes sparkled above her pink cheeks, and the skin of her neck, shoulders, and arms looked milky smooth as it glistened in the torchlight.

"Esther, it is so fine to see you. How did Mordecai ever release you from his talons? Look at you now. I've always seen you as a frightened rabbit skittering about." Nazanin held her at arm's length. Her blue eyes glowed with excitement.

Was it just Esther's imagination, or did her friend speak with even more sophistication than before?

"Nazanin, you look so lovely." Esther squeezed her arms. "So different."

Nazanin tilted back her head, and laughter spilled out, sounding like tiny bells. Then she eyed Esther with one cocked eyebrow. "They care for us well here. Even before I met the queen, I had to undergo a month of beauty treatments. Even though we are mere handmaidens, we cannot look like beggars on the streets. The palace has standards. Come, you must meet the queen."

Even as women continued to flow around her and Nazanin tugged on her arm, Esther's feet remained planted. "Now?"

Nazanin laughed again. "As soon as she arrives. She will wait to present herself after almost everyone is seated, including her guests, the king's concubines, and his lesser wives."

Esther's mind swirled, trying to take in all the information. Her stomach pinched, and she suddenly questioned how she'd ever believed she could be a storyteller to the queen.

Ahead, just beyond the first courtyard, men's laughter and music filled the air. The warm breeze carried the rich aromas of wine and roasted meat.

Esther glanced into the banquet room and spotted the raised platform where dozens of jeweled women lounged in fine robes and flowing veils. Were those the lesser wives and concubines? Esther had heard about them but hadn't given them much thought. She remembered Mordecai telling her that Xerxes had married a Persian princess. Within two years, she'd already given him sons.

Esther's brow furrowed, wondering what Queen Vashti thought of that. She also realized that if she were to become a storyteller to the queen, she'd most likely have a larger audience than just one woman. Esther's stomach tightened even more.

"Esther." Nazanin's smile faded, and her eyes narrowed. "Is there a problem? I went out of my way to tell the queen about you. I also dared to ask her to send one of her eunuchs to deliver that message to you. You're not going to back down, are you? Do you understand the position that would put me in?"

"No, uh, yes," Esther sputtered. "No, I don't want you to look bad. Yes, I understand what an honor this is and how you went out of your way to help me. But you said you had to undergo a month of beauty treatments before meeting the queen. I'm afraid of how I'll appear to her."

Nazanin released her hold of Esther's arms, placed her arms to her sides, and let her jaw drop. "You cannot be serious. Please tell me you aren't. Why, Esther, you're the most beautiful young woman I know, even without beauty treatments. Your perfectly heart-shaped face, large dark eyes, and soft pink lips. And in that gown. All the other women would be jealous, maybe even Queen Vashti herself. I knew that even if you wore your simple frock, you'd still be exquisite. That is not something to worry about."

Heat rose to Esther's cheeks, and she softly touched her face. "You flatter me, but that does not make me feel better about this. I feel so insignificant." She glanced around the room. "I don't fit in."

Leaning in closer, Nazanin locked eyes with Esther again. "And that's why the queen will love you, beautiful and humble." She reached forward and took Esther's hand. "Now, come. I have seats waiting for us near the queen's throne. The first round of fruits and drinks is already being served."

I don't belong here. This is a mistake. Esther glanced around again. The music, the chatter, the shuffling of bodies around the room. Her knees trembled. She slid her hand down the waist of her fine gown, feeling like a fraud. "Maybe we should do this another time. I don't know if I'm ready."

Nazanin grasped Esther's hand and pulled her forward. "Nonsense. I have told her about you. About your wonderful stories."

Blowing out a slow breath, Esther allowed herself to be led. "Will the queen be coming soon?" She asked only loud enough for Nazanin to hear.

Esther didn't need to wait for the answer, for at that moment, the room's chatter stilled to near silence, and then like the ripples of water spreading out, the sea of people lowered to their knees.

CHAPTER FOUR

One woman walked through the sea of people toward an exquisitely carved chair. She wore a blue gown of the finest linen, and her raven hair was braided where an iridescent veil was pinned. Her dark slanted eyes reflected wisdom, and her slight smile held mystery.

Esther saw the ripple reach them. Nazanin lowered herself onto one knee and bowed her head. Esther did the same, lowering herself to the ground and forcing her eyes to follow.

From the corner of her eye, Esther saw that every knee was bowed out of respect for the queen. Glancing up, she saw that the only ones not kneeling were the lesser wives and concubines, who still lounged on cushions. A mix of boredom and disdain was displayed on their faces.

An uneasiness settled in the pit of Esther's stomach as a new realization came over her. All was not well within the palace walls. From the outside looking in, the luxury, music, and feasting seemed enviable. But did the lesser wives envy Queen Vashti? And what would it be like to be one of the king's concubines, knowing you could never live a normal life with a husband and family of your own? An ache tugged in Esther's heart at the thought.

A tap on her shoulder caused Esther to glance up. The other women around her had stood again or were seated. Esther also noted Queen Vashti sitting regally in her carved chair.

While most women now moved toward banquet tables filled with food, Nazanin motioned to Esther. "Come, let us not delay. I know the queen will be eager to hear your stories."

They approached the queen, and Esther's breath caught. Queen Vashti's skin was as smooth as cream. Perfectly shaped eyebrows, coral lips. Her body was long and sleek, and the blue gown dipped low at the neckline and fell in smooth waves over her curves. Her proportions looked to be perfectly carved, like one of the statues of the false gods.

Nazanin approached and then paused ten feet from the queen. Two eunuchs stood by the queen, one on either side.

Noting their approach, Queen Vashti met eyes with Nazanin and offered the slightest nod. Nazanin clutched Esther's hand again, and they continued forward, pausing within arm's length of the queen.

Vashti looked past Nazanin and stared down at Esther with kind eyes. "You are such a beauty. Are you new to the city?"

"No, your Majesty. I have lived across the bridge at the King's Gate for these last ten years with my cousin after the loss of my parents."

"And your cousin, does she care well for you?" The queen's voice was like a purr.

"My cousin, he—Mordecai—is a kind man. He is a father to me and has always treated me kindly. Mordecai imports goods and sells them to the palace. He's at the gate daily."

"Mordecai. Yes, I have heard of your cousin. Now, please, tell me a story."

Esther's lips parted slightly as she realized Nazanin was right. Vashti had been expecting her.

A hundred stories filled Esther's mind, yet one rose above them all. It was a story she heard in various forms from men and women across the provinces. It was the Hebrew story she heard on her cousin's knee. Tonight, she chose to tell the Persian version.

Taking a deep breath, Esther stretched her hands outward, lifting them slightly. Then she projected her words with drama and emotion.

"The world, all that we see and that which we do not see, was birthed by Ahura Mazda, the source of all good and all life. The one who's always been and will be forever. He made all we know in seven steps because of his goodness. First the sky, and then came water. The sky was an orb suspended amid nothingness. Within the atmosphere, Ahura Mazda released water and then separated the waters from each other by the earth. The sky rose high above the world and passed beneath it.

"Land formed next, followed by every plant. Ahura Mazda spread all kinds of vegetation upon the earth and instilled it with its own life. Then Ahura Mazda created Gavaevodta, the Primordial Bull, who would give life to all other animals which would feed on and fertilize the vegetation. Next, Ahura Mazda created human beings, and in the seventh step, Ahura Mazda made fire." Esther's hands lifted higher and danced as if her fingers were flames of fire. Her eyes remained fixed on Queen

Vasthi as she spoke. As she ended the story, quieted her voice, and lowered her hands, Esther realized that she'd held the attention of everyone around her.

Vashti's lips curled in a smile, and pleasure danced in her eyes. "Who taught you this story?"

"I wish I knew a name, but dozens—if not hundreds—of men and women have been my teachers. We have an extra room, and my cousin does trading near the King's Gate. Weekly he welcomes guests and offers a bed for the night and a simple meal in exchange for their stories and legends." Esther shrugged. "I have a knack for remembering the stories, but I am not keen on remembering the storytellers' names."

"You have quite a gift, and along with your beauty, I am surprised you have not already been claimed as a bride."

Esther touched a hand to her warm cheeks. "My cousin is as protective as he is proud. Or at least that's what my neighbor Sarai says. He has not yet chosen a suitable husband."

"I see." Vashti's nose wrinkled, and she waved a hand to the sound of music and men's voices beyond their banquet room. "Hopefully, your cousin does not look among my husband's guests."

"No, my cousin did not attend Xerxes's banquet." Esther bit her lower lip between her teeth, quickly wondering what to say that would not reflect poorly on the king. "My cousin is weary after a day's work...and truthfully does not favor the dancing girls."

Laughter spilled from Vashti's lips. "Your cousin is wise indeed. Yet he allowed you to come?" She leaned forward slightly, her eyes on Esther's face, waiting for an answer.

"My cousin has always spoken well of you, your Majesty. Our grandfather served your father in Babylon. My cousin says he remembers you as a child."

Emotion flashed in Vashti's gaze. If it was longing or sadness, Esther could not tell. Maybe a mix of both.

"I was glad to be allowed," Esther answered simply, and then remembering her friend, she looked over her shoulder at Nazanin and then back to the queen. "Thank you for the personal invitation."

Vashti's hands slid down the arms of the chair and then motioned Esther forward. "Come, you must sit by me. I would love to hear more of your stories. I have met many storytellers, but none as young as you. You do wish to sit next to me, don't you?"

Esther's mouth grew dry, but she nodded. "Yes, of course. Thank you for the honor." A thin bench stretched beside the carved chair, and Esther settled upon it. Esther looked at Nazanin and patted the bench beside her. Nazanin shook her head with the slightest motion possible, and then Esther understood. She had not been invited by the queen to sit. Instead, Nazanin took a few steps back and reclined next to a small table.

A servant approached and offered Esther a plate of food and a goblet of wine. She accepted both and set them next to her on the bench. Esther eyed the rich food, much of which she couldn't name, and chose a few grapes instead. Though Esther had spent months dreaming of these banquets, her stomach was far too knotted to eat.

The feast continued around them, and Esther watched the women select food items from the tables and the servants who milled around, adding the choicest delicacies to their plates. The music played, and Vashti spoke with noblewomen who approached. She didn't turn anyone away, but she wasn't talkative either. Then, after at least a dozen women had stepped up to speak with her, the queen waved her hand. The finely dressed eunuchs understood, and they asked the remaining women to disperse.

Then with her eyebrows lifted, Queen Vashti turned her attention again to Esther. "Did you not enjoy the food?" Vashti asked, eyeing Esther's plate.

"I am certain it tastes wonderful, but I cannot eat." Esther shrugged. "I lead a simple life…." She smiled, breathed, and placed a hand on her stomach. "I think all of this is too much to take in."

"What is your age?" Queen Vashti asked, turning slightly in her seat to give Esther her full attention.

"I am nearly sixteen years old." Esther smoothed her dress across her lap. "In only a few months."

Vashti smiled again at this. "And you know many stories?"

"Yes, many. Stories from all corners of the kingdom. I could tell you another. Perhaps you would like to hear another Persian tale?"

"Please." Vashti clasped her hands on her lap. "Although maybe just a short one." Vashti rubbed her temples. "The rising volume of this room is giving me a headache. If my husband hadn't requested I put on this feast, I'd already be in my chambers. Still, maybe you could return? Tomorrow or the next day, perhaps? I will pay you for your services, of course. I will work it out with my eunuchs to beckon you within a few days."

Heat climbed Esther's neck, and she couldn't help but smile. Her heart fluttered with hope, yet she worried about what her cousin would say. Would it make her undesirable as a future Jewish bride for her to become a storyteller to the Queen of Persia? Or would Mordecai see it as a blessing from Yahweh—a way for them to obtain the money they needed to travel to Jerusalem? Was this a curse or a blessing in disguise?

Esther stood, preparing to tell another story. "I must speak to my cousin about—"

A swift lift of Queen Vashti's hand halted Esther's words. Esther followed the queen's gaze to the back of the banquet hall.

The music stilled as the door opened, and seven eunuchs in fine white robes approached. The lantern light reflected on their bald heads. Behind the eunuchs, two other men walked. The men's eyes landed on Vashti, and their gazes displayed the hunger with which Esther imagined wolves would look upon their prey.

A quick flick of her wrist made it clear that Queen Vashti wished for Esther to sit. But instead of returning to the bench by the queen's side, Esther hurried over to the cushion where Nazanin sat and situated herself by her friend's side.

Nazanin grabbed Esther's hand like a vise and fixed her eyes on the queen as if making eye contact with the men would lead to their harm.

Seeing her friend's reaction, Esther instinctively scooted closer to Nazanin's side. "Who are those men with the eunuchs?"

Nazanin leaned closer, whispering in Esther's ear. "Those are the lower officials of King Xerxes himself."

"Lower officials?"

"They work for senior officials running the royal household."

Queen Vashti rose as they approached. Ignoring the lower officials, she turned to the eunuchs. "Mehuman, Biztha, Harbona, Bigtha, Abagtha, Zethar, and Karkas," she said, naming the king's eunuchs individually, "I am surprised to see you at my banquet and not serving your king. By the looks on your faces, it appears you've come due to an urgent matter. Is all well with my husband?"

From the corner of her eye, Esther saw a stirring among the lesser wives and concubines. Worry was etched across the faces of some. Others gloated to see the fierce looks in the chamberlains' gazes that focused on the queen.

The eunuch closest to the queen cleared his throat. "The king commands that you come," Mehuman's words projected loudly enough for the guests to hear. "He wishes to display your beauty before his guests."

"Come with your crown," one of the chamberlains sneered.

"Only your crown," the lower official closest to Esther said.

Esther's stomach lurched as she saw the man's dark smile brighten with those words. The man laughed and swayed slightly, and she was sure that he had already had much to drink.

A look of horror crossed Vashti's face. She touched her hand to her neck. "The king commands?" Her gaze narrowed. Anger flashed like lightning in her eyes. "I am the queen."

"Who is that official who speaks in such a way to the queen?" Esther asked her friend, staring at the tall man with a narrow face, sharp cheekbones, and dark, close-set eyes.

"That is Haman the Agagite," Nazanin said, voice trembling. "He is a diviner and claims to know the ways of the gods. For some reason, the king trusts him."

It was clear from Queen Vashti's face that she did not. The queen tugged the hem of her gown down lower to cover her legs. Looking past the eunuchs, she glared at Haman. "How can the king ask such a thing? Xerxes would not suggest that."

Queen Vashti jutted out her chin. "The king commands that I veil myself whenever I leave the palace. He has told me he does not wish commoners to gaze upon me. And now these eunuchs say the king wishes for me to display my *beauty* before the common men in his banquet hall? He would do no such thing." Queen Vashti's eyes bored into Haman's. Then her head jerked, and she focused on Mehuman's pale face again. "Tell me, is this truly the king's request?"

"I speak for the king. This is not my request or that of any other." Mehuman's eyes darted to Haman and then back to Vashti's again. "It is the desire of King Xerxes," Mehuman replied meekly.

Striding closer to the throne, Haman nodded once and slowly licked his lips. He pressed them together and then pulled his lip between his teeth, releasing it with a smile. "And you know the request of any Persian king cannot be denied."

"Can it not? I am the queen, and I refuse." Queen Vashti lifted her goblet and tilted it back and forth slightly as if spinning the wine in a slow circle. "No doubt my husband is drunk. He would never ask such a thing in his right mind. Perhaps my refusal will sober him. Then he will realize that such a thing should not be asked."

"The king will not be pleased," Mehuman said, bowing slightly and stepping backward. At that exact moment, Haman crossed his arms over his chest and stiffened his neck in defiance.

Vashti held her head higher. Then she looked away from the men and fixed her eyes on Esther.

As she did, the eunuchs and officials also turned and looked at Esther. Tears nearly sprang to her eyes under their intense gazes. Esther focused on her queen's calm gaze instead. She would have believed that the men's demand left the queen unfazed if it weren't for the slight twitching in Vashti's jaw.

"Esther, do you know the story of the great flood?" Queen Vashti asked without the slightest hint of emotion.

"Yes, of course." Esther swallowed and then spoke louder. "It is one of the great stories of Persia." Although Esther's knees quivered, she rose to her feet.

Vashti motioned Esther forward. "Can you tell me that story?"

"Yes, your Majesty," Esther said as she stepped through the men to stand before her queen. Again, Esther lifted her arms and cleared her throat, forcing herself to think of the queen alone, not the men with their eyes on her.

"After the creation and expansion of the world, there came a time when Ahura Mazda beckoned the angels who did his will. Also invited were Yima and all the best men of Airyanem Vaejah. When they had all assembled, Ahura Mazda lifted his voice. 'Listen, Good Shepherd, Yima. You have cared for the earth well, but now winter will cover the world with snow. Two-thirds of the cattle will die, and the rushing waters will wash everything away.'"

Esther moved her hands in long sweeping motions, mimicking waves. "Son of Vivahvant, O Yima, I beseech you to make a safe place for the people and the flocks. Make a safe place for the animals and the birds. Create a vessel with four sides. Make each side the length of the stadium. Gather the finest of the flocks and people who are unmarred by disease. Bring dogs and birds—two of every kind. Gather seeds from plants, crops, and trees. Also, bring within a red, burning fire. Within the structure, men will live happy lives, and each year will seem like a day. A river will run through this structure, and there will be no strife, poverty, or disease."

There was more to the story, but from the empty look in Vashti's eyes, it was clear she was not listening. Esther let her voice trail away.

The room grew silent.

Without turning, Esther heard the footsteps of the men behind her as they retreated. Not a person dared to speak because they all knew matters did not bode well for the queen due to her refusal.

One minute passed and then two more. Esther lowered her hands, unsure of what to say or do.

"Winter has come." Vashti's voice was flat. "Just like the rushing of water—the coming of the great flood—this is the beginning of the end."

CHAPTER FIVE

This is the beginning of the end. What did the queen mean by those words? Was it the end of the banquet, or something more? Esther scanned the room. All eyes were on the queen. Vashti straightened her back and squared her shoulders once again. She motioned for Esther to sit and for one of her eunuchs to come to her. She spoke quietly to him. He bowed his head to listen, and when the queen had finished speaking, he lifted his hands to the room.

"Your queen says, please do not mind the matter at hand," the bald man said loudly. "Great effort was made to prepare a feast for all the kingdom's women. Please enjoy the banquet and the entertainment prepared for you." Then he ordered the musicians to continue playing.

Women's voices rose once more, mixing with the music. Yet it was not the happy chatter of before. Instead of butterflies dancing in her stomach, Esther's gut ached as she remembered the hungry, menacing gazes of the two senior officials. The way they eyed the queen caused Esther's skin to crawl. She brushed a hand down her arm as if she could brush away her uneasiness.

Nazanin sat silently next to Esther. The food on her plate was untouched. Every few minutes, she glanced back over her shoulder in anticipation.

Esther grasped Nazanin's hand. It felt as cold as ice. "What is wrong?" Esther asked, even though she knew the answer. Every subject in the kingdom knew of the king's wrath.

"If I weren't required to stay with my queen, I'd leave. I do not want to see what's to come. If I were you, I'd go when I still had the chance. There may be a danger to anyone connected to the queen. It may be good that Queen Vashti has not already declared you her royal storyteller. But as for me..." Nazanin's voice trailed off.

"I will not leave. I'm staying with you. Surely the king will come to his senses. Surely." Esther's words stuck in her throat. She didn't continue, and Nazanin remained silent. Esther's only comfort was Vashti, who sat regally upon her throne.

Esther had to believe the king's wrath would not fall on his first wife—the one he'd named queen. The one who'd given him an heir, a son. Perhaps Xerxes would not treat the queen so harshly.

Indeed, his drunkenness caused him to make such a request in the first place. Perhaps a part of him was in his right mind enough to remember his love for his queen. His wife's response might bring him to his senses. Yet even as Esther hoped for these things, the thumping of her heart feared the worst.

Is Nazanin right? Should I go? Am I in danger?

It didn't matter the answer. Esther remained rooted on her cushion. Queen Vashti had asked her to return. She had to know if there was even the slightest possibility that the queen remained in the king's favor.

Not thirty minutes later, Esther heard the pounding of men's footfalls on the tiled floor. She turned, as did everyone else in the banquet hall, and her heart sank. It wasn't only the seven eunuchs and two senior officials who approached but a dozen soldiers with them.

Esther gasped and wrapped an arm around Nazanin's shoulders as if protecting her friend would save the queen too. "Surely the king will not have the queen killed for disobeying his drunken request."

Nazanin's face paled. "He has done so to others for much less."

The men approached. The queen stared at Memucan and lifted one eyebrow in question. "You return so soon?" Even though the music continued, the queen spoke loudly enough for the closest groups of women to hear.

"The king burns with anger, as you no doubt expected," Haman hissed. He motioned for the musicians to stop. To Esther's surprise, they did.

"King Xerxes consulted with his wise advisers who know all the Persian laws and customs, for he always asks our advice." Haman swept his arms, motioning to the other official with him. "As you know, we meet with the king regularly and hold the highest positions in the empire." Haman's cruel smile curled up as he spoke, but Vashti's gaze remained on his without a hint of emotion.

"Did you say *we*? I know my husband's advisers: Carshena, Shethar, Admatha, Tarshish, Meres, Marlena, and Memucan—the seven nobles of Persia and Media." She glanced at the two officials before her. "But I have not heard that Haman and Hormoz are among them."

Harsh laughter spilled from Haman's mouth. "You speak boldly for someone no longer in favor of the king."

Hormoz stepped forward with his hands clutched in front of him. "The king insisted on knowing what must be done to his queen—what penalty the law provides for a queen who refuses to obey the king's orders, properly sent through his eunuchs. Memucan himself reminded us of the truth of the matter. You, Queen Vashti, refused to appear before the king. And you did so before all the women. Before this day is out, the wives of all the king's nobles throughout Persia and Media will hear what the queen did and start treating their husbands the same way. There will be no end to their contempt and anger." Hormoz turned and scanned the sea of women that stretched in every direction.

"So it pleased the king to issue a written decree, a law of the Persians and Medes that cannot be revoked," Haman added.

Pushing up from the armrests, Queen Vashti stood. From her place on the raised platform where her chair sat. Peering down her nose at them, Vashti sucked in a slow, controlled breath. "And I am sure you've come to inform me and my kingdom subjects of what the decree said."

Before Haman or Hormoz could speak, the eunuch Mehuman stepped forward. His features softened, and his eyebrows drew together. A pained expression crossed his face. Mehuman lifted his face and kept a steady eye on the queen. "An order has gone out that Queen Vashti be forever banished from the presence of King Xerxes and that the king should choose another queen more worthy than she."

Banished? Forever? Esther's mouth fell open. *Surely not.*

With the proclamation, a murmur rose among the king's lesser wives and concubines. Voices also rose around the room, mixing with gasps of disbelief. Only Queen Vashti stood, unmoving.

"When this decree is published throughout the king's vast empire, husbands everywhere, whatever their rank, will receive proper respect from their wives," Mehuman continued, his voice rote as if speaking from a script in his mind. "Even now, letters are already being sent to all parts of the empire, to each province in its script and language, proclaiming that every man should be the ruler of his own home and say whatever he pleases."

The two officials looked at each other and smiled before turning their attention to the queen. Mehuman, the eunuch, raised his hands as if to silence the room. When it was quiet, he approached Queen Vashti. "A caravan is being prepared even now." He cleared his throat and lowered his gaze. "I bid you farewell, my queen."

The room stilled, and a collective hush fell. As did the rest of the room, Esther leaned forward, waiting for Vashti's response. Still, the queen's face reflected no horror, only sadness. She scanned the room slowly, taking it in one last time. The queen's gaze stopped on Haman and Hormoz, and bile rose to the back of Esther's throat as she noticed pleasure on the faces of the two officials. Haman's eyes especially feasted on Vashti's beauty even as his eyebrows lifted in smug approval of her fall from the king's favor.

Esther had never hated a man or woman in her life, but her heartbeat quickened, and her stomach roiled at the sight of Haman. If he was someone King Xerxes trusted, she knew she wanted nothing to do with the king either.

Esther stood and stepped back slowly, putting as much space between her and the official as possible.

Ignoring the gawking of the two men, Vashti stepped down from the platform and gracefully strode out of the room. In one line, the queen's eunuchs followed.

It was only as Vashti and the eunuchs exited that Esther released the breath she'd been holding. Deep in her gut, Esther knew that Vashti would never enter this banquet room again. Soon, she'd be gone from the palace. Maybe even Susa. In a quick turn of events, Esther no longer needed to worry about what Mordecai would say about the honor the former queen had wanted to bestow. There was no chance she'd be an official storyteller to the queen.

Esther turned back to Nazanin, who still sat. The color had washed from her friend's face.

"If she's leaving, do I have a position here?" Nazanin asked, rising. "What am I to do? Should I follow her?" Nazanin covered her face with her hands. "How could things have come to this?"

"Maybe things will change," Esther soothed. "Maybe tomorrow Xerxes will wake up and change his mind," Esther offered, yet the words sounded hopeless even to her.

"You know as well as I that can never be the case. If it is written in the laws of the Medes and Persians, it cannot be revoked." Nazanin's voice was flat. Her blue eyes filled with tears.

"Then we both do not have positions here, do we?" Esther wrapped the gold cord of her belt around her hand. At least she'd had a chance to dress beautifully once in her life. And tomorrow, she'd return to her simple life. Tomorrow her heart would be full of questions about her future, without answers.

Before Nazanin could respond, one of the eunuchs returned. With quickened steps, he approached Nazanin. "Come. The queen requests you." He moved through the room, speaking the same to Vashti's other handmaidens and servants.

Nazanin stood unmoving for a moment as if she hadn't understood the eunuch's words. Then, with slow moments, she adjusted the skirt of her dress, spun slowly, and peered down at Esther. "Can you tell my mother and father that I love them? Tell them not to fear. I will try to let you know where I will be going with my que—with Vashti." Nazanin's lower lip trembled. "Tell them not to think otherwise. No matter what happens to Vashti, urge them to believe that I live and am happy. Yes, tell them to think about that."

Then with quickened steps, Nazanin moved toward a cluster of the other young women who now served a queen removed from her title. A former queen who would soon be deposed from her home.

As she moved among the crowd of other women toward the banquet hall doors, Esther whispered a prayer to Yahweh that nothing worse would come of them.

Yahweh, though they walk in the shadow of death, may Your hand protect them. Even though they are removed from the king's favor, show Your favor to them. Even though there are tales of many gods, may they somehow learn of the one true God, greater than any king. Where others seek destruction, may You provide hurting hearts with hope. Yahweh, You are Shahanshan, King of Kings, just as my cousin says.

Yet even as she prayed for the queen and her women, Esther's anger at the officials rose. With balled fists, she continued out of the banquet room, pursing her lips and shaking her head.

How could the impulse of a drunken king lead to this? And how could the king's trusted officials gloat? The muscles tightened around her mouth and nose, and she scrunched her face. The only good thing was that Esther would never have to see those officials again as long as she lived.

CHAPTER SIX

Morning light filtered in through the window opening. As Esther stretched, memories of the previous night crashed around her. *The palace. The sea of women, rich foods, wine. Storytelling. The delight in the queen's eyes at her tales. The approach of the eunuchs and officials.*

Although it seemed like a nightmare, Esther knew that every memory of last night's events was accurate. She rubbed the sleep from her eyes, wondering if Nazanin was still in the city. Had they escorted the queen to some distant land even last night? Had Nazanin been forced to go with them?

Ignoring the delicate gown folded in a bundle on the stool in her room, Esther dressed in her simple tunic. She walked into the main living area, feeling like one of the palace's stone columns rested on her chest. Although she'd expected Mordecai to be waiting up when she'd arrived back last night, their home had been dark and silent. Even though her mind had swirled with worries of the banished queen, to her surprise, she'd fallen quickly to sleep.

She peered out the front window, noticing more people than usual hurrying toward the marketplace. Had word already gotten out about last night's events? Would Mordecai know? Or would he be shocked when she relayed all that had happened leading up to the queen's banishment?

Mordecai sat on the cushion in the main living area with a bowl of porridge before him. His back was to her.

Esther hurried into the room. "Mordecai, did you hear about last night? I was sitting not five feet from the queen when some of the king's eunuchs and high officials entered. They said they had a message from the king. According to them, Xerxes commanded Queen Vashti to come before the men's banquet to show off her beauty."

Esther moved to the shelf that held last night's bread, baked by Sarai, and broke off a piece. She turned. Mordecai's shoulders straightened, and she knew he was listening. Still, he did not turn.

Esther placed her bread in a bowl and added some dates. Then she moved to sit across from her cousin. "We could hear the men's revelry from the women's banquet. The laughing. The cheering. You were right—the room was filled with dancing girls and concubines. Can you believe that environment was the one King Xerxes asked Queen Vashti to enter? It was the type of environment any man would want to protect his wife from."

Esther sighed as she sat. "For the queen to go would make her like a common harlot." Esther broke off a piece of her bread. "Then one of the commissioners told Vashti to wear her crown. *Only* her crown." The words spilled out, yet her cousin's silence caused her to pause.

Mordecai looked down at his bowl, and she saw that the porridge was untouched. His shoulders trembled, then his hands lifted and covered his face.

"So you have heard." Her voice was no more than a whisper. Esther licked her lips and swallowed. She took a deep breath and released it, wondering if she should tell him more.

Esther's mind filled with the image of the elegant queen, so noble and kind. "How could he ask such a thing?" Esther placed a hand over her heart. "To be humiliated like that."

Mordecai lowered his hands. "I have heard, and rumors are spreading that someone—maybe one of his advisers—put the king up to this." Mordecai threw his hands in the air. "Get the king drunk and then stroke his ego. 'My king, do you not have the most beautiful woman in the world as your wife?'" Mordecai lowered his voice as he spoke. "'The men have heard as much, but their respect for you, oh king, would grow if you show them her beauty.'"

"Yes. How could one do this to a queen?" Esther returned the piece of broken bread to her bowl, her appetite gone now.

Mordecai lifted his spoon and stirred his porridge, although it was clear he had no intention of eating it.

"You do not understand, Esther. It was more than simple humiliation. There is a tradition that cannot be revoked. The king's wives are only supposed to be seen by him and those who serve in the palace. Last night was different because only women were invited to the queen's banquet. This tradition also includes the king's other wives and concubines. Any time the queen, the other wives, or the concubines go before ordinary men, they must be covered with veils or hidden behind screens. Their beauty is only for the king's eyes."

"But last night…" Esther pressed her lower lip between her teeth. No wonder the eunuch seemed so uncomfortable with the request.

"Yes, last night Xerxes was acting like a fool." He sighed. "Not only do I know, but the word is spreading through all the kingdom about the queen's disposal, a decree written in the laws of Persia and Media. It cannot be repealed."

Esther's trembling fingers touched her lips as Mordecai continued. "The decree says that Queen Vashti can never again enter the presence of King Xerxes. Her royal position will be given to someone better than she."

"Do you think the position will be given to one of his lesser wives?"

"I do not know. We may not know for some time. What was speculated before is true. The king, his elite soldiers—the Immortals—and the rest of his army will ride out in a few days. We were right to believe the queen's banquet was a way to honor the women who'd soon be losing their husbands, brothers, and sons to this campaign." He pushed his bowl to the side and stood. "But the light has already left our city. I wasn't here when you arrived home because I'd been beckoned to gather supplies for the leaving caravan. With her handmaiden and servants, Vashti has already ridden out under cover of darkness."

"Already?" Esther gasped. "And where are they going?"

Mordecai moved to the window. He peered at the growing masses walking toward the King's Gate and shrugged. "Some say Persepolis. Others say to the farthest part of his kingdom in Egypt." He ran a hand down his face and then stroked his beard. Since Mordecai worked near the King's Gate, he chose to wear his beard like a Persian rather than in the way of the Jews. He'd told her it was better not to be noticed for standing out. She'd never questioned that. She also didn't argue when he'd started calling her Esther, the Persian version of Hadassah. Nazanin's family had acted the same, and Esther knew her Hebrew name to be Naomi.

Esther's eyes welled up, and she wrapped her arms around herself, squeezing. *This can't be happening. Gone already. Poor Nazanin.* Her comfort was that no matter where Nazanin traveled, Yahweh would be with her.

An orb of emotion lodged in Esther's throat, and she told herself she'd visit Nazanin's family soon. Esther's chest and stomach clenched as she also remembered the queen. So beautiful. So noble and worthy of respect.

"How can it come to this?" Esther pushed the words out. "This is not right. This is not fair. Xerxes wanted his wife to prance around in front of drunken men. It makes me ill just to think of it."

Mordecai turned. He crossed his arms severely over his chest, and his face burned red with anger.

"I have a feeling the king's noblemen are behind this. I read the decree, which stated that Queen Vashti has done wrong, not only against the king but also against all the nobles and the peoples of all the provinces of King Xerxes." He pointed his finger in the air. "The queen was the scapegoat. When the king's edict is proclaimed throughout his vast realm, all the women will have no say in their husbands' whims," Mordecai scoffed, "from the least to the greatest."

He approached Esther and placed a hand on her shoulder.

"That makes me concerned for you." His voice softened, and he released a heavy sigh. "That is why we must pray to find you a good husband—someone who will treat you with respect."

"And a man who also wishes to travel to Jerusalem?" Her voice raised an octave. "That would be best, don't you think? Then we'll no longer have to live by the whims of nobles and kings."

Mordecai's stomach growled loudly, causing his eyes to widen and breaking the seriousness of the moment.

A soft laugh slipped from Esther's lips. "I suppose this is something we can talk about as we eat." She returned to her bread and dates. "Or your stomach will continue to protest louder than your words."

"It's easy to talk about returning to Jerusalem, but it's still a barren place with no walls of protection and numerous enemies." Mordecai returned to his seat. "It's no place for a beautiful young woman like yourself, although Susa might not be either soon." He lifted a spoon and took a bite of his now cold porridge.

"What do you mean?"

"I mean, we must obey the laws of our ruler—whoever he is. You were not alive during the Babylonian captivity. The strongest and most handsome Jews were taken from Jerusalem to serve in the royal palace, my father being one of them."

"I know the stories of Daniel, who survived after being thrown into a den of the lion, and the three Hebrew men thrown into the fire for refusing to worship Nebuchadnezzar's carved image. Those are some of my most popular stories. I'm starting to get more requests at the marketplace when people see me. Sometimes they even reward me with a few coins."

"They make great stories, but to live through them is another matter." Mordecai shook his head.

"I can't imagine." Esther took a bite of her bread.

"My father knew Daniel well, and the prophet was a target by many who served the king."

"It makes sense. Daniel's interpretations and dreams took honor from the other seers." Esther lifted a date to her lips. "Although they sought their gods for answers, Daniel alone was bestowed answers and wisdom from Yahweh, the one true God."

"Yes, and when the Persians and Medes captured the Babylonians, those who served in the palace were brought here to Susa to serve in the city. Some were even taken into the palace." Mordecai took another bite of food and sighed. "In Babylon, all—from the least to the greatest—were forced to worship the king, his idols, and his gods. Here in Susa, Jews and everyone else can worship as they please.

"While it is better for us, I'm afraid we've become too comfortable. You're right, Esther, to say we should seek to return to Jerusalem. If only the Holy City weren't so dangerous—surrounded by enemies on all sides—perilous for beautiful women."

Esther nodded. Susa was a pagan city filled with many nationalities, each worshiping their gods. But at least she could walk to the market and back without fear of an outside enemy swooping in and violating her or kidnapping her to be a bride in a tribe of pagans.

She took another bite of her bread and pondered her cousin's words, thinking of the dangers she'd witnessed last night. Those dangers might not be as evident as kidnappers with swords, but the officials she saw should be feared just the same. A shiver ran down her spine. "You said that some of those from Babylon who served in the palace serve here too? Do you know this to be true?"

"Yes, many of the seers and astrologers that serve Xerxes come from Babylon. Of course, those who served at the time of my father have passed now, but I have heard of their sons taking their places. Haman and Hormoz being two."

"Haman and Hormoz!" Esther gasped. "They entered with the eunuchs to deliver the king's request." Esther dropped her bread into the bowl. "I saw them just last night."

Mordecai nodded once. "I am not surprised. Men like that will stop at nothing to gain power." He clenched his jaw. "They use trickery, darkness, and the evil arts."

Even the taste of the sweet date grew sour in her mouth at the memory of those men, and she quickly swallowed it. "But what would be the purpose of disposing of Queen Vashti?"

"Vashti is descended from royal Babylonian blood. Perhaps they think she knew too much of their ways while also having the ear of the king. Or maybe they did not want her to comfort Xerxes when he went to war. Persian kings take their wives, children, and sometimes concubines with them. A wise wife is worth more than the finest armor or even an army of Immortals. If Xerxes is lost on the battlefield, perhaps these men believe they will have a shot at the throne."

Esther ate her bread in silence, taking in her cousin's words. She shuddered, remembering the evil, hungry look in the eyes of the two lower officials. Mordecai was right. They'd do anything to gain power and control.

Before yesterday, the happenings of the palace seemed distant and out of reach. After last night, Esther understood more about the evil and the power struggles within the walls. Her cousin told her that Persia would soon be engaged in a war. As unpopular as Xerxes was with his impulsive actions, high taxes, nonstop building projects, and continuous expansions, at least his vices were known.

The memory of Haman's eyes filled with evil surfaced in her mind again, and she found it hard to swallow as her stomach churned.

"We must pray that Xerxes finds victory," she stated simply. "We should also pray for Jerusalem, that Yahweh will raise men and women to rebuild its walls and make it a haven for our people." Esther wiped a tear from the corner of her eye. "As long as we are here, we will continue to be subject to the whims of a king or any of his officials." Esther folded her hands on her lap. "Perhaps this is happening so we don't remain comfortable—"

"Such wisdom from one so young." Mordecai reached forward and patted her hand. "Although many believe I came to your rescue, I often realize you have come to mine. Let us take to heart your words, young cousin, and pray for Jerusalem and a plan for our return. Let's pray for Xerxes—the king of the Persians and the Medes—for his war and safe return."

CHAPTER SEVEN

Three days later

A commotion outside drew Esther's attention to the window, and she guessed the reason for the excited crowds. The army was assembling. King Xerxes was leading his troops to Greece, and it was time to head out.

The hot breeze blew in through the window, and she quickly tied on her sandals. She stepped outside and spotted men and women lining the roadway. In the distance, she heard the stamping of feet marching in unison on the cobblestone.

Esther did her best to move through the crowd, maintaining a view of the King's Gate. She wanted to get as close as possible to watch the king and his entourage exit through the gate to join up with his army.

Weaving her way through the crowd, she found a spot to wait and watch near her cousin's office. It was as good a view as any. Yet, for some reason, his door was shut, and he was nowhere to be seen.

The crowds grew, older men and young ones, women and children, from many nations. Their colorful garments and head coverings filled the marketplace and roadway with vibrance. While children jumped around amid all the excitement, the faces of the women were pinched, and their eyes downcast. Esther guessed that many were saying goodbye to husbands and sons. She was thankful that Mordecai was needed in his position. She couldn't imagine what it would be like to care for all her own needs with him gone. Or to think of her cousin on the battlefield in harm's way.

Down the roadway, she spotted groups of marching soldiers approaching. She'd heard Mordecai talking with a friend last night that forty-six groups were coming together to fight for the Persian empire. Did Greece have a chance against such an army? Esther held her breath as the first columns of men approached.

Black-bearded Assyrians led the columns, wearing brass helmets and cuirasses with red cording and pleating in the front and back. Their hands grasped iron clubs, lances, and daggers.

Shorter than the Assyrians, the Scythians wore trousers and pointed hats. The Scythian weapons looked more fearsome—composite bows and battle-axes that looked like sharp, hooked hammers.

The sounds of horses' hooves filled the air, and chariots approached, carrying bronze-skinned Indians wearing light cotton garments. Mounted Bactrian archers rode behind them with composite bows made of cane. Although the Bactrians were not huge in number, Esther had heard of the archers' powerful determination and their intense training.

Ethiopians with dark skin and curly hair wore leopard and lion skins. Some carried long reed arrows tipped with sharpened stones. Others held bows nearly as tall as themselves, crafted from the stems of palm leaves. Still others carried spears tipped with antelope horns.

Esther's feet grew tired from standing, and the rows of soldiers marched forward in line. Caspians wore goatskin, and Colchians marched with shields of cowskin. Saragian horsemen followed next with lassos, and Thracians donned fox-skin caps.

The noblest of all were the Arabian archers who rode on camels, their robes multicolored in different patterns. After these columns of soldiers passed through crowds of cheering older men and reverent women, the sound of marching came from the direction of the King's Bridge.

The Persian, Mede, and Kissian infantry strode forward from the palace, over the bridge, and through the King's Gate to meet up with the advancing army. The Persian officers and nobles glittered with adornments of gold body armor and headdresses. The cavalry followed next, wearing leather helmets. The fighting men on horseback wore leather helmets, colorful garments, belts, and their highly decorated shields, shining in full display. Esther had heard a description of the wicker shields before, but this was the first time she'd seen them. It amazed her that wicker could be woven tight enough to stop any arrow or sword and be light enough not to weary the soldiers.

Behind those soldiers, litters carried women, wives, and concubines hidden underneath veils. Servants bore the weight of the litters, and beasts of burden plodded forward, their bodies loaded with supplies.

As they passed, Esther's heartbeat quickened when she spotted King Xerxes's elite troops. *The Immortals.* Her breath caught as she eyed the handsome men who numbered ten thousand.

The Immortals wore breastplates of bronze set in overlapping rows like the scales of fish. Shoulder straps held the breastplate in place over bright blue tunics. The soldiers wore loose-fitting cotton headdresses on their heads to protect their faces against dust, wind, and dirt. They carried short spears with golden apples at the tip and oval wicker shields.

Time dragged on as seemingly endless rows of men paraded before the crowds. Esther was about to pull herself away to start dinner when a hush settled over the people. Behind the columns of men, one lone man rode in a fine chariot. Not just any man. From his erect back and regal form, Esther knew she looked upon the king. *Xerxes.*

Beside the king, a group of magi walked, carrying torches of sacred fire from their altars. Behind the king, the empty chariot of Ahura Mazda was drawn by eight white horses, with the charioteer following on foot. Last in the parade came Xerxes's carriage with ten sacred Nisaean horses pulling it. The carriage was available whenever Xerxes grew weary of riding his chariot on the long journey.

Esther remembered a story about the Persian tradition of taking along the empty chariot of Ahura Mazda, the Persian creator, whenever they headed out to war. The inclusion of this chariot invited their Lord of Wisdom to accompany them into battle. The glory of the horses and chariots was exquisite, but the king took Esther's breath away.

Xerxes wore a uniform similar to that of his Immortals. Yet, underneath the golden breastplate, he wore a white linen tunic with gold braiding. Even though she'd seethed over Xerxes's treatment of his queen only days ago, seeing him standing regally in his chariot caused her heart to quicken and her mouth to grow dry.

The king's features were chiseled, as from the hand of a fine craftsman. Dark wavy hair framed his face, and the curls of his beard glistened in the blaze of the afternoon sun. His shoulders were broad, and his body was tall and lean. Rings of gold and gems sparkled on Xerxes's hands as he gripped the horse's reins.

The crowds around her knelt as the king passed, and Esther instinctively went to her knees. The man beside her did the same, and she glanced sideways to see her cousin. The anger of days prior no longer flashed in Mordecai's eyes. Instead, she saw reverence. Esther understood. Even though the king's actions toward his wife had been wrong, seeing King Xerxes's glory displayed him in a different light. Despite his indulgences and quick temper, Xerxes had to be a man of wisdom and power to have already put down rebellions in the outlying regions of his kingdom and to have such a diverse army under his leadership.

The king's profile gave Esther a glimpse of his set jaw as he passed. A warmth grew in the pit of her stomach, and she quickly looked away. She had never had such stirrings within her for any man. Yet the warmth spread from her belly, up through her chest, to her limbs.

She touched a hand to her face and hoped her cousin did not notice the pink that surely tinged her cheeks. Daring to glance at the king again, Esther vowed to pray for Xerxes's safe return. His kingdom counted on it, and the truth was, her heart ached at the thought that she'd never see his form again.

Voices around them lowered to no more than a whisper, paying respect. Then with a flourish, Xerxes lifted a hand and waved to the crowd. Acknowledged by their king, the throngs raised a deafening cheer, and the crowd returned to their feet, stretching their hands high.

Mordecai stood and reached a hand toward Esther. She took it and accepted his help as she rose. Then Esther pressed her hands to her ears, sure the King's Gate would crumble under the shouts.

Even as celebrations filled the air, worried thoughts swirled in her mind. *What if these brave soldiers are overcome? What if the king is killed in battle? Who will rule the kingdom then? And how could the Jews endure in a land intolerant to the worship of Yahweh, the one true God?*

As the cheering died down, Esther leaned close to her cousin. "With such a grand kingdom already, is there any purpose for returning to Greece? Surely a king such as this would be satisfied with one hundred and twenty-seven provinces."

Mordecai opened his mouth to answer, but an older man on the other side of Mordecai responded first.

The white-haired man shook his fist in the air with elation. "Not only will our king fulfill his promise to his father, Darius, to strike down the Greeks, but our kingdom will become richer for his conquest!"

"A king satisfied is no king at all, but rather a glutton and a coward," another man blasted proudly as if he were the right-hand man of Xerxes himself. "Our army will bring back the splendor of Athens. Just you watch."

Esther's shoulders drew back, and her chin lifted. The memory of Vashti's downcast gaze and slumped shoulders slipped away as she focused on the king's power on display.

A chill ran down her arms as she better understood the purpose of the king's feasting with nobles from every province, which had lasted one hundred and eighty days. For half a year, she'd believed the music and the food had been for relaxation and entertainment. But a display such as this hadn't evolved overnight. A war council had taken place within the palace walls, and today was the culmination of their planning.

Esther pushed the worries out of her mind and allowed herself to be swept away with the crowd. "Surely no opposing army can stand up to power like this." Her words escaped with a breath.

Hearing her exultation, Mordecai grasped her wrist. "Do you not remember the story of Gideon?" Mordecai lowered his voice so only Esther could hear. "Yahweh decreased Gideon's number of fighting men so Yahweh would get the glory. The winner isn't always as expected. And the true glory of the man is not seen at the beginning but at the end."

Esther placed a hand over her heart and gasped. "Are you saying that they will be defeated?"

"Cousin, lower your voice." Mordecai glanced from side to side. "A man's true strength does not come from chariots. Yahweh gives, and Yahweh takes away." He shrugged. "The next few years will tell the tale. At least we have time to save all the money and resources we can for our journey to Jerusalem."

Years? Esther placed her fingertips to her temples, trying to imagine their kingdom without a king.

Days ago, Mordecai had said the light left Susa when Vashti was driven from town, but Esther disagreed. She realized more than ever that Xerxes was the light of the Persians and the Medes. Yes, Yahweh was the Lord of lords, but for the people of Susa, this king was all they knew.

Nearly as much as Esther wanted to travel to Jerusalem, she wanted their king to return. She wanted the music of rejoicing and the aroma of feasting to soothe her to sleep again. She wanted to know that she could continue her worship of Yahweh even if she remained.

CHAPTER EIGHT

Three years later

Esther knelt in the courtyard, remembering Sarai. Even though the sun had just peaked on the horizon, rays of heat bore down. She wished she had her old friend to converse with as she baked her bread. Esther missed how Sarai joked about how servants and maids would tend to Esther. *She was such a dreamer. Always looking to what could be someday.*

Two years had already passed since the older woman's death. Three years, since the march to Greece. How could that be so?

For a time, it seemed the Persian army would defeat the Greeks. The first year King Xerxes's army had captured, looted, and burned down Athens and the sacred Acropolis. Victory appeared inevitable, but the Persian forces faced a loss in Salamis, causing much of the army to retreat to Persia.

While some soldiers remained to fight, word had come that Xerxes would soon be returning. Although some citizens of Susa claimed that burning Athens had been victory enough, Esther guessed the king would not think so, especially after the clear display of his power upon leaving.

Not a day passed when Esther didn't remember the night she walked through the King's Gate, across the bridge, and into the palace courtyards—striding as if she belonged.

During quiet nights, she still missed the music and laughter. For that first half a year, she couldn't imagine life without music. Now she tried to remember if it had been real, or if it had just been a dream.

The bread finished baking, and Esther quickly lifted it from the coals, tossing the thin loaf into the basket. In the last three years, she had baked her bread in the morning and spent nearly every day telling stories at the marketplace. In the afternoons, she and Mordecai had often walked home from the market together after his day's work.

After visiting the palace and watching the grand procession that went to war, Esther had difficulty waiting for what would come next. She wanted to go to Jerusalem. She wished for her cousin to find her a husband, yet daily, Mordecai waited and prayed.

"What good is prayer if you do not get an answer, Cousin?" she often asked him.

"I do get an answer, Esther. For now, Yahweh says we must wait." He pushed a fist against his chest. "Sometimes, it does not make sense to me. For now, I will do my job at the gates."

"And I will tell my stories," she added, and so she did.

On most days, she visited the marketplace and told her stories to all who would listen. For someone who wanted more, she had only to look at Mordecai's growing coin purse to feel as if their dreams for Jerusalem were possible.

She hurried inside, eager to get to the marketplace. In addition to earning a few coins for their savings, Esther also listened closely for any news of the returning king.

After placing the bread basket on the shelf, Esther slid her sandals on and ran a comb through her long, dark hair. Then she tied on her headscarf. She no longer wore simple dresses. As a storyteller, Mordecai now insisted she wear the colorful patterned dresses he'd given her as gifts.

Esther grabbed her empty coin purse and tied it around her waist. Hopefully, by this evening, it would be half full of coins.

With a smile, she strode to the marketplace. The cobblestone roads shimmered with the heat of the midmorning sun, and the air was filled with the exuberant bleating of lambs being herded toward the market stalls.

A messenger boy jumped over sheep droppings on the road, even as his eyes fixed on the looming King's Gate—with its carved bull figures—that jutted into the sky. The white carved stone starkly contrasted with the roughly built market stalls where buyers and sellers milled about. The imposing structure provided a hint of the luxury that waited behind it when one walked through the gate to the king's palace.

Also called the Sublime Porte, the name referred to both the physical palace gateway and the place ordinary citizens could go to petition the king or hear his judgment. In addition to court officials' offices, benches lined the walls for petitioners to use. There was also a throne platform for the king or his representative. Today, already a dozen men sat, waiting to be questioned by the guards before they could be admitted into the courtyard beyond.

Since Xerxes's expedition to Greece, his nobles took his place, governing the people of Susa and all the king's other provinces. Messengers carried information from the people of the city to the gate, and eunuchs conveyed missives between the courtyard and the audience hall.

Esther's steps slowed as she approached the platform near Mordecai's office door. Seeing an opposing figure up ahead, she felt her smile curl down into a frown. Near the arched entrance of the King's Gate, a familiar palace eunuch stood. Esther's stomach tensed as she recognized Bahar, Haman's faithful servant. Was Bahar there to deliver a message? Or had he come with Haman? The day's vibrancy faded with the palace official's presence.

Even though Esther had hoped she'd never have to see Haman again after the queen's banquet, she hadn't been so fortunate. With Xerxes in Greece, Haman had set himself as one of the nobles. He lived in a fine villa outside the King's Gate with his wife and numerous children and passed by the gate daily. There were even days when Haman sat upon the throne chair, acting as if he were the king himself and demanding the people give him honor.

Esther had noted the evil intent in his eyes the first time she'd seen Haman at the queen's banquet. These days, it was as if those wicked intentions seeped into every part of his body.

Haman's face had grown thinner, causing his sharp, hawklike features to look more intense. And with funds from the king's bank, Haman had special garments woven to denote his role as an astrologer, as well as an official. Purple snakes and other idolatrous images were embroidered on his garments and headpiece. Esther's flesh crawled whenever she saw the man.

Yahweh, if I can get through the day without one glimpse of Haman, I will have peace. Perhaps it wasn't the holiest prayer, but it would make her labor easier.

A small crowd had already assembled, waiting for her. Instead of standing to tell her tales, as she'd done before the queen, Esther settled onto a brown woven cushion that Mordecai had set out for her. She placed her skin of water beside her, thankful the shade from the tall, stone gate protected her from the sun's intense rays.

Coins jingled in one young man's money pouch as he sat before her, always a good sign. He eyed her with a flirtatious smile.

Esther's face grew even warmer in the desert heat. She adjusted her headscarf and looked away. While she liked to believe all came to listen to her stories, her cousin joked that for some, it was hard to listen to her tales when they were focused on her raven hair, kind brown eyes, and ready smile.

Behind her, distant travelers carried building materials through the King's Gate. A line of caravans also loaded grain, jars of oil, and baskets of produce into stone storehouses.

A man's voice rose above the others from the line by the storehouses, his accent clearly Indian. "Where is Adin, the head storekeeper?" he called. The sharpness in his voice drew Esther's full attention.

A young storekeeper—Hebrew, she could tell from his hair—cowered slightly under the Indian's glare.

"Adin and his kin left for Jer-Jerusalem," the storekeeper stuttered.

The Indian scoffed. "Ha, I would not waste my time! Zerubbabel's temple is a poor replacement. If it's a reflection of the Hebrew god, they must not have much of a god at all!"

The comment caused Esther to cringe. Although their conversation continued, the men's voices lowered, and Esther returned her attention to her audience.

The young man's gaze turned back to hers, and he had a far-off look in his eyes. Esther saw him swallow, and then he gave her a weak, pensive smile. "Do you agree?"

"You can remove a people from their land, but you cannot remove a land from its people." Esther's eyebrow lifted, surprised by how easily her cousin's words slipped from her lips.

"I suppose there is always that," he said, adjusting his turban. Then he settled back, resting against one elbow to listen.

"What story do you have for us today, Dido?" an older woman asked.

Dido, "beloved one" and the first Phoenician princess. It was the name she went by in the marketplace.

"What type of story would you like today? A Babylonian tale? Or perhaps an Ethiopian legend?"

"Hebrew," a voice called from the cobblestone roadway.

Esther glanced over and spotted a familiar man approaching with a woman by his side. Esther's lower lip puckered as she recognized Nazanin's parents, Jabez and Mara. The last time she'd talked to them months ago, they were preparing for their journey to Jerusalem. Sadly, they hadn't heard from their daughter since the day of the queen's banquet. They didn't know whether Nazanin lived or died, but they had other children to consider. The family toiled to leave Susa before King Xerxes's return, and with the announcement that the king's armies were on their way home, there was no time to waste.

Esther jumped to her feet, hurried to them, and embraced the couple. Pulling back, she looked into Mara's eyes, noting sadness. "Is today the day?"

Nazanin's mother nodded. "Yes, but we both agreed we'd come by for one last story."

"Well, I won't keep you then. Come."

Esther returned to her seat. Nazanin's parents sat before her, as did others in the crowd. Remembering Haman's eunuch, who stood behind her, Esther's throat tightened, and the taste of bile rose. Thinking again of Haman, she immediately knew the story she would tell.

"There are many Hebrew stories you may have heard. Of a young man named David, who defeated a giant, or a woman named Deborah, who led an army," Esther started. "But there are less common ones you may not know."

Her eyes moved from face to face, making eye contact with the dozen people who sat before her. "Perhaps the story I share today, about a Hebrew king named Saul, will be new to you. It's a story about a time Saul disobeyed Yahweh and what resulted from it."

Pausing her gaze on Nazanin's father, Esther noted his wrinkled forehead, lifted brows, and worried look. Did Jabez already guess the story she prepared to tell and its connection with the impious noble, Haman, who walked through the King's Gate daily?

Esther cleared her throat. "During the time of Saul, the discord with the Philistines was fierce. Knowing how great an enemy he had, Saul enlisted men for the king's service whenever he noticed any strong or brave man.

"It was during this time that Samuel, Yahweh's diviner, came to Saul with a message from Yahweh. 'Thus says Yahweh,' the prophet Samuel said, '"I will punish Amalek for what he did to Israel, how he ambushed the populace on their journey out of Egypt. Now go and attack the Amalekites and devote to destruction all that belongs to them. Spare not men, women, or children. Put to death even their ox and sheep, their camels and donkeys."'"

As Esther spoke, more men and women gathered, and she lifted her voice louder. Perhaps the people were drawn in because they'd never heard the story. Or maybe they were intrigued to hear how the Hebrew god, Yahweh, directed a great king.

"King Saul gathered his army and went to the city of Amalek and set up an ambush in the valley. Saul warned the Kenites—another people in the land—of the battle to come, for they had shown kindness to the Israelites. Heeding the warning, the Kenites fled.

"Saul then slaughtered the Amalekites from Havilah all the way to Shur, east of Egypt." Esther waved her hand as if slashing with a sword. "And while Saul devoted himself to destroy all the people with the sword, he took King Agag alive.

"King Saul spared Agag's life and kept the best of the sheep and the goats. The king tried to hide his misdeeds, but Yahweh's word came to Samuel, 'I regret that I made Saul king, for he has turned away from following Me and has not carried out my commands.'"

As if punctuating her story, the sounds of sheep bleating and doves cooing came from the marketplace.

"Early the next morning, Samuel went to find King Saul. When Samuel found him, Saul greeted Samuel cheerfully. 'Blessed be you to Yahweh, for I have carried out Yahweh's commands.'

"But Samuel said, 'What then is the bleating of sheep in my ears and the lowing of cattle?'" Esther frowned and set her hands on her hips, mimicking the prophet. Then she paused and tapped her chin. "Saul made the excuse that the sheep and the cattle were spared to be offered as *sacrifices* to Yahweh, but Samuel was not fooled. 'Does the Lord delight in burnt offerings and sacrifices as much as obedience to His voice? Behold, obedience is better than sacrifice, and to listen than the fat of rams.'"

Esther paused her words, and a hush fell over the crowd. Then she pointed beyond the crowd, lowering her voice. "'Because you, Saul, have rejected the word of Yahweh, He has rejected you as king.'"

She expected the crowd to gasp at the decree, but instead, they hunkered down as if they were the ones being scolded. And, instead of their eyes focusing on her, their now fear-filled gazes looked to someone behind her.

The hairs on the back of her neck stood on end, and though she opened her mouth to continue, no words came. Esther knew, without looking, that Haman the Agagite stood behind her— Haman, the descendant of King Agag from the story. The pagan king whom Saul had failed to kill. Haman was also Amalek's descendant. Haman's ancestors, the Amalekites, attacked the weary Israelites on their desert sojourn out of Egypt.

A throbbing in Esther's temples warned her not to continue her story. For even though Saul failed, Samuel the prophet ensured Agag's death.

Esther wished she had the bravery to turn around and look Haman in the eye. She imagined herself turning and pointing at his chest, at the idolatrous images. *Agag, your ancestor, died by the prophet's hand, and God decreed that all of your family—with its evil practices—would be blotted out of remembrance.*

She eyed the waiting crowd and breathed in. Then Esther looked at the faces of Nazanin's parents. Even though Haman's presence was a threat, her friends needed this story of hope for their journey. Jabez and Mara needed to be reminded that even though evil may seem to win for a time, the people of Yahweh would receive victory in the end.

Esther opened her mouth, and an urgency to finish the story propelled her to her feet. "Knowing Yahweh's request must be kept, Samuel said, 'Bring me Agag—'"

"Esther, no!" A shout filled the air, and a man's hand circled her arm. Attempting to keep her balance, Esther jerked her arm away. Everything within her told her to run from the wicked Haman. It was only as she realized the man had called her Esther—instead of Dido—that she knew who'd grabbed her.

Hot tears filled her eyes. She turned to see Mordecai, pale and hunched as if expecting a blow at any moment. Haman stood next to her cousin with a dark glare fixed on her.

Esther's first instinct was also to cower. Instead, she straightened her shoulders. Before her, Haman's narrowed gaze flashed both anger and fear. *Fear?* Yes, he knew the story too.

Her brows furrowed, and her eyes widened as the truth became clear. Despite his power and prestige, Haman no doubt was tormented by the knowledge that the Hebrew god had twice marked his people for death. Even though Haman did not know her and Mordecai to be Jews, did he sense it? Or maybe the evil one in him rose against Yahweh's chosen children.

With a snarl, Haman stepped forward, yet Esther held her ground. She gently pried her cousin's hands off her arm.

Even as Haman's eyes blazed and his hands balled into fists, Esther lifted her head higher. She then raised one eyebrow in a question as if she did not know what the official was angry about.

Just when she expected Haman to lift his fist to strike her or order one of the nearby soldiers to do the deed, the gentlest touches brushed her chin. Mordecai's quivering hand touched her face and then turned her chin to face him.

Mordecai's lips pressed tight, keeping his face motionless until he had her attention. "Esther, Storyteller, do not finish your tale. As the saying goes, silence is a fence around wisdom." Although he no longer cowered, fear flashed in her cousin's eyes. Mordecai forced himself to be strong for her when he could not be strong for himself.

From the corner of her eye, Esther spotted Haman tugging at the hem of his tunic shirt and gritting his teeth.

Esther pulled back from his touch. "My name is Dido, sir. You must have the wrong person." Then she swept her arm toward the crowd but paused when she saw two guards approaching. "A Hebrew story was requested, and that's the first one that came to mind."

"Are there no other stories you can tell?" Haman snapped. "Or perhaps it would be better if my guard removed you from this marketplace once and for all."

Before she could answer, Mordecai moaned and placed a hand on his chest.

Seeing her cousin's distress, Esther relaxed her shoulders. As much as she wanted to finish the story—to remind Haman that Yahweh's will was the destruction of the Agagites—it would just bring more pain than good.

Looking at Jabez and Mara, Esther noted tears were filling their eyes too. They'd come for a story; the last thing they needed was to see her dragged away. Hadn't they already faced enough pain?

Blowing out slowly to still her pounding heart, Esther knew she must submit. Even though she wanted the story to take a jab at Haman, she wished for peace for her friends and cousin even more.

Her eyes flashed to Mordecai and then back to Haman. She pressed her hands together, touching her fingertips under her chin, and bowed—first to Mordecai and then to Haman. "I—I'm sorry. I meant no offense."

"Do not..." Haman's breathing was labored. "Do not continue." His growl was more evident with each word.

Esther bowed even lower. "No, I will not continue with that story, sir. I regret any offense."

Looking down at the cobblestone under her feet, Esther waited for Haman to leave. Instead, he strode around behind her and paused. *What more does he want from me?*

Her eyes fluttered closed, and she whispered a quick prayer, seeking Yahweh to give her the right words to escape this situation. Faster than she imagined, the answer came.

Tears filled Esther's eyes as she looked again at Mordecai, ignoring Haman's glare.

"I am sorry, Mordecai, *my friend,* but this story was a reminder. And a warning. Our king, Xerxes, is returning, is he not? And even though he did not fully conquer the Greeks, he is our king."

She placed a palm to her chest just over her heart, fingers splayed. "All of us, from the least to the greatest, must still give reverence to our king." Then looking away from her cousin, she turned to the crowd. "Obedience is better than sacrifice. It is what our returning king will desire."

Behind her, Haman took a step closer. With a tug, he yanked off her headscarf. Then he lifted her hair and let it slide through his fingers. Haman's breath was warm on her neck. Dropping her hair, he reached his fingers around, sliding against her neck. Then with another soft growl, Haman stroked her cheek with two fingers.

Esther closed her eyes, and it took all her self-control not to recoil from his touch.

"I'd suggest another story to relay the importance of obedience," Haman hissed in her ear.

Esther's eyes fluttered open. "Yes, of course," she managed to whisper. She stared straight ahead. Still, she refused to turn, refused to shrink back. Finally, with mutterings she couldn't make out, Haman strode away.

A collective breath released from the crowd, and Esther felt her shoulders droop. She'd been a fool. She hoped her weak explanations had been enough and that she didn't now wear an invisible target on her back.

The crowd dispersed as soon as Haman's form disappeared through the King's Gate. Even Nazanin's parents slipped away without a word to her, and Esther didn't blame them.

Casting a look over her shoulder, she saw Mordecai locking the door to his office. And even though Haman had left, his eunuch still studied her intently.

Shivers raced down Esther's arms. The last thing they needed was for the eunuch to realize the true connection between her and Mordecai. She didn't need her cousin to be considered an enemy of Haman too. Crossing her arms over her chest, Esther strode away.

She walked toward home. Then the sound of footsteps behind her caused her to quicken her pace. *The eunuch, he follows.*

She hurried to a near run, and Esther's breathing grew labored from the movement and fear. If she cried for help, would anyone come? The citizens of Susa knew better than to stand up against one of the palace guards.

The footfalls sounded closer, and Esther knew it was no use running. Pausing her steps, she turned, closed her eyes, and lifted her hands to cover her face, preparing to block the blows.

"Esther."

Her eyes opened, and she saw the face of Mordecai.

"Oh, Cousin." Her knees grew even weak, and she fell into his arms. "I'm sorry. So, so sorry."

Instead of indulging her, Mordecai pulled back—holding her at arm's length. He spoke to her between clenched teeth. "Why in the heavens would you choose to tell that story? You must have seen his guard. You must have known that Haman, the *Agagite,* was in the marketplace."

Regret washed over her, and Esther's chin trembled. "He and his people are enemies of Yahweh." Her voice was low. "And it's not right that first he has a part in deposing the queen, and then he acts as if he's the king himself—as if his judgments would be of any use to the people." Her blood seemed to simmer in her veins as her words continued to flow. "I remember the lustful, greedy look on his face the night of Queen Vashti's banquet," she continued, her voice low. "I know Haman had something to do with what happened to the queen. And to Nazanin. I wanted Haman to feel even just one prick of pain after all the heartache he's caused."

Mordecai placed a finger to his lips. "Esther, please, you cannot speak such things in public." He looked over his shoulder and scanned the roads. Seemingly satisfied that they were not being followed, Mordecai took her elbow and led her the rest of the way to their door, guiding her inside.

Once the door was closed, Mordecai sank onto the nearest stool as if his legs no longer held him.

Esther clenched her hands together and paced. "I saw the guard, but I didn't see Haman—not when I started the story. Part of me knew telling the tale would be dangerous. Another part wanted Haman to hear—to remember that his ancestors' wicked deeds have not been forgotten. And maybe remember that his actions will also be judged."

Her cousin lowered his head and ran his hands through his hair. "Do you not see the problem you have caused?" Then his red-rimmed eyes peered up at her. "I've told you that my father worked for the Babylonian kings. Haman's father did too. And while I have always known Haman was an Agagite, he's never known me to be a Jew." Mordecai's eyes squeezed shut.

What had he seen in Babylon—lived through? Had the treatment of the Jews been so horrendous that Mordecai still chose to hide his identity after all these years?

Esther's eyebrows puckered. "Why would he think you were a Jew now? Why would he think either of us was?"

"Only a Hebrew would know that story of Samuel and Saul. Only a Hebrew would understand the meaning of Haman being a descendant of the Amalekites and that Yahweh has demanded their destruction." Mordecai released a low moan. "Haman is an enemy of the Jews, just as his ancestors have been, yes?"

Esther nodded. "And if Haman is quick to bring pain to others like Vashti and her maids, how much more will he do so to anyone he knows is a Jew." Esther swayed at the realization that one man's offense could put an end to all their dreams, all their plans. "The last thing we need before we journey to Jerusalem is to stand out as problems to Haman."

"And to the returning king," Mordecai added. "Haman is an official in Xerxes's court. He has the king's ear."

Esther paced the floor as Mordecai talked. "I understand your worries, but just because I told one of the Hebrew stories doesn't give anything away. I tell many tales from many lands. The first story Haman heard me tell was the story of the great flood. It was that night I stood before the queen."

Mordecai wiped his hand across his face and then pinched his brow. "I hope you are correct. I hope I am making too much of this." Mordecai spoke through clenched teeth. His face pinched as if he were holding back tears. "But you were not in Babylon, *Hadassah*. I was just a child, but still, I remember the targeted abuse. The stories of Daniel and Hananiah, Mishael, and Azariah—or as the Babylonians called them, Shadrach, Meshach, and Abednego—are just two of many experiences."

Mordecai's jaw clenched as he spoke. "I remember Haman's father, Hammedatha, an astrologer like Haman. But more than an astrologer, Hammedatha was an enemy of the Jews. Haman, too, is an enemy of the Jews. If we are known, we are no longer safe. It would not be far enough even if we travel to Jerusalem." Fear radiated in Mordecai's gaze as she'd never seen before.

Esther searched for the words to calm his fear. "You say that Haman sees the Jews as enemies, but there are many Jews in Susa, many more than us."

Mordecai again ran a hand through his dark hair, making it stand on end. "Yes, but Haman isn't concerned with all Jews, only those of importance—like an official at the gate. Or those he deems a threat—like a storyteller who makes him look like a fool before a listening crowd."

With her cousin's words, the severity of what she'd done punched her like a fist to her gut. Esther staggered back, pressing against the wall. Feeling her strength give, she slid down the wall onto a cushion on the floor. She placed her hands on her head and shivered, remembering how Haman had tugged off her headscarf. Had he dropped it? Had he kept it? Her stomach lurched, thinking he had.

Did he keep it as a reminder of her insolence? Was Mordecai correct? Had she just placed herself and Mordecai before Haman as problems to be crushed?

"Maybe you're making too much of this," she said again, even though her words held no hope. "And our people should have listened to Yahweh and obeyed His laws, just as Saul should have. Because of our lack of repentance, we were exiled to Babylon—an exile that Yahweh said would last seventy years. And though that time has passed, many Jews have chosen to remain."

Mordecai tugged on his beard as he often did when distressed. "Just as Agag is Haman's ancestor, don't forget, Esther, that Saul is ours. We are Benjamites in Saul's lineage. Although we are from the smallest tribe, our ancestors were once known for their courage. As much as I'd like to think that someday our tribe will redeem itself from Saul's sin, yet again, an Agagite is in a position of power."

Esther pressed her hands to her forehead, allowing his words sink in. Her mind swirled, seeking any threads of hope.

"We still do not know if Haman understands we are Jews— or even related. Perhaps you were just an official helping a friend." Esther's voice rose. "More than that, the king returns tomorrow or the day after. Haman will be too busy securing his own position of power under Xerxes to think about us."

Mordecai sat silent, and Esther guessed he was replaying the day's events. She looked to the shelf with their bread and considered cooking the artichokes she'd purchased from the market yesterday, but she knew it would do no good. She doubted either of them would eat their evening meal tonight.

"Your position will be given to your fellow who is worthier than you," Mordecai muttered, seeming to speak more to himself.

Esther tilted her head. "Yes, those were the words of the decree written against Queen Vashti."

"I know." Mordecai nodded once. "They are also the words of the prophet Samuel which he spoke to King Saul, 'Yahweh has this day torn the kingship over Israel away from you and has given it to your fellow who is *worthier than you.*'" He sighed. "Will we ever be considered worthy enough, Esther, to rise to the favor and status God once designed for our people?"

Esther's heart sank, hearing those words. Mordecai knew the truth. Even in Susa, a city that tolerated all religions, the Jews were never truly free. Not when Yahweh required they live set apart. Not when their history was full of enemies. And not when one of the descendants of those enemies had even a shred of power.

CHAPTER NINE

Three days later

Esther walked over the cobblestone to her familiar spot on the platform near Mordecai's office, by the grand staircases that led up to the king's palace. It had taken her days to get up the nerve to return. She scanned the marketplace for any sign of Haman or his eunuchs.

The hot wind ruffled her hair, carrying with it the sweet aroma of cut flowers and the intense odors of dried fish and herbs. A steady mingling of voices was punctuated by shop owners calling out to buyers to come and view their wares.

On either side of the staircase, which led up through the King's Gate, scribes and accountants had set up their booths, doing their official work translating documents and collecting taxes and tributes.

Soldiers guarded the gate and milled around buyers with watchful gazes. One guard was especially interested in a thin beggar who eyed a piece of ripe fruit from a pyramid of oranges. Of course, he'd be a fool to try to steal it, no matter how hungry he was. The usual punishment for such a crime was the loss of fingers or even a whole hand.

Market stalls stretched in both directions, and a cacophony of animal sounds and voices rose. Merchants built stools and tables from wood brought in from distant lands and worth nearly as much as gold. Hammers pounded against the cedar, adding to the noise.

Persian women moved from stall to stall, purchasing their daily items. Their bright tunics swished as they walked.

Vendors sold apricots, eggplants, oranges, and limes. One woman and her daughter stood behind a table filled with small clay spice jars. The wind carried the aroma of cinnamon, cardamom, cloves, and saffron, but even those wonderful smells didn't lift Esther's spirits.

The marketplace was the same but also different. Although the sun shone brightly, a dark shadow seemed to hover over the place.

"Have another story today, Dido?" An older woman, a jewelry vendor, angled Esther a glance as she passed.

Esther paused. "What's a day without a story to bring excitement?" She gave a rueful laugh.

The woman nodded. "Of course, maybe you should stay with Persian tales of bravery, eh? It seems even the stone statues have ears at the gate these days."

The woman reached out her hand, offering Esther something she clutched in her fist. Esther stretched an open palm to the woman. Her eyes widened as the vendor placed a red bead in the shape of a rose into Esther's palm.

Esther gasped, studying its intricate design. "Is this for me?"

The woman nodded. "Yes, a gift." She waved her hands in front of her. "There is no need to pay. But..." The woman leaned toward Esther, lowering her voice. "You must remember, Dido, that she who wants a rose must respect the thorn."

Esther opened her mouth to ask the woman to explain, but a customer hustled up, drawing away the vendor's attention. Esther continued on.

The woman had called her Dido and had heard her stories. No doubt she had witnessed the recent confrontation with Haman. While storytelling had always been a delight, for the first time, Esther truly understood the power of her words.

Yahweh, help me to watch my tongue and only to speak as I should. Please. Let my words be used for the good, not the harm, of my people.

Weighted dread settled in her chest as she approached the platform with her cushion. What if those listening sought a double meaning behind her words? What if other officials took offense to her stories? What if Haman returned? She'd never be able to live with herself if harm came to her cousin because of something she said.

Thankfully, no one gathered at her feet today. Maybe word had gotten out about the confrontation with Haman. Not that it mattered. Mordecai had told her just last night that they'd have enough money saved up within a few months to travel to Jerusalem. And even though Esther had longed for the Holy City since childhood, a new reality hit. She'd be leaving behind all she knew. Even more, she had no husband to go with her. Would she ever marry? Mordecai tried to assure her that he could find a husband in Israel, but Mordecai's face had flushed as he spoke, and he didn't seem convinced with his own words.

As Esther watched, a new group of women walked among the Persians. The Elamites were the native women of Susa before Cyrus the Great made them Persians. Even though

Elam was no longer a political power, Elamite was still one of the three official languages of the empire and was used in administrative texts. And the people still worshiped the Elamite deities, including the mother goddess Kiririsha.

Esther considered calling out to the women and offering a story about their "mother of gods," but changed her mind. Even if it could make a few coins, she just didn't have the heart for it today.

More shoppers gathered at the next stall, eyeing the luxurious fabrics. One woman glanced in Esther's direction and smiled. Then she tugged on the arm of someone who looked like her mother and pointed. "Look, the storyteller is here."

With a look of delight, the older woman hurried to Esther and motioned for her daughter to follow.

"Dido, can you tell us a wonderful story? Last time you told us of the building of Zerubbabel's temple in Jerusalem. And the time before that how the Medes and the Persians conquered the world."

Esther forced a smile. Remembering her talk with Mordecai, she knew what story she wanted to tell. "I can tell you about the night Darius the Mede conquered the Babylonian empire, and the handwriting on the wall." She clasped her hands together and forced a smile. "It is a wonderful tale."

The women sat down in front of her, wrapping their skirts around their legs.

White fluffy clouds dotted the blue sky, drifting lazily on the gentle breeze. Esther adjusted her new headscarf and pulled her black braid around to the front, running her fingers along the end.

As the women leaned forward to listen, Esther noticed a figure approaching. She didn't have to look over to know it was her cousin. He undoubtedly acted as if he were drawn to her words, but Esther knew the truth. Mordecai worried. Perhaps his presence would cause her to be more careful with her words.

"The great king of Babylon, King Belshazzar, held a great banquet for thousands of nobles," she said with a smile. "Preparing for a feast, he ordered his servants to serve wine in the gold and silver goblets that his father Nebuchadnezzar had taken from Solomon's temple in Jerusalem. The servants brought out the goblets. The king and his nobles, wives, and concubines drank from them. As they drank, the king's guests praised the gods of gold and silver, of bronze, iron, wood, and stone."

Next to her, Morecadi's body stiffened. Without having to look, Esther knew that Haman was striding through the gate. As she continued her story, she glanced over to see four guards flanking him. Without hesitation, Haman marched in their direction. Esther's words caught in her throat as Mordecai jumped to his feet.

"Why hasn't the new shipment of stones reached the palace?" Haman's voice cut off her words. "Our building project has been put on hold, which does not make King Xerxes happy. He wishes to know the reason for this delay this very day."

King Xerxes? Is he home? Even though Esther hadn't been at the market for the last three days, she still would have expected to hear the news.

Mordecai's wide eyes and dropped jaw told her he hadn't known either. Had the great king slipped in last night? Surely he could have guessed what joy it would have brought his people to have their king home.

Then again, Xerxes didn't return as a conquering warrior. Esther's heart sank thinking of him arriving under cover of darkness to keep from drawing attention to himself.

Mordecai pulled in a deep breath, motioning to the line of offices and storehouses built along the wall. "Are there not a dozen other officials you can ask the same question?" And even though her cousin spoke bravely, Esther noted a glint of fear in his eyes.

"Do you dare question me, dog?" Haman bared his teeth and seethed. "Do you not realize that I could have you torn limb from limb with one snap of my fingers?"

Mordecai cocked an eyebrow. And Esther knew then that the king's presence had changed matters in her cousin's eyes. "Really? A meaningless death, and the outrage of the people at the market. Is this how you wish to welcome *our* king home? He just arrived last night, did he not?"

Haman's lips pressed together. He blinked as if mulling over Mordecai's words.

"Would you rather continue threatening me, or would you like your answer about the stones?" Mordecai jutted out his chin.

When Haman didn't respond, Mordecai pointed to the west. "Word came that the shipment of stones will be here before nightfall. A messenger sent word of their upcoming arrival."

"Yes, very well." Even though Haman spouted no more threats, he looked at Mordecai as if he were a hungry jackal and her cousin a piece of meat to be devoured.

Esther's cheeks burned at the sight.

Then, as if remembering something, Haman's eyes brightened. "Yes, I will meet you back here at nightfall." Even as Haman spoke to Mordecai, his gaze turned to Esther. "A new decree is being written up even now. One that will be of interest to both of you."

A decree? King Xerxes had just arrived home. What order could he possibly have for all his subjects when he'd only had one night of sleep in his bed?

Esther never had the chance to finish her story. Within no time, word had gotten out that Xerxes had returned and a new decree would soon be posted.

The marketplace filled. The people's voices rose with questions about the decree and opinions about the king's silent return. As she remained on her mat, voices assaulted her from every direction. With so many ideas and opinions, it was hard to know who to listen to, as everyone talked at once.

"The king has returned? Why were we not informed?"

"Xerxes burned Athens, yet he leaves his highest commander to fight while he's given up and returned to Susa?"

"Maybe the king has returned to build up his army once again. Xerxes is not one to be afraid. Fear, for a Persian, is the equivalent of slavery."

The voices around Esther buzzed, but she could think of nothing else but the decree. What were the king's wishes so soon after returning home?

The hours ticked by, and still no word. Esther remained on her cushion, but no one asked for a story. One couldn't think of legends when their returning king would soon post a new rule.

The sun lowered to the horizon. Just when Esther believed Haman must be lying about the decree, the sound of soldiers marching sounded from the direction of the bridge. She stood and moved to get a better look, and then an arm wrapped around her shoulders, spinning her away from the view of the gate. She cried out, and then she realized it was Mordecai. He pulled her toward him in the opposite direction of the surging crowd.

With frantic movements, Mordecai pushed through the crowd. He pulled her away from the gates, moving down the road to their home.

"Stop! What are you doing?" Esther's feet struggled to keep pace. As he pulled her, Esther's body slammed into one person and then another, but Mordecai still rushed ahead. Dodging an older woman with a cane, Esther stumbled and barely caught herself.

She pulled harder on her arm, trying to break free. "Cousin, stop. Let go! What is this about?"

But still, he moved on without turning back or giving her a reason for his frantic pace.

Finally, the crowd thinned, and Mordecai's footsteps slowed slightly. Esther tried to pull her arm from his grip one more time, but it was no use. "Mordecai, please stop. You're hurting me."

As if hearing her for the first time, Mordecai paused. Though his face was red and his breaths came in heavy panting, he did not release her arm. "We need to get you home. You have to hide."

Esther shook her head, not understanding. "What do you mean I have to hide? Does this have something to do with the decree? Have you heard?"

His trembling chin and lips told her he had.

An icy sensation washed over her. She had been there when Xerxes's decree had been proclaimed against Vashti. Even though the edict had been unreasonable, no one questioned it. Within a few hours, the queen had been gone. Yet if Mordecai's rasping breaths were any indication, this had to be worse.

"Yes, let's go. Now let go of my arm."

Mordecai's fingers released. Esther rubbed the red marks on her skin and darted to their home. This time, it was Mordecai who struggled to keep up. As soon as they entered their home, Mordecai closed the front door while Esther secured the window.

Mordecai's labored breathing filled the room, and cries carried down the road from the marketplace. Esther wasn't sure if they were happy cries or ones of sadness and shock, but it was clear that whatever Xerxes required from his people on his return had struck the people to their core.

CHAPTER TEN

Esther was in front of her cousin in three quick strides. She reached up and grasped his upper arms. "Please, Cousin. Tell me what's going on."

Mordecai's lower lip trembled. He glanced around. "We should have left. Maybe it's not too late. If we leave tonight…" He mumbled, not making any sense.

Esther knelt before him. She placed her cheek on his knee as she used to when she was a child. "I need you to tell me what the decree said and why you are so worried."

Coming to his senses, he stroked her hair. Then Esther pulled back and noticed tears rimming his eyes.

"I overheard two of the king's eunuchs talking." His words came out with a shudder. "The king is searching for a new queen."

"A new queen?" His fear made no sense. She flinched back slightly and shrugged. "Well, that is to be expected. I don't understand why terror has ahold of you."

He reached for her face, holding it tight. "You do not understand." Mordecai again awkwardly stroked her hair. "The king has appointed agents in each province to bring beautiful young women into the royal harem. These women will be given beauty treatments, and each will go to the king's bed. The young woman who pleases the king the most will be made queen to take the place of Vashti."

"So that is what concerns the king on his first day back, his need for a queen?" Esther pushed away and rose to her feet, shaking her head. "It makes sense. I'm sure many young women wish for such an opportunity. The chance to live in the palace, even in a harem, would be welcome by some. Then there is the possibility of becoming a queen."

"You don't understand." Mordecai's voice was harsh as he lowered his head into his hands. "These young women will not have a choice."

"Are you saying they will round up young women to take to the king, whether they like it or not?" Esther gasped, placing a hand on her neck.

"Yes." The word choked from Mordecai's mouth. "Guards are being sent out even tonight." He lifted his gaze to her, tears filling his eyes. "And I heard the guards at the gate talking. They know all the beautiful young virgins of Susa. After all, they watch them come and go from the market."

He stood and turned toward the bolted door, clutching his fists. "I heard the men joking about the luck of their king, and I heard..." His voice trailed off.

Esther stepped forward and placed a hand on his back. "What did you hear?" A sinking feeling in her gut warned her of the truth to come.

"One of the guards stated that if he had a choice, Dido, the storyteller, would be at the top of the list. One guard said you visited his dreams at night." Mordecai shook his head. "And you do not want to know the rest."

A gasp escaped Esther's lips. "They mentioned my name?" Her nose wrinkled. "But that's not what I want. We have plans to go to Jerusalem. I want a husband who shares my belief. I want children." Her eyes narrowed. "The last thing I want is to be part of the king's harem—just a body to..." Esther pressed her lips tight, halting her words.

Mordecai fumbled with his outer tunic and then held up a small purse. "If we leave now, we might be able to get out of the city before they realize you're gone." He glanced around the room. "We'll have to leave almost everything behind except food and extra clothes." Mordecai pressed his hand against his head. "But once out of the city, we can find a caravan. We can work on how to gain more funds...."

"But your position at the gate, what of that? Someone will miss you. Someone will come looking for you. Even more, will we be able to slip out? Perhaps even now, the guards are stationed on the roadways."

The guards. She'd once seen them as protectors but not anymore.

Esther crossed her arms over her chest. She felt ill that the guards had noticed her at the gate in such a way. To know what they thought of her, dreamed of her.

All these years, she thought her stories drew the crowds. Her stomach turned. Had the guards ever listened to her stories, or had they just filled their minds with lustful thoughts?

Yes, it was better to leave, but to do so would mean leaving everything.

"Do we just leave our home? All we have?" she asked. They did not have great wealth, but this was the only home she remembered.

"Staying is not safe for you. After others read the decree, they might wish to leave too. We need to get ahead of them. I imagine many fathers may feel the same as I—Xerxes's bed is not our dream for our daughters."

Tears filled Esther's eyes to hear Mordecai refer to himself as her father. She felt the same about their relationship—loved him as a daughter would—but sometimes she worried she was more of a burden than a joy. She was thankful Mordecai didn't think of her that way and didn't want her to go. Yet what choice did they have?

Esther nodded and moved toward the shelves where they stored their food. "We can make two bundles, one for food and one for clothes—"

The pounding on the door interrupted her words. Esther froze.

In unison, she and Mordecai looked to the back door. It was their only way of escape.

"Dido! Open up," a guard growled on the other side of the door. "You are requested to come to the palace by the king's edict."

Sucking in a breath, Esther looked at her cousin. "Do we leave now? Leave everything?"

Without hesitation, he pointed to the back door and nodded. Then, Mordecai rushed to her and pressed the money bag into her hand. "Esther, go. I will find you."

Before Esther had time to respond, the back door opened. A form stepped inside. The light of a torch flickered on the guard's face.

The guard strode forward, placing his free hand on the dagger that hung on his belt. This was no ordinary guard from the King's Gate. He wore a woven tunic with a golden collar. Fine robes flapped behind him as he walked. He was one of the palace guards.

The soldier paused before her. As he hovered over Esther, she noted a fresh scar on his cheek. *Has he just returned from Greece with the king himself?*

Mordecai shuffled to the man with arms stretched out as if welcoming a guest. Finally, her cousin lifted his eyes and met the guard's gaze. "Can I help you?" Mordecai cleared his throat.

The pounding on the front door continued, but the soldier gave it no mind. He clucked his tongue. "Mordecai, correct? I'm told that is your name. You don't seem surprised to have one of the palace guards enter your courtyard and walk through your back door."

Then the guard's face scrunched with mocking. "*Can I help you?*" he mimicked. "Ha! You don't seem surprised because you no doubt know why I'm here. Well, yes, you can help me. The beauty of your cousin has been noticed and appreciated. A decree has been posted just today declaring our king's desire—I'm sure you have heard."

"Decree?" Mordecai rubbed his brow, feigning confusion. "Is that also what the pounding on the door is all about?"

The guard's hand moved to the dagger in his belt. Esther's lips drew tight, and she slowly breathed, resisting the urge to plead for him to leave them be. A guard—a soldier fresh from the battlefield—would have no patience with her pleas.

Glancing over his shoulder at her, the guard smiled. Then he flexed his hand, moving it away from his dagger and back to his side. "Yes, well, since we are playing a game of ignorance, King Xerxes desires a new wife. He decrees that all the beautiful virgins be gathered up and brought to him."

"Gathered up? Do you mean to become part of his harem?" Esther placed a hand over her heart. Even though Mordecai had said the same thing, it was hard to believe.

"What more could a poor girl ask for than to be brought into the royal harem?" The guard offered a crooked smile, and she noticed a few missing teeth. "In the king's harem, there will be no concerns about who to marry. You will no longer have to clean or bake bread."

Esther smoothed her frock and squared her shoulders. "I do not mind my tasks. It is an honor to serve in all the ways I can."

Again, a knock sounded at the door. Releasing an impatient grunt, the guard moved forward and unbolted it. The door swung open.

Another guard, wearing the same uniform, stepped inside. "Let me guess. Is this one resisting? Is Dido weaving a tale to stall?" The guard widened his stance and placed his hands on his hips, looking more impatient than angry.

Mordecai took a step forward, bowing and spreading his hands before both men in a plea. "My cousin needs time to consider."

With the swoop of his hand and a flick of his wrist, the first guard withdrew his dagger and pressed the blade against Mordecai's throat. His movements were quick, and Esther knew one wrong move would end her cousin's life. Watching, the second guard lifted his brows in amusement.

"No, please," she dared to whisper, reaching out a hand.

"Your beautiful cousin has no choice," the guard growled near Mordecai's ear. "Why fight it? Many young women will find great joy in being loved by the king." Then he returned the dagger to his belt and shrugged.

Loved? Is that what he called it?

"Can you have no mercy?" Mordecai asked as the guards turned toward Esther.

She felt her legs growing weak under her.

Mordecai lifted his hands to the men, palms up, bowing and prostrating before them. "What becomes of the women in the harem if something happens to the king? And what kind of life is that, being one of many lovers instead of being a wife and mother—having her own home? What type of life?"

The second guard looked at Esther, and she noted no hint of compassion in his eyes. "That does not matter now," he shouted. "It's a mandate from the king that cannot be revoked."

"What is the problem?" A new voice called from the doorway—a voice that made the hair on Esther's arms stand on end.

Haman strode through the front door, and an icy coldness dropped into the pit of her stomach. In the flickering torchlight, the demonic beasts embroidered into Haman's garments swayed as if mocking her.

"It has already been decided that your cousin, Dido—or, should we say, Esther—is to be brought before the king," Haman continued. "King Xerxes has requested the most beautiful women of his kingdom, and I know of no beauty as great as this one."

Then, pausing before her, Haman reached into his robe and pulled out a cloth object. At first, Esther did not recognize it, but as he slowly unfolded it, Esther saw that it was her head scarf. Her neck muscles tensed, and her stomach threatened to heave as Haman lifted the scarf to his face and brushed it down his cheek, breathing in deeply. "Who am I to withhold what the king requests?" Haman cooed.

Esther glanced at her cousin, noting helplessness and shock on his face. Then the look in Mordecai's eyes evolved from desperation to resolve. His hands at his sides balled into fists.

Cousin, no!

She knew, at that moment, Mordecai would fight for her, even if it resulted in his death.

Yahweh, calm him. Protect him! Silent words flew up in urgent prayer.

Turning back to Haman, Esther took a step forward. Her knees still trembled, but she relaxed her shoulders and forced herself to calm down. "I will go," she stated plainly. Pleasure brightened Haman's eyes.

"Esther, no!"

"But first," she continued, ignoring her cousin's cry, "before you take me, I'd like a few minutes with my cousin…to reassure him."

The first guard strode toward her small bedroom and glanced around. Seeing there was no door and that the window was too small to escape through, he nodded in that direction with his chin.

Her legs seemed to weigh as much as the cedars of Lebanon as she walked into the room. Mordecai followed. And as she faced him, Esther saw that his fight was gone.

They both understood the truth. Esther had no choice. They'd waited too long to leave, and now it was impossible to travel to the Holy City together.

Esther desired to throw herself onto her sleeping mat and weep for the unfairness of it all, but she knew that would only make things harder for her cousin.

Swallowing down her emotion, she hugged her arms around her waist. What she needed now was strength.

Esther looked around the room that had been hers for as long as she could remember. She was rocked on that same sleeping mat by her father before he passed. And she had the faintest memory of her mother sitting beside her, telling her stories by the window. She and Imma had dreamed of someday going through the King's Gate and across the river together. Never had they dreamed the palace beyond would be her home, her prison.

She turned to the slump-shouldered man who looked much older than his years.

"Cousin, why this?" Her voice was low. "How can I live in such a way?"

Being part of the harem. Being away from the only father I've genuinely ever known. Being taken to the king's bed…

"How can I live in such a way?" she repeated, the words choking out. Esther blinked back tears, trying to stay strong and refusing to let them flow.

"How can you?" Mordecai's voice lowered to a whisper. He lifted his chin and offered a sad smile as if knowing that while he could not save her, perhaps he could send her away with crumbs of hope. "As you've done, *Hadassah,* living as a Jew in a captive land."

"What do you mean?" Her eyes searched his face.

"Faithfulness to Yahweh is a seed that grows in our hearts, no matter the soil it is planted in. You water it with truth and trust." A tear broke loose, and Mordecai pressed a soft fist against his lips before reaching out to take her hands.

"Even though we may not understand, *daughter,* we both have to believe that Yahweh has a purpose. As you are placed with the king's harem, know that you do not have to be concerned with the deeds of others, only yourself."

Esther squeezed his hands, focusing on his words, knowing they were what she needed to get through.

"As far as you are concerned, you will faithfully attend to your husband," Mordecai continued. "As a wife—the king's wife—keep your eyes focused. It does not matter if you are the least loved or if you are chosen as queen. Be the faithful one I have always known you to be, before your husband and before your God." Mordecai lifted Esther's hands and pressed them to his lips. Then with great resolve, he released them.

As if a memory stirred within him, Mordecai's eyes flickered. "Your mother told me to tell you this one day." His eyebrows lifted. "Daughter, do you know what your name means?"

"Esther, yes. It means Star."

"In Persian, yes, but in Hebrew, the root means 'to be hidden.' Think of that. And Hadassah?" he asked.

"Hadassah in Hebrew means myrtle tree."

"You are correct." Mordecai nodded. "And it symbolizes peace, love, and prosperity, which can be summed up in compassion."

Esther looked to the door, knowing that guards would come for her at any moment.

"And in Persian?" Mordecai asked, drawing her attention back to him.

"Hadassah in Persian? I do not know."

"In Persian, Hadassah means *bride*," he whispered.

"Compassion bride..." The words slipped from her lips, and an unexpected peace settled in her heart.

The sound of footsteps neared, and she knew their time together was done.

"Remember this, Hadassah," Mordecai said with his parting words. "The best and most holy place is where God has assigned you. The place where He planned for you to be, even if this place first seems like captivity."

CHAPTER ELEVEN

The echoed cries of young women filled Esther's ears as she walked through the arch of the King's Gate and moved onto the bridge. Dozens of young women shuffled along with her, each one leaving family and home. All chosen for their beauty. And their reward for being stripped from their homes and families? The slim chance to become King Xerxes's queen.

Her hands hung empty at her side. What did she need that the king couldn't provide? Nothing. She needed nothing from her old life now that her new one stretched before her.

Esther walked across the long bridge over the deep ditch, which the people referred to as a river, even though water rarely flowed beyond the King's Gate. Up ahead, the palace complex was divided into two parts—the official section and the private residence. The official section, Apadna, was where the king appeared in formal ceremonies. As for the private residence… Esther never thought, in all her days, that she'd ever visit that part of the palace, let alone call it her home.

Guards surrounded the young women on every side, warning them if they slowed or stopped. Months ago, some of these very men had fought against the Spartans. Now they herded young women no older than girls to their retreating king.

One guard pointed ahead to a part of the palace lit by no less than a thousand oil lanterns. "Over there is the king's residence. Adjacent to it is the House of the Women."

"How many women are there?" the young woman who walked next to Esther dared to ask. Soft reddish-brown curls framed her heart-shaped face.

He scoffed. "There may be one queen, but the king has dozens of concubines—and soon that number grows. Young women will come from every part of his kingdom. Xerxes demands it in his search for a bride."

As she walked, Esther thought of her cousin's words, which she'd heard when she was a child. *"Remember who you are. Remember who our people are. No matter where you go, Yahweh is with you."*

The young women's cries stopped once they entered the outer courtyards of the complex. From the looks of the faces of the other young women, it appeared their fears were forgotten as they took in the extravagance and opulence of the tile floors, sky-high columns, cedar beams, intricate statues, and detailed mosaics.

Beyond the long courtyard, they walked through one guard room and then another. The guards' eyes followed them, some gazes mocking but most guards showing approval with their cocked smiles.

The guards paused on the other side of the guard room, gathering the women into a tighter circle.

"Ahead is the king's chambers and the throne room," the guard explained with a flick of his hand in that direction.

From a glance at the private residence, it was clear Xerxes had spared no cost. The doors were closed, but down the hallways, decorations of Lebanese cedarwood, Egyptian linen curtains, and gold furniture with purple cushions filled the space.

In the marketplace, Esther had seen small trinkets made from these materials. Yet the cost was too great even for a small wooden box, a linen head covering, or a small plush pillow. She couldn't imagine the price of the items in just this one hall. She shook her head, unable to think what it looked like beyond those doors.

"I shall rush there now and tell the king that he need not worry about all the other young women. His new queen, Anahita, is here," a young woman called out. Her blond hair was intricately styled, and she wore a fine robe. "Once Xerxes sees me, the king will know his search is over." Even though she joked, the pink that rose to Anahita's cheeks hinted that she wished it could be so.

The guards laughed almost in unison.

"Try it," one guard teased, "and we'll return your head to your parents this night."

Gasps arose all around Esther, and one young woman began crying again.

"No one is allowed to approach the king unless it is by his request," the guard explained. "Many have tried it, and most have died." He ran his finger across his throat, imitating a knife's swipe.

"Is there no way to approach him and not lose your life?" Anahita asked.

"If the king extends his golden scepter to you, you can live. But he insists on no interruptions. Surely every man, woman, and child in the kingdom of the Persians and the Medes knows of Xerxes's temper. Dare to test it? Try to find Vashti to see how that worked out."

The young woman beside Esther tucked a strand of curly hair behind her ear with a trembling hand.

Esther wrapped an arm around the young woman's shoulders, stooping slightly due to the young woman's petite frame. "Do not worry. There will never be a need to approach the king's throne without being requested, now will there?" She spoke in what she hoped was a soothing tone.

"No, I suppose not." The young woman forced a smile.

"I am Esther," she whispered in the young woman's ear as the guards led them forward.

"I am Leila."

The group, which Esther guessed was at least thirty young women, was led through the first courtyard and then passed beyond the grand banquet hall where she'd feasted with Vashti.

After walking down a long walkway, decorated with cedar and colored tiles, they saw another large hall open before them with a portico facing a spacious courtyard to the north. Tall pillars, topped with capitals, held the roof up.

As they entered this grand room, a dozen eunuchs replaced the soldiers. The eunuchs wore long white linen robes and had shaved heads. Seeing the kindness of the faces of the men put the young woman at ease. Esther saw many of them wiping their tears.

"Please line up," one of the eunuchs asked. Other eunuchs approached, handing out warm, wet towels for them.

"These are to wash your tears," one of the eunuchs stated simply.

Accepting the towel, Esther wiped her face. Then she lifted the cloth to her nose again, breathing in the aromas of jasmine and myrrh.

Pulling in a deep breath and attempting to swallow down the knot of emotion in her throat, she pushed thoughts of Mordecai out of her mind. If she'd learned one thing growing up in Susa, it was that the king's edict was impossible to change. To try meant to lose one's life.

Esther lined up with the other women according to the directions of the eunuchs. Minutes passed, and nothing happened. Finally, a set of doors before them opened. A tall man in a white linen robe hemmed in blue and purple strode in.

This eunuch walked with authority and also with grace. His feet glided over the floor in silver sandals. As he moved, his sleek body reminded Esther of a tall tree in the wind. His muscular form was clear under his robe, and his face was chiseled like one of the statues in the front courtyard.

As he approached the line of young women, Esther got a closer look and guessed he was a few years older than her cousin Mordecai. There was intelligence in his gaze. Immediately, Esther thought of him as someone she could consider a friend.

He sauntered down the line of women with his hands behind him, eyeing each one. Each young woman looked up at him and smiled as he passed, no doubt realizing this man was in control of her fate.

Will he accept me or reject me? Esther didn't know why it mattered, but she longed to see his approval.

Step by step, the man moved closer, his gaze gliding over each young woman. Then the eunuch paused as his eyes met hers.

Esther couldn't help but smile broadly. Her eyebrows lifted slightly, waiting for a response. He took a step to the side as if to get another look. Even though her heart pounded, Esther held his gaze. She was used to meeting the eyes of those in her audience when she told stories, and she knew the strength of a spirited look.

Instead of continuing, he waved her forward. "What is your name?"

She took one step out of the line. "Esther, my lord."

"From your accent, it seems as if Susa is your native home."

"Yes, my lord. You are correct. I've lived my whole life, barely a stone's throw away, not far from the King's Gate."

He nodded once and then stepped back to address all the new arrivals.

Esther returned to her spot in line.

"This wing is for the harem, where the royal ladies live. This wing will be your new home." Even though he didn't raise his voice, he spoke with authority. His eyes moved over the young women with interest and compassion. His gaze paused briefly on Esther again and then moved on.

The two young women flanking Esther eyed her with curiosity. Esther simply shrugged. Maybe he had seen her telling stories in the marketplace? It was the only thing she could think of.

"I am Hegai, the king's eunuch in charge of the harem," the man continued. "I will see that each of you receives the prescribed beauty treatments. You will also be taught court and palace life. After that, each of you will have one night with King Xerxes. The young woman who most pleases the king will be made queen instead of Vashti."

Hegai clasped his hands in front of him. "You are the first group of young women—those found worthy in Susa—but more will come. More young women will be taking the journey to the citadel of Susa, and each province shall be represented. The king's guard has to ensure every beautiful virgin, even from the farthest reaches of Persia, will be brought as an offering to Shahanshah."

As he continued stating his expectations of their obedience and cooperation, Esther's gaze moved around the room, noting the four doorways that entered the hall. Each of the doorways had jambs decorated with stone-carved reliefs. The frame closest to her depicted Xerxes entering the hall. The larger-than-life image of Xerxes was followed by two attendants, one carrying a fly whisk and the other holding a parasol over the king's head.

Esther tilted her head, studying it and remembering a story. Only when she felt an elbow to her ribs did she notice all eyes were on her. She quickly swung her head back to Hegai and noted humor in his gaze.

"I am sorry." Esther dipped in a bow. "Please forgive my inattentiveness. Did you ask me a question, most-honored Hegai?"

The man's brow lifted, causing lines to spread across his forehead. "I do have a question. First, please tell me what you find of interest in that relief you were staring at so intently."

Esther pressed her lips together and nodded. "Yes, of course." Then she took two steps closer to the image. "This is our great king, Xerxes, and his two attendants. One attendant covers the great king with a sunshade. The other holds a fly whisk. The fly whisk is used to keep insects away, but I've heard that in some ritual ceremonies, fly whisks are also used to scatter evil spirits."

Esther opened her mouth to continue, but then she closed it again as she heard murmurings among the other young women. They likely had no interest in hearing more of what she had to say.

The rap of a cane on the floor by one of the lesser eunuchs quieted the women's voices.

Hegai's eyes stayed on Esther. "Did you have more to say?" His face displayed pure interest.

"If you are certain." Esther glanced at the other young women. Some seemed interested, others angry. Still, some appeared not to be listening as they struggled to hold back their tears.

"Yes, of course."

Taking a deep breath, Esther chose to continue. "I know many of the builders of Xerxes's palace are craftsmen brought here after the conquest of Babylon. My cousin's work includes importing supplies, and he's welcomed travelers to our home for meals.

"In Babylon, flies represent Nergal, the god of death," she continued. "Including the fly whisks in the relief is a way for the craftsmen to give honor to Xerxes, king of kings. A physical representation of keeping evil from these walls. More than that…" Esther's voice trailed off until Hegai's nod urged her to continue.

"The solar deity Dibbarra is often associated with Nergal. I was told they represent the midday sun and the summer solstice, which the Babylonians believe brings destruction. So you see…" Esther pointed. "The images on those reliefs can be considered a double blessing for King Xerxes." She nodded once, showing she was through. Pressing her lips into a thin line, Esther tried to ignore the many sets of eyes fixed on her.

Esther reached behind her neck and pulled her braid forward, stroking its ends with her fingers. Then she set her gaze on Hegai again. "That is just what I was thinking. Now, sir, can you please repeat your question?"

With slow movements, Hegai threw back his head. Laughter spilled out. "Is that all you were thinking?" He crossed his arms over his chest and tilted his head toward her. "I asked if anyone had been to the Palace of Susa before. These young women shook their heads, letting me know they hadn't. And so I looked to you, seeking your answer."

Esther's fingers clenched the end of her braid as the memory of Queen Vashti's feast, and her proud exit, filled her mind. Esther had never forgotten the queen's quiet grace as she strode from the banquet hall for the last time.

"Once, years ago now," Esther answered pensively. "A hand-maiden of Queen Vashti told the queen of my stories, and I met the queen on the night…on the night of her last banquet." Esther paused, wondering how much she should share.

"And you told our queen a story." It was a statement, not a question. Hegai nodded in remembrance. "What is your name?"

"Esther," she stated simply.

"Yes, Esther, I was there that night, serving Xerxes's harem." Hegai's voice trailed off. Then, remembering his purpose, Hegai motioned to one of the other eunuchs. The young man hurried toward him.

"Take these young women to the rooms we have prepared. All of them except Esther. She will remain with me."

Esther's hands grew clammy. She grasped them before her, hoping to hide their tremor, as she watched the other young women leave. Her knees trembled, and she looked around for a place to sit. Seeing her distress, Hegai pointed to a chair along one of the walls.

Esther moved in that direction and then sat. Images of the guards arriving at Mordecai's home earlier that evening filled her mind. Haman had shown up too. Why? Why had he shown up at her house? The room dimmed around her, and she lifted her face to the breeze blowing through the open window, sucking in big gulps.

This is all a ruse. Had Haman used the king's edict as an excuse to pry her away from Mordecai? She had humiliated him before that crowd at the market, and now he would make her pay for her deeds.

If Haman tries to seek revenge on me—for that story concerning his ancestor Agag—Mordecai will never know. He will think I'm part of the harem.

Esther clenched her fists, and her knuckles turned white. What would be worse for her cousin—that she was part of a harem or imprisoned in the palace by one of the officials? Then again, the only difference was that one lived in luxury. Neither had an ounce of freedom.

The wind blew in through the window once more. The feel of the breeze ruffling her hair stirred the memory of Haman's breath on her neck. Her stomach lurched, and Esther lowered her head, daring not to look at Hegai.

Another set of footsteps approached. She glanced up and saw a younger eunuch carrying a goblet. Hegai took the cup from the man and offered it to her.

Esther eyed the goblet, wondering what type of drink it contained.

Hegai offered a sad smile. "It is only water, I promise. Are you all right? Do you feel ill? I know a lot has happened tonight."

"You aren't taking me to him, are you?" Esther's fingers trembled as she took the goblet from Hegai's hand.

"No one is going to the king tonight. No one will be presented to the king for a long while—a year at least. There are physical preparations. Much to learn. A lot to know."

"Not to the king. I mean, you're not taking me to Haman, are you?" The goblet trembled in her hand.

"To Haman?" Hegai spit the name. "Why would I do that?"

"I don't know. Maybe because Haman was the one who came to my home tonight."

"He came to your home?" Hegai sat on a bench beside her. He rubbed his brow. "Have you had many interactions with Haman before?"

"I—I first saw him at the queen's banquet. He and another official accompanied the eunuchs when they delivered the king's request for Vashti to present herself at the men's banquet. Now, I don't wish to speak ill of any of the king's officials..." Esther lowered her voice and rushed her words. "But I was close enough to Haman to see the *intent* in his gaze." Esther chose her words carefully. From the scowl on Hegai's face when he'd spoken the name of Haman, Esther guessed his dislike of the man, but it would be too risky to make assumptions.

"You said that was the first interaction?"

Esther shifted under his gaze. "I've seen him going through the King's Gate, of course. And recently..." She waved a hand in front of her heated face. "I told a Hebrew story in which things didn't go favorably for Haman's ancestor Agag."

"I see."

Something told her his eyes were closed, and she could hear him swallow. Her thumb circled the goblet's edge. Part of her still wondered if she could trust this man.

"When you told me I wouldn't be going with the other young women, I worried that you had a—a different purpose for me."

Hegai cleared his throat, and she turned to him. Close up, she saw his eyes were blue. Compassion radiated there. "Esther, you do not have to worry. You are safe here with me." Hegai scowled. "Especially from Haman's grasp." He opened his hands, palms up to her as if offering a peace treaty. "But I will say, I do have a different purpose. A good purpose."

"You do?" Esther finally took a drink from the goblet, and her eyes widened as she swallowed the fresh, cool, sweet water—like no other water she'd ever tasted.

"Yes, a good purpose, I promise you that. I remember being impressed with the young storyteller who stood before our queen and spoke with such confidence." He looked to the relief on the wall of King Xerxes. "And your comments tonight proved my first impression was correct. You are no ordinary woman."

Esther took another sip from her water, not knowing what to say. Then pulling the goblet away from her lips, she shrugged. "I enjoy stories and interesting facts—hearing them and sharing them."

Hegai's smile widened, showing white, straight teeth. "Yes, I can see that, and I have plans to give you an audience."

"An audience?" Esther laughed.

Hegai stroked his chin. His eyes squinted as if he were looking into the future. "Tomorrow morning, I will bring seven maids to tend to you. They are efficient young women, and I'm sure they will also enjoy your stories."

"But how can seven maids care for only one person?"

"Oh, don't you worry." Hegai swept his arm and motioned for her to follow him through one of the tall doors. "There will be much preparation. Like I mentioned to the other young women, you must learn royal etiquette. And there's a year's worth of beauty treatments. We will teach you our Persian customs and provide language studies. A special diet will also be required. Yes, Esther, there is much to do to prepare for your one night with the king."

CHAPTER TWELVE

Every moment of the next hour, Esther told herself that she needed to wake up from the dream. Hegai led her to a private room with instructions that a handmaiden would soon arrive to tend to her and prepare her for bed.

"Your beauty treatments begin tomorrow after you break your fast. Tonight, there will be only one maid to attend to you. Tomorrow, six more will join her."

"Thank you." Esther didn't know what else to say.

Hegai left, and Esther glanced around the room.

"It's larger than Mordecai's whole house," she whispered to no one.

The glazed brick walls shone like gems. A large bed platform covered with linens and cushions was situated against one wall. A colorful woven rug lay in front of the bed. A dressing table was set up with a bronze mirror and ivory brush set. A carved chair sat in front of the table. Never had Esther seen such fine things.

The door opened, and a young woman walked in. She looked to be Esther's age. She was tall and lean with ebony skin and cropped curly hair. High cheekbones and a broad fore-head gave her a regal look as if Esther should be tending to her, not the other way around. She wore a simple blue linen tunic with a white belt.

"Welcome," the woman said simply, flashing a smile. "I am Tawana. I am your assigned handmaiden. Have you come far?"

"I am Esther. I live not too far away." She cringed. "Or should I say, *lived*?"

Tawana nodded a response. Then she approached Esther, walking around her in a slow circle. Tawana lifted her eyes in curiosity as if measuring Esther up. It reminded Esther of men buying livestock at the market.

Esther laughed. "I didn't think I was that interesting."

"Fair skin, raven hair, and light brown eyes speckled with gold." Tawana nodded. "Yes, I heard the eunuchs speaking of your beauty. I was pleased that Hegai chose me to serve you." She paused and pressed her palms together. "First, we'll bathe, and then we'll dress."

She led Esther into a tiled room with steps going down to a pool of water that looked large enough for her to lie in.

"Is that for me?" she gasped.

Esther had never seen such a feature. With water scarce in their desert city, she and Mordecai only took baths every few weeks with a bucket of water. They used cleansing oils more often, as did most people she knew. Esther had heard of tubs to bathe in, but she'd never seen anything like this.

"I'm sorry it is small. The other young women have a larger bath, but they have to share."

"I do not mind."

Tawana helped Esther to undress and then assisted her in bathing, rubbing her body with cleansing clay, rinsing it off, and then covering her with oil before helping her dress in a thin linen gown. Esther yawned as Tawana combed and braided her hair.

"It's late," Tawan said, rising. "You should get some sleep. Your beauty treatments start tomorrow."

Esther moved to her bed and sank into the cushioned surface. Her eyes started drifting closed as Tawana laid a thin linen sheet over her.

"I will be sleeping in the other room." Tawana pointed to the door. "Tomorrow, new beds will be set up for your other handmaidens. We will be close enough to hear you when you call."

"Thank you, Tawana. I look forward to getting to know you better."

Esther's heart still ached with all she'd lost, but the fear she'd had when Haman arrived at the door had mostly subsided. While she didn't want to think of going to the king, Esther consoled herself, knowing that wouldn't be anytime soon.

Hegai said the beauty treatments would last over a year, and if tonight was any indication of what was to come, she looked forward to them. Her skin had never felt so soft, and sinking into the warm bathwater was something she could get used to.

Tawana turned down the oil lamp and then went into the attached room, closing the door behind her. Esther's room was dark except for the moonlight coming through the tall windows. She had almost drifted off to sleep when crying stirred her to wakefulness. It wasn't the loud wailing like when they'd walked across the King's Gate. Instead, it was more like a gentle whimper.

Sitting up, she scanned the room. Moonlight had transformed the tables, couches, and tiles into shades of gray. She rubbed her eyes. *Where was that lamp?*

There. An oil lamp sat on one of the tables. She left her bed and shivered when she stepped from the rug to the cool tile—so different from the hard-packed dirt floor at her cousin's house.

With the lighted lamp in hand, Esther headed in the direction of the whimpering. Peering outside the door, she saw a hall with three doors on either side. She listened intently as she walked down the hall, searching for the sound.

Then she heard it again. On the second door to her right. Esther opened that door and looked in. The room had six beds. On two of them, young women were sleeping. The other three young women sat on the beds and stared at the distressed one.

Esther immediately recognized Anahita, with her blond hair, sitting up straight in her bed. Leila, with reddish-brown curly hair, lay prone on her bed, cries shaking her body. The young women looked like they'd also been bathed, with their hair braided—other than Leila. Her curls rose like a halo around her head.

Esther moved toward Leila and put the lamp on the table. Leila looked no older than fifteen or sixteen—the age Esther had been when she first came to the palace. Seeing Leila's blotchy skin and red-rimmed eyes rekindled Esther's anger at the situation.

Who was this king who demanded that young women be dragged from their homes and held captive for his pleasure?

Leila sat up, providing Esther a place to sit beside her. As Esther wrapped her arm around Leila's shoulders, Esther remembered Xerxes as he had been in his fine armor, riding out with his army to conquer Greece. According to the war reports, things had not gone as planned. So was this his next conquest—young women who couldn't fight or resist?

Outrage burned within Esther, like a hot flame licking up oil. What type of king would rip young girls from their fathers and mothers? What kind of man would fulfill his lust by taking them into his bed? If Xerxes wanted a queen, surely there had to be a better way.

Yet how would her anger help this young woman? It wouldn't. What use was it to fight? Nothing could go against the king's edict. She knew that. The best she could offer was to help calm this young woman's fears.

Esther leaned in slightly toward Leila. "It's all right," she soothed. "I know it is hard being away from your family. Since we can't change things, maybe changing our hearts is better."

The young woman's shoulders stiffened, and she turned her face away from Esther. "It's easy for you to say that. You probably wanted to be here." Leila jutted out her chin. "You look like someone a great king would choose as a queen. You are so beautiful. But me? There is no chance I will be chosen, and I will miss out on the one I love."

"The one you love?" Esther sat back slightly, removing her arm from around the young woman's shoulders.

"I have a friend. I have known him my whole life. My father said he would approach Ashkan's father next year. It was all planned." Sobs wracked her body again. "Not only do I have to leave the one I love, but I'll also be forced to go to the king's bed. I have no desire for that man. This is not what I wanted for my life."

Esther placed a hand on the young woman's back, moving it in slow circles. "I know this is hard," she whispered. "But now that we are here, we can choose to bring more pain to ourselves, or we can make the best of things." And as Esther spoke those words, she knew she was trying to convince herself as well.

"Who are you to talk?" A tall, bronze-skinned woman stood from one of the beds. She crossed her arms over her chest and took two paces toward Esther. "What did you do to deserve such honors to be given your own suite?" she asked, pointing a finger at Esther's chest.

"Soraya, please, sit down," Leila called to her.

"Do you think you are smarter than we are, Esther?" Anahita rose from her bed, standing next to Soraya. "Who told you those things about the carvings of Xerxes on the walls?"

"*No one* told me, or you can say *everyone* told me." Esther drew about a breath, attempting to stay calm.

Anahita wrinkled her nose and glared. "What do you mean by that?"

Esther scooted away from Leila and turned to face the blond beauty. "I was raised by my cousin, Mordecai. He worked with imports at the King's Gate. He has many friends from all parts of the kingdom, and he'd often invite them to stay in our extra room. But there was always a price for their stay." Esther lifted one eyebrow.

"A price?" Soraya asked. Her voice was gruff, but Esther noticed her shoulders soften and her defiant chin tip down.

"Yes, Mordecai always told our guests they could stay for the price of a story. Would you like to hear one of them?" she asked. "I can tell you one of my favorite Persian tales."

CHAPTER THIRTEEN

Esther stretched and opened her eyes, blinking against the bright morning light of the room. The floors and walls had been crafted of glazed bricks more dazzling than jewels, and linen curtains hung from the high ceiling by silver hooks. Yet even more stunning was the view out the window.

Esther moved to peer out. From her vantage point, she noticed an outdoor courtyard. And beyond that, the hills of Susa led away from the city. She'd never looked upon their land from such a vantage point. Her eyes followed the sand-colored hills as far as she could—where the earth met the sky. How long would it take to get to that point? A day's journey, perhaps. Yet the King of Persia's lands went farther beyond—to new lands with people who looked different than she did, spoke various languages, and worshiped gods other than Yahweh. Yet the king ruled over them all. *And I will go to him someday.*

Last night she'd resigned herself to that fact. Although she longed to return to her home and cousin—to talk to him about the plan to move to Jerusalem—that was no longer a possibility. Like flowers that bloomed in the desert and soon faded from the burn of the sun, their plans were dead. A single tear ran down her cheek.

Esther yawned and turned away from the window. Was Tawana still in the adjacent room? Should she go to her maid to ask what the day held or wait until Tawana arrived?

Settling back onto her bed, Esther decided to wait. Perhaps the young woman slept. It made sense, for she had awakened to tend to Esther during the night.

After telling the other women a story, Esther fell asleep on the end of Leila's bed. Tawana had come for Esther when the night was darkest, stirring Esther awake.

"Esther, you must stay in your quarters," Tawana had whispered. "Do you want us to both get in trouble?"

Esther had fallen asleep immediately after returning to her own room.

Now, lying on the soft cushions with the delicate, smooth linens, Esther felt like she was floating on a cloud that lifted her into the heavens. So different from the thin reed mat and the coarse blanket she had back home.

Still, her heart pinched when she thought of Mordecai. Esther pictured him sitting in their main living area with a bowl of barley porridge before him, growing cold. Her cousin could never eat when he was upset.

Tawana quickly dressed Esther, sliding a yellow gown over her frame. After styling her hair, Tawana led Esther to an open portico where food was laid out to break their fast.

Esther walked into the portico area, noting all eyes were on her. She wanted to turn, to leave, but she had no choice. All the other young women were already eating at a long table, and Esther didn't see an open space to join them.

Pausing her steps, Esther turned to Tawana. "Am I late?"

"No, Esther, Hegai has ordered a different menu for you." Tawana motioned to a small table with a single chair. Fresh fruits and vegetables had been laid out—far more than Esther could ever eat.

Esther's stomach growled. She had eaten many of those foods, but she'd never seen them displayed together in such abundance. "Pomegranates, cucumbers with dill, apricots. These are some of my favorite foods, but why is my menu different?"

Tawana shrugged and turned her back to the other young women, who now eyed Esther's special table and were whispering among themselves.

"I did not ask why your food is different, and I wouldn't either if I were you. Hegai always has his wishes, and it is best to obey them. Please, Esther, sit down and enjoy your meal."

Esther ignored the other young women as she sat down. Mordecai had always said the Jews were set apart. Yet until this moment, she didn't understand how hard it was to be so. It would be much easier to join the other young women and enjoy their conversations and friendship.

What is the purpose Hegai has for me? Esther lifted an apricot to her lips and took a bite. The fruit was fresh and sweet, yet all she could think about was how she wished to share it with Mordecai. He'd done so much, given so much, and now she had no way to help him.

Hegai waited until all the other young women exited the room before he turned his attention back to Esther. "They will start their first beauty treatments today, but I have other plans for you.”

Esther tapped her foot, waiting for him to continue.

“I will give you a tour of the palace. I know you’ll appreciate it, and you’ll only be able to focus on your lessons if you’ve had a chance to look around.”

“All of the palace?”

“Everywhere except the king’s wing. No one can enter that part of the palace unless they are summoned. To do so is to risk your life.”

“Has that happened?

“More times than you want to know.”

“Thank you. Can we start with the other reliefs in the main hall?”

“Give us time. You must dress first.”

Esther glanced down at her fine linen tunic. “Am I not dressed?”

“That gown is fine within these walls. But you are not a servant. You are destined for the king.”

Tawana helped her dress in a creamy white gown and then layered a tunic over it. A veil covered Esther’s face, and a golden cuff was placed on her wrist. Only then was she able to join Hegai, journeying outside the women’s quarters.

The echoes of men at work carried down the halls as Hegai showed her additional banquet rooms and porticos. Colorful glazed tile bricks decorated the halls with backdrops. The scenes showed palace life and various nations bringing tribute to the king. Then Hegai led her to a large flowering garden.

The aroma of fresh flowers, trees, and shrubs took Esther's breath away. "I've heard of oases in the desert. I didn't realize one was so close." Then she peered back over her shoulder at the expansive complex. "There is more than enough food for all the king's needs. Why does he continue to build?"

"Xerxes started plans for renovations to his palace from the day he became king, and by the time work is finished, it will be twice the size of his father's residence." Hegai chuckled. "Then again, I should say *if* it is finished. Even when those plans are complete, there will be new ones. Xerxes loves architecture as much as he enjoys talks of war—maybe more."

Esther allowed her fingers to trail up the stem of a red rose, and as she did, the vendor's words came to mind.

"She who wants a rose must respect the thorn," Esther whispered, a chill racing up her arms.

"Excuse me?"

"She who wants a rose must respect the thorn," Esther repeated louder. "It's something a kind woman once told me."

"That is for certain." He nodded. "And I have never heard a truer sentiment concerning our king." Hegai met Esther's gaze. "The king has much to give to someone willing to look past his…thorns. And I speak not of wealth and power alone." Hegai sighed. "But one must be patient, wise, and compassionate to discover that."

Esther nodded, understanding that is what Hegai expected of her. She liked to think that perhaps that is why Hegai set her apart. "I understand," she stated simply.

"Good, there is more to see." He clapped his hands together. "I will show you the work still in progress. Even though it is too dangerous to approach this work, I'd like you to see the vision of our king."

As they walked, Hegai explained how Xerxes's predecessors had established a tradition of impressive building projects that became a mark of effective kingship. He related how artisans worked on the palace, coming from all four corners of the Empire—India, Ethiopia, Cappadocia, and Sardis.

They paused at the end of a long hall, and teams of laborers looked as if they were close to completing walls that rose even higher the those in the inner court.

Esther's mouth gaped open. It amazed her how sun-dried brick could be formed into such opulence.

"The roof will be made of Lebanese cedars, the finest known wood, first acquired by King Cyrus. The gold was bought from Sardis and Bactra. Precious stones from all over the kingdom. The silver and ebony from Egypt. Ornaments from Ionia." He pointed to men chiseling stones in the distance. "The stonecutters are Ionians and Sardians themselves. Those who brought gold are Medes and Egyptians, and the men who brought the wood are Sardians and Egyptians. Medes and Egyptians also work to adorn the walls."

Goose bumps rose on Esther's arms as she watched their magnificent work. She wished she could tell her cousin of these experiences or relay a message that she was well. Did he worry? She knew he did.

Esther hugged her arms to her chest, but she dared not ask Hegai for the favor of relaying a message—not yet.

"The palace craftsmen and workers remind me of the king's army," she finally said.

"What do you mean?"

"Instead of forcing each of the different people groups to conform to one standard, these men are each allowed to do the work they do best." Esther adjusted the sleeves of her dress as she continued, still in disbelief that she wore such fine clothes.

"My family came here from Babylon," she confessed. "I hear things there were not the same. Men were forced to work as the king desired—and worship as he desired."

"I was just a young man when we moved from Babylon to Susa during the reign of Darius the Great," Hegai told her. His eyes flashed in pain for just a moment before disappearing. "We, meaning all the palace workers."

"And what was the purpose of the move?" Esther asked.

"To be more centrally located." Hegai eyed her. "Did you know the tomb of the great Hebrew prophet Daniel is here?"

Esther placed a hand on her heart and couldn't help but gasp. "In Susa?"

"Yes, the burial spot is Sush-e Daniyal. He was a highly respected and distinguished member of the Babylonian diaspora."

"My cousin says my grandfather knew him well."

Hegai smiled to himself. "I expected as much. You remind me of him—of Daniel. Your presence and wisdom. Unexpected for one so young."

Did he guess that I'm a Jewess? An icy shiver traveled down Esther's spine.

Had she said too much? Was this a trick? Although Mordecai was proud of their heritage, he continually urged her to keep their identity hidden.

There are many enemies of God's people. Better to be safe, my cousin, than face the wrath that has simmered for generations.

Both were silent as they walked back into the main hall, and Hegai stood silent as Esther studied the reliefs. On the jamb of the eastern doorway, there was a relief showing Xerxes fighting with a lion-headed monster. The reliefs on the western doorway showed the king in combat with the lion. Then Hegai led them back to the women's quarters. South of the columned hall, the main wing contained six apartments in two rows.

"Each apartment consists of a large pillared room and smaller rooms." Hegai pointed. "The west wing contains sixteen additional apartments."

"And all of them are filled with women?"

"Not currently, but they will be."

"All for the king?" she dared to ask.

"Yes, of course."

Hearing that was a hammer's blow to Easter's heart—so many young women had been taken from their homes, all in search of a new queen.

"So many lives upended."

Hegai didn't answer. He didn't need to. They both knew it to be true.

How can a man like that offer love to one woman when his affections are spread over so many?

A painful stirring, like pinpricks jabbing her heart, radiated from Esther's chest. *Still, I cannot think of that.*

She remembered Mordecai's words. Her job was not to consider the other women or to compare herself to them. Even as just one member of King Xerxes's harem, she would tend to her husband, for that is what he would be to her before the eyes of God—her husband.

And I will be his compassionate bride.

CHAPTER FOURTEEN

The next day, Esther lined up with the other young women. Most of the others ignored her. Only Leila gave Esther a soft smile and moved to stand by her side. Hegai stood before them once again.

"Before you are taken to the king's bed, you will be given the prescribed twelve months of beauty treatments—six months with myrrh oil, followed by six months with special perfumes and ointments." Hegai eyed the women. "Their purpose is to cleanse you, exfoliate your skin, and bring healing to sunburns, skin diseases, and sores. Only those with unblemished skin, free from disease, may go before the king."

Hegai walked the row of young women, who had grown in number overnight. "When you approach the king's bed, you will appear as a goddess to him."

Eunuchs separated the young women into groups. Three maidens were waiting in the room as Esther and the others entered.

Tall windows in the room opened to one of the smaller gardens, and sweet aromas of flowering bushes wafted in. In the center of the room stood platforms covered with mats. After the women undressed, they were given a wrap and told to recline on the mats. Esther lay down, and one of her new hand-maidens, Tiamat, approached with a jar of oil.

Working efficiently, the young woman poured oil onto Esther's arm and began to rub it in. Her touch was gentle, and the aroma of the oils was unlike anything Esther had ever smelled—sweet and yet spicy at the same time. As the young woman worked, Esther soon felt her eyes drifting closed.

Some of the young women chatted with their handmaid-ens, but Esther's mind drifted to thoughts of the marketplace and home. Had Mordecai gone back to work? Did he wonder about her fate in the palace? Surely he did.

A sandstorm picked up outside, and two eunuchs rushed into the room to cover the window. Esther grabbed her linen, attempting to cover as much of herself as possible, but the men didn't glance in her direction.

Tiamat tried to hide a grin, but Esther noticed two dimples on her cheeks that hadn't been there before.

"Do you find it humorous that I am uncomfortable with the eunuchs' presence?" Esther asked.

"No, it is always this way with the young women at first. Of course, the last group of women came years ago, before the king went to war." She shrugged. "But the young women now are the same as they've always been."

Esther's back stiffened at those words. She didn't want to ask any more about the king's women. She'd seen the harem lounging at the queen's banquet over three years ago, and she guessed all those women were still around.

Funny, Hegai hadn't shown her that part of the palace. It still made her wonder why Xerxes didn't choose one of them to be his queen, especially those who bore his children.

"Have you worked in the palace for a long time?" Esther asked, feeling it was a safe enough question.

"Since I was a child."

"A child?" Esther drew in a breath.

"I was sent as a tribute to the King of Persia from Babylon." Tiamat moved to Esther's other arm. "My brother also."

"Your brother?"

"Yes, he was one of the five hundred young men who became eunuchs paid to Xerxes as a tribute. And I was one of the young women."

"Five hundred?" Esther suppressed a gasp.

"Yes. Soldiers collected young men over time. The guards forced parents to do their part. With seven children in our family, my parents had a hard choice of who to send. I do not blame them. Alam and I were two of the oldest. Schooled in the ways of Persia, we've become hard workers. There could be worse things than being a servant in palace life."

"I have no brothers or sisters," Esther stated. "My mother died when I was just four years old. I only have a few memories of her. My father died less than two years later. I remember him better."

"So you are alone?"

"I have one relative. He's older and raised me as a daughter."

Tiamat poured more oil. "Is he married or with children?"

"No. He's had the opportunity. More than one father approached him about marriage for a daughter, but my adoptive father knew both of the young women well. He said they saw me as a burden rather than a gift. So he declined."

"From the way you speak of this relative, it is clear that you love him very much. And he must care for you the same."

Tiamat poured oil from another jar as she moved to Esther's legs, and the aroma hinted at myrrh, honey, and lime.

"Yes, and the worst part is, he lives so close. It is just a short walk from my cousin's home to the King's Gate."

"Perhaps you can send a message to him?" Tiamat's eyebrows lifted in question.

Esther shook her head. "Hegai is in control of everything that happens. He's made it clear we must forget our former lives. It must be as if they were no more. Hegai would never allow a scribe to write and deliver a message."

"Who said anything about writing it?" Tiamat shrugged. "My brother is a messenger and has a wonderful memory. Surely it would be no problem. We would be happy to help." The lyrical cadence of Tiamat's voice gave Esther pause. The young woman's smile was too bright, as if she had another motive for the offer.

"That is thoughtful." Esther smiled and closed her eyes again. "That's something I'll have to think about."

Tiamat continued to rub the oils into Esther's body. Did Tiamat press a little harder than she had before? Esther wasn't sure, but something inside told her Tiamat could not be trusted. If Yahweh wished for her to communicate with Mordecai, Esther would trust Him to make a way.

———

The weeks passed, and Esther discovered how important it was to listen rather than talk. If a young woman shared a secret during a meal or a massage, it would be passed through the whole group of young women by the end of the day.

Esther appreciated the talents of Tiamat, especially her massages with the oils. Yet no doubt the young woman and her brother had ulterior motives for doing favors for the other young women—most likely to earn their appreciation. After all, one of these young women would be queen. Who knew the ranks that a handmaiden and messenger could rise to together if they both had the new queen on their side?

Late one evening, nearing the end of her first month of beauty treatments, Esther sat on the patio outside her room in the cool of the evening. In the distance, a flock of birds rose and fell in the sky.

She wished she could be one of those birds, sweeping down to see her cousin. She'd spent every day with him for most of her life. It felt strange not to be able to share this experience with him.

Behind her, a man cleared his throat. Esther jumped, placing the hand over her pounding heart. She turned and saw that Hegai stood there. Her shoulders softened with relief.

"I am so sorry, Esther. I did not mean to startle you. I've wanted to talk to you for a while, but more young women have come in from our territories. They speak various languages, and getting them to understand bathing and beauty treatments has been a lot of work. I would love to talk to you."

Esther patted the bench beside her. "It is lovely to have someone to converse with. I shouldn't admit this, but sometimes it gets lonely. I miss…" Esther's voice trailed off. She pressed her lips together. *No, I can't confess.*

She had to think of what was best for Mordecai.

"You miss your cousin, Mordecai?"

Esther gasped, and her eyes widened. "What do you mean? How do you know?"

"It becomes apparent when this man walks near the harem's courtyard to find out about a young woman named Esther. Numerous times a day, he asks the guards, servants, anyone who will talk to him, for word of his cousin Esther."

Hegai paced with his hands behind his back. "They know him, of course. They know you. The men and women near the King's Gate have heard your stories. They are not supposed to give information about the king's women—to do so could lead to severe punishment. That's when I decided to speak to Mordecai myself."

Esther raised her hands to her lips. "You did that? You went and spoke to Mordecai? Please, sir, tell me that he heeded your warnings. He is a good man. He cares about me. I am like a daughter to him. And he is like a father."

Hegai sat back and folded his arms over his chest. "Who said I went to give him a warning? I talked with him because I have compassion for the man. Even though I cannot share the details of what happens inside Xerxes's palace, I assured Mordecai you are being tended to with great care. I am not certain that will change things, though. Your cousin is persistent."

"If anything, he is that." Esther's heart ached with missing him. She patted her face, urging herself not to cry. Then she turned her attention to the birds again.

A few from the flock had ventured onto the patio and hopped on the stone. They pecked on the ground, checking for crumbs. The birds reminded her of one of the psalms of Asaph that Mordecai had sung, especially the line that said, "I know every bird in the mountains, and the creatures of the field are Mine." Her cousin would always pause after that line, reminding Esther that Yahweh knew her, too, and considered her, Esther, His own.

"Thank you for talking to my cousin. I hope that puts his mind at ease."

"I even told Mordecai that you are highly favored. You should have seen how his face brightened to hear those words, *highly favored*. I said I believe you to be the most beautiful young woman—and the brightest too."

Esther's eyes widened as she looked at Hegai. "Is that why you have set me apart again?" she whispered.

Hegai opened his mouth in surprise, and then he laughed. "Esther, why else would I have given you seven maidens? Why else would I keep you apart from the other women if I didn't believe you deserved better treatment—if I didn't have great hopes for you?"

Great hopes? Her heart soared from his words, which didn't change the emptiness that echoed within.

"I didn't fully know why things are different for me, but sometimes it feels like a curse." She rose and moved to the stone rail that separated her patio from the garden. "I am not able to have friendships like the other young women. I—"

"Friendships? Is that what you call them?" Hegai asked, interrupting her. "I hear more fighting than gentle conversation. One says that others dress more beautifully, so she demands something better. Another complains she did not get as many beauty treatments as her friends." He sighed. "There are complaints about snoring, table manners, and those who sing off-key." Hegai shook his head. "I guarantee, Esther, you should appreciate the quiet more. Besides, the maids say you enjoy entertaining them with stories."

"Oh yes, I do."

"Perhaps consider them as friends. They will move with you during your transition into the harem. Even though it is hard, enjoy this time. Change comes soon enough. Soon it will be your time to go to Xerxes, and then you will be moved into the harem unless…"

The small birds lifted again to the sky, and Esther turned to look at Hegai. "Unless?"

Hegai stood and approached her, patting her hand. "Never mind that. Just use this time to think and to pray to your gods—whoever they may be. Things will change after your night with the king. Whether he chooses you or not, you will be a different woman with different responsibilities. Take this time, Esther, to find your courage for whatever comes."

CHAPTER FIFTEEN

Esther lay upon the cool sheets and closed her eyes, yet her mind wouldn't be still. How had a year also passed since she'd been taken away from Mordecai and her home? It didn't seem possible, yet it was true. The first young women would be going to the king within a week.

Anahita hounded Hegai about going to King Xerxes first. Esther was almost sure he'd allow it—just to get her to stop the constant whining. Anahita was beautiful before, but her blond hair glistened like the sun's surface after the beauty treatments. Her eyes, wide and blue, appeared like gems, and her skin glowed milky white. Yet, in Esther's opinion, her beauty was matched by Soraya's, who was the opposite of Anahita in every way.

Where Anahita had seductive curves, Soraya's skin was bronze, and her body stretched tall and thin. Dark brows contrasted with her blue-gray eyes, reminding Esther of the sky after a storm. When Soraya had first arrived at the palace, her hair had been twisted in braids. Over time, and because of the beauty treatments, it had grown to touch her shoulders and fell in gentle waves.

Out of all the young women, Leila had changed the most. Her curls took on a deeper copper color due to the henna treatments. She had appeared as a child in her first weeks, but the abundance of fine food and drink transformed her into a woman. Like Anahita, Leila's curves made her look like one of the Greek goddesses, even in a simple tunic. And the young woman's kindness to Esther and the others gave her a ready smile, which brought out her true beauty. The rosebud had bloomed beautifully, and Esther had no doubt the king would notice.

Dozens of girls now filled the women's wing, each as different from the other as flowers in the garden. Most provinces were represented by young women who spoke many languages. Some had brought idols or other symbols of their gods. Hegai allowed these to be set up next to their beds. If anything, the diversity caused Esther to appreciate Xerxes's kingdom even more. No mere king could rule the four corners of the world more effectively, in her opinion.

Yet now, the question that rose most often in her thoughts was how Xerxes would be as *her* husband. She was one new woman among hundreds. While Esther's life now centered on him, the opposite wasn't true. Xerxes did not need anything she offered. *Yahweh, please help me not feel I'm giving my life for nothing.*

Esther turned over in bed as sleep evaded her. She also couldn't help but consider her parents' marriage. When had they met? What drew them to each other? How had their families responded?

She also imagined the conversations her parents had with each other about their faith and their future. Mordecai had told her that her parents planned to take the journey to Jerusalem. Before illness struck them, it had been their greatest wish.

Had they pictured living in a land where everyone knew Yahweh by name, and they no longer felt a need to hide their identity? Had they dreamed of Zerubbabel's temple or pictured life in the Holy City? Had they mourned their ancestors' sins? Sins so great that Yahweh had decided the only way to change their hearts was to strip away all their hearts longed for other than Him.

She thought of her mother, who—as Esther had heard—found great joy in her only daughter.

Esther thought of her father. His dream had always been to return to Jerusalem, even if it was considered a wild and dangerous place. He'd been a devout man who'd learned the ways of the Torah from *his* father, who'd been taken into captivity as a boy. Their lives had been simple. Now Esther was living in the palace of a great, powerful ruler.

Yahweh, I am one woman, but I pray my influence may be great—not because of who I am alone but because of who You can be in me and through me in this place.

As if in response to the prayer—that she'd spoken only in her mind and heart—there was stirring on the mat next to her bed. Moonlight streamed down through the high windows, and Esther turned to see one of her handmaidens looking up at her. Aafreen's wide eyes reflected fear.

The youngest of her handmaidens, Aafreen, had arrived in the palace as a tribute from Babylon, just as Tiamat had years before. Yet, while Tiamat had accepted her fate, Aafreen still longed for her life back in Babylon, and Esther understood.

"Are you having trouble sleeping too?" asked the young woman lying on a mat near Esther's bed.

"Yes, I am. Today marks nearly one year that I've been away from my family," Esther confessed.

"Just a few months longer for me," Aafreen whispered. "My sister told me I was the lucky one after being chosen to come, but I would give anything to still share my sleeping mat with my younger siblings in our small dwelling." Her lower lip pouted. "Is it wrong to say I wish I did not have to be here? I do like serving you, but—"

Esther held up a hand, halting Aafreen's words. "I understand." She sighed. "I was just thinking of my parents. They both died of sickness years ago when I was a child. But that doesn't mean I don't miss them. I think of my cousin, too, who raised me. While your family lives far away in Babylon, my cousin lives close—so close I picture walking out of the woman's hall, through the banquet rooms and inner court, to the King's Gate. He lives not far beyond that."

"Could you?" Aafreen sat up. "Would you?"

Esther shook her head. "No. It's too great of a risk to him or myself. Once chosen to be one of the king's women, the only way to leave is to be banished, such as Queen Vashti herself."

Aafreen clutched her linen sheet to her chest. Esther could see the color drain from her face, even in the moonlight.

"What do you know, my friend?" Esther tried to keep her voice gentle.

Aafreen looked down at her hands in her lap. "I should not—"

Then, meeting Esther's eyes again, Aafreen looked away, but not before Esther caught a glimpse of knowing.

It was Esther's turn to sit up now. She scooted closer to the edge of her bed, adjusting the cushions and peering down at Aafreen.

"Do you know anything about Queen Vashti? Do you know where she was taken?" Esther wasn't sure why this was so important. Perhaps because what happened that night changed everything. It was why Esther was here.

Esther could hear Aafreen's heavy swallow, and then her handmaiden pressed her linen sheet to her lips as if attempting to keep the words inside.

"You know something, don't you?"

Aafreen glanced at the sleeping maid behind her. While the other maids slept in an adjoining room, Aafreen and Parisa slept by Esther's bed. They'd used the excuse that they wished to be close to Esther to better tend to her. Esther believed they liked being close to her because both were young and far from home.

"Would it help if I told you a story?"

Aafreen's eyes flickered up, even as her forehead wrinkled. "You still will, whether it helps or not."

"Yes." Esther nodded, emotion filling her throat. "I will soon face Xerxes. If there is something important about the former queen that I should know, you will tell me." Then, even though her stomach felt tied up in knots, Esther lay back up on her pillows and lifted her face to the cedar ceiling, deciding to tell the first story that came to mind.

Esther closed her eyes, picturing the scene and the young woman in a situation she never wanted to be in. "There was once a young Moabite woman named Ruth, who had a mother-in-law named Naomi. Naomi lost her husband, Elimelech, and she was left with her two sons. Naomi's other daughter-in-law was also a Moabite named Orpah. After they had lived in Moab about ten years, both Mahlon and Kilion also died, and Naomi was left without her two sons. Since she now had no means of caring for herself, the older widow packed up to return to her hometown of Bethlehem, in the hill country of Judea.

"Naomi urged Ruth to return to her mother's home, yet Ruth refused. Instead, she told Naomi, 'Wherever you go, I will go; wherever you lodge, I will lodge; your people shall be my people, and your God my God. Where you die, I will die, and there I will be buried. Thus and more, may the Lord punish me severely if anything but death separates me from you.'"

Esther paused and listened to make sure Aafreen was still awake.

"Is that all?" Aafreen asked.

"No, it is just the beginning." Esther turned her face to the window, taking in the stars that seemed almost close enough to touch tonight, and then continued. "After a long journey, the two of them came to Bethlehem. They arrived in the late spring, during the barley harvest.

"But once there, the women had to provide for themselves. Ruth told Naomi, 'Let me go out into the harvest fields to pick up the stalks of grain left behind.' Ruth went out to gather behind the harvesters. As it happened, the field she chose belonged to a wealthy relative of Naomi's named Boaz. While there, Boaz arrived at the field and discovered Ruth and her loyalty to her mother-in-law." Esther smiled and turned to peer at Aafreen. "I'd like to think he believed her to be beautiful too."

Aafreen sighed. "I imagine she was."

"Approaching her, Boaz asked her to stay in his field and drink from his well. Boaz also ordered his workers to leave extra grain.

"That night, Ruth showed her full basket to Naomi, and Ruth continued working with them through the wheat harvest in early summer.

"Later, seeing that Boaz's interest in Ruth was promising, the older woman told Ruth to go to the threshing floor and lie next to Boaz's feet while he slept. Boaz awoke, startled to find Ruth at his feet. Then Ruth asked him to spread his robe over her—a symbolic act of espousal. The next day, Boaz went to the city gate and became Ruth's redeeming kinsman to carry on Elimelech's line. And Boaz took Ruth into his home, and she became his wife."

"Did they ever have children?" Aafreen asked.

"Yes, Boaz and Ruth had a son, Obed. Obed was the grandfather of David, the great Hebrew king." Esther sighed. "It's a beautiful story. And just think, a Moabite became the grandmother of a Hebrew king."

Aafreen brushed her hair back from her face. "How do you know the story?"

"My cousin tells this story when the harvest is brought in."

"Are you Hebrew?" Aafreen's voice sounded sleepy.

Esther's heart pinched at the question. *Had she said too much?* "Why do you ask?"

"Because you know this story."

"I know many stories," Esther hurriedly answered. "You know this. You've heard many of them."

"Yes, but there was something different about this one."

Esther tucked her hands under her pillow, uncertain how to respond.

"Or maybe it is not because you are Hebrew," Aafreen stated simply. "Maybe it is because you will go to Xerxes soon and—" Her words caught short.

"And what?" Esther placed a hand on her chest, feeling her heartbeat through her nightgown, knowing why it pounded and wishing it were not so.

"Xerxes is not like Boaz." Aafreen's voice sounded different. "I did not say so before, but the travelers who brought me from Babylon to Susa work for the king. At night after their drink, the men told us of Queen Vashti and how they took her from Susa."

"Is she no more?" The room's air pressed on Esther's being as if pressing her into her bed. "And her handmaidens?" She thought of Nazanin.

Aafreen remained silent as if weighing her words. "Wine is like a snakebite, separating life and death." Aafreen's voice trembled.

Esther covered her mouth at Aafreen's words, yet hadn't she always known? The darkness in the eyes of Haman and

Hormoz. If Xerxes's excess of wine was like a snakebite, they were the fangs.

Pressing her eyes shut, Esther tried to pray, but the ache of finally knowing of Queen Vashti's demise caused her mind to race.

Each young woman would go to their king, seeking his approval—more than that—his favor.

The favor of a man like Boaz meant a home, a family, and a life. The favor of King Xerxes? It could mean the opposite. The king was prone to rash decisions, and he had the power to enforce them.

As Esther fell into a fitful sleep, she knew the truth. Stepping into what was to come over the next week depended on Yahweh's wisdom, Yahweh's strength. Though Xerxes was a great king, Esther knew she couldn't step forward unless she trusted that Yahweh was greater still.

CHAPTER SIXTEEN

On the first anniversary of their entrance into the palace, the young women were escorted through a door they'd never entered. From where she stood, near the back of the line, Esther heard squeals of delight from those who'd entered through the doors ahead of her. Their joy was quickly followed by bickering.

"I saw that necklace first." Anahita's voice rose.

"Of course you did," Leila protested. "You always must have the best."

Esther looked to Hegai and shrugged and then tentatively entered the room. A gasp escaped her when she saw the luxurious items spread before them—gowns, jewels, shawls, sandals, headdresses, hairpieces, and more. The colors and fabrics took her breath away.

Esther had often gazed with interest at the market booths. Vendors brought materials from the four corners of the kingdom. She was used to seeing tunics and trousers for men, in addition to wool skullcaps. There were always colorful layered skirts and matching vests for women. Some of the vendors stocked colorful robes and shawls, but never in the number of colors and patterns displayed before them now.

Her eyes widened to see the display of jewels. Numerous tables were filled with them. Gold and silver ornaments were intricately decorated and adorned with gems. Even though Esther had never longed for such things, it quickened her heart to see such a display.

A cluster of young women circled a table covered with necklaces and arm cuffs. Passing them, Esther walked over to a table of shawls ranging from thick plush drapes to near-transparent veils. She lifted one yellow veil that felt as light as a feather and brushed it to her cheek. Softer than a chick's down.

All the young women talked at once until a short staccato clap from Hegai silenced their words. In an instant, all the young women silenced their voices and turned their attention to the head eunuch. Esther, too, returned the veil to the table as Hegai strode to the center of the room.

"These clothes and jewels are provided for your use as you go to the king," Hegai declared. "Each young woman may choose what she desires, and when she is moved into the harem, the chosen items will be sent with her as a gift from your king."

Gasps and pleased whispers rose from all the young women. Hegai waited for them to quiet themselves once again before he continued. "Xerxes believes—as I do—that your choices say much about you. So consider all your options and choose wisely. Feel free to try on garments or jewels that you'd like. These doors will be open to you for the reminder of your days until you go before your king."

Hegai left the room, and the loud conversations started once again. Some young women hurried to grab their hand-maidens to help carry chosen items.

The noise and the frantic movements of the young women caused Esther's shoulders to tense. Pressure moved from her temples toward her forehead as she considered all the choices. *Should I dress the part of a queen?* She wrinkled her nose and winced, thinking of Vashti's elaborate gown, jewels, and veils. She could do so, but it would not feel like her. It would be hard enough going to Xerxes without trying to portray something she wasn't.

Esther paused at a flowing dress with an intricate pattern around the hem. It was lovely, but it reminded her too much of the loud-talking noblewomen who visited the marketplace. They loved to wear such brightly colored garments.

Another simple white gown reminded Esther of the beautiful apparel Sarai had given her when she attended Vashti's banquet. Only this one had a hem of purple fringe.

Her heartbeat quickened to see armfuls of gowns and headpieces being hauled away. She moved even faster around the tables, trying to decide what to choose before it was gone.

As her eyes filled with tears, Esther paused, lifted her face to the cedar ceiling, and closed her eyes. *Yahweh, show me the way. Help me honor myself and my husband. Show me the correct choices for me. I don't know how to decide alone.*

Then, deciding to get a fresh breath of air, a new thought hit her. She didn't have to choose independently, did she? Excitement stirred her heart. With quickened steps, she hurried past the young eunuchs at the doorway, moving toward Hegai, who lounged in a chair just outside the door.

Hegai's eyes lifted in surprise, and she noted humor there. Esther smiled as she saw wisdom too. While the young women filled their arms with what appealed to their eyes, Hegai knew the king.

With slow movements, Esther paused before Hegai and bowed her head.

"Yes, Esther? Do you need something? Your hands are empty. Are not those gowns and jewels to your liking?"

"There are many beautiful things." She lifted her head and met his gaze. "But can I ask you a question?"

"Of course."

She'd gotten used to Hegai's simple tunic and shaved head. To the other young women, they might just see the king's servant in charge of their beauty treatments, but Esther knew there was more to him. Hegai was insightful and caring too.

The voices of the other young women rose in volume, and Hegai motioned for two of the young eunuchs to tend to them. Then Hegai stood and clasped his hands behind his back. "Come, let us walk to the patio. Then we can talk without the constant squeals in our ears."

Esther followed through double doors and breathed in the fresh air that smelled like jasmine. She approached the flowers' blooms and deeply breathed in the aroma.

As Hegai strolled through the manicured trails, Esther walked in step with him.

"Tell me, Hegai, have you served the kingdoms all your life?"

"I knew Darius the Mede. I served Cyrus, the King of Persia. I still serve Xerxes." He looked at her curiously.

"You may consider me a foolish young woman, but I have never known the care of a mother. No one took me to look at items like these in the market. I never paid attention to jewelry and such—or longed for these things. I'm not sure if I'm making any sense." Esther bit her lip, trying to put her feelings into words.

Hegai continued his slow pace, pausing every so often to appreciate a delicate bloom or to breathe in an enticing scent.

"I have some memories of my mother and father," she continued. "But after their deaths, I lived under the care of my older cousin, as you know. I have been taught that strength is with the young but wisdom with the old. So may I dare ask, what would you recommend I wear for my one night with the king?"

The old eunuch tipped up his lips in the slightest of grins and nodded. Then he paused and faced her, waving his hand toward where they'd just come from. "So many voices and opinions among the other young women, aren't there? Such valuable garments and jewels at their disposal have stirred up many emotions and rivalries. All those young women do is talk and fight as it is. I can't imagine the days to come." He tilted one eyebrow. "I'm not sure how they argue so well, even when they don't fully understand each other's languages."

Esther pressed her lips into a tight smile, knowing he spoke the truth. Yet she didn't move—not even when the eunuch turned back to face the way they'd come. Hegai hadn't answered her questions, yet Esther felt that if she were patient and waited, he would.

Finally, Hegai leaned over, plucked a flower from one of the jasmine bushes, and winked. "Because your older cousin raised you—and you are more willing to listen instead of talk— the gods have favored you indeed."

"Not once have I ever considered the loss of my mother as a favor from the gods." The words were released before she had time to consider them.

"It is something to consider." He motioned Esther to follow him and slowly strolled down the return path. "When you sleep tonight, without the sounds of the other women's voices buzzing in your ear, like mosquitoes, then you might consider its truth. Who you became because of your losses and your gains—being raised by a cousin who treasures knowledge and stories—caught my attention. You are not an ordinary young woman, and I know the eunuchs in charge of the harem will discover as much.

"Even if King Xerxes does not choose you as queen, your life will be different in the palace," Hegai continued. "You'll have access to the scribes and their writing systems. Perhaps you can even start writing down the many stories told to you."

Hegai's words lightened Esther's heart, but still she waited to know the answer of what to wear to go before the king. She needed to know the answer, even if it meant strolling the gardens all night.

Pausing again, Hegai lifted a jasmine flower to his nose and breathed in the scent. His eyes fluttered closed for a moment. Then he looked at her.

"You want my advice?"

"Yes, what should I wear? What should I take? I do not want to choose alone."

He nodded. "I will help you, but perhaps the answer isn't as far away as you think." He turned to face the palace behind him. "Esther, what do you know about Xerxes already? What does he favor?"

Esther turned, too, her eyes moving over the palace complex. Although the expansive building was filled with ornamental things, many decorations were similar. "Much of the furnishings, curtains, and drapes are dark blue. Persian blue, as my cousin calls it when he works at the King's Gate."

Then her eyes moved from the complex to the garden. "The gardens are filled with numerous flowers, mainly jasmine and roses." She stroked her chin. "Also, the king's wealth is beyond measure, yet he still chose to ride to the fight with his men. He's a leader, but he knows the lands he rules." Esther's voice rose slightly. "And when he left for Greece, Xerxes honored the custom of having the empty chariot of Ahura Mazda, drawn by eight white horses, with him. I could tell that meant something to him."

"You have come to your conclusions, then." Hegai's eyes sparkled.

"Yes, but can you still help me choose? I will only take what you tell me to."

"Of course." Hegai continued his pace. "If you trust me, I will gather only the things I think are necessary and have them ready for your visit."

Esther clapped her hands together as excitement bubbled up, warming her. "Yes, I trust you." She brushed her hair back from her shoulder. "And when will my visit be?" Her voice trembled when she asked.

"Seven days, Esther. One week until you leave my care. But I am happy to know that my work was not in vain. I know you are ready for this task. And for whatever is to come."

CHAPTER SEVENTEEN

Esther awoke to the sound of Tawana's movements in the room and the song of a bird just outside the window. Her rapid pulse was her first reminder of the importance of the day. But as she stretched and rose, so much felt the same—like the hunger that gnawed her stomach and the whispered prayers to Yahweh that sprang from her heart. How could those things feel so ordinary when, today, everything would change?

Aafreen drew a bath, and Tawana folded Esther's linens and blankets. Two of her other maids set out a few simple foods on her dining table. Her three other maids entered, carrying the bundles that Hegai had prepared for her.

As Esther rose, Tawana moved to her mattress and folded it. It, too, would be moved. By tomorrow her room would be cleaned. Would a new occupant soon fill it?

Esther's brow furrowed. She would not think about that too much. Ignoring the additional young women brought to the castle was the only way she could settle the pounding of her heart.

Instead, Esther took Mordecai's advice and considered Xerxes her husband. Even though she did not yet know him, she had still dedicated her heart to him.

Esther focused on their relationship, not those of his other wives, concubines, or others in his harem. She didn't allow her mind to wander, considering their experiences and whether or not they pleased the king.

Over the last six days, Esther had planned to stay in her room when the others exited their rooms, dressed and ready to meet the king. But after a few days, she couldn't help herself. She wanted to see too, when she heard the murmurings of the others in the hall as they watched one of their friends leave for the king's quarters.

Esther had stepped out to see Anahita dressed in splendor. The layers of fabric, veils, and jewels shone, causing Esther to suck in a breath. Anahita wore long layered colored skirts, a long flowing veil, and a headpiece of rubies. Jeweled bracelets wrapped around her arms like vines, sparkling with precious stones.

"You look like a queen."

Surprisingly, the words had come from Esther's lips.

"Of course I do," Anahita had answered simply. Then the blond beauty met each of their gazes before she strode away as if saying, "This is how it's done."

Anahita had yet to return. None of them would. After each young woman spent a night with the king, she was moved into the harem.

How did things work there? Did the women talk among themselves about their exploits with the king? She hoped not. To think of Xerxes as her husband alone, and dedicate her heart to him in that way, was the only way she'd live a contented existence within these palace walls. And today was her day. Now was her time to prepare.

Hours later, Esther looked at her reflection in the polished bronze mirror. She closed her eyes and slowly opened them again, scarcely believing it was herself she was seeing.

Following Hegai's suggestions, Esther bathed, and her hair was washed with henna. She then received a massage with olive oil, cassia oil, myrrh, and honey. Her maids used pomegranate juice for her lips. They did not stain her cheeks or apply kohl to her eyes at Hegai's suggestion.

"You have a natural, simple beauty," he'd told her. "Restraint is often the greatest jewel." Esther knew he'd spoken those things aloud not only for her sake but also for her attendants. They must not do too much.

Her dark blue gown was simple, and her white cape, which fastened at her shoulders, was embroidered with gold thread. Instead of tassels, white feathers cascaded over her shoulders, reminiscent of Ahura Mazda's wings.

The front of Esther's hair was pinned up and adorned with jasmine, while the rest cascaded down her back. In her hand, she carried one single red rose.

Even though days had passed since she'd seen Anahita in all her sparkling glory, tension still tightened around Esther's chest like a rope that hadn't eased. Tonight was her turn, and her simple garments couldn't be more opposite from Anahita or—from what she'd heard—the others who'd gone before her. *Am I making the right choice?*

Esther pushed feelings of insecurity out of her mind as she slid her feet into simple sandals.

"Would you like a fan? A handpiece? More jewels?" Tawana asked, her eyes narrowed and her brow wrinkled with concern.

"I am confident," Esther stated simply. *I will only take what Hegai suggested,* Esther reminded herself.

Then, when all was ready, Esther strode out of her room to the waiting audience of eunuchs and other young women.

Hegai smiled broadly and nodded his approval. He approached and leaned close, speaking only loud enough for Esther to hear. "Your body will be as a goddess before him, but do not be afraid to speak. The king should know of your mind."

"What should I say?" Her mouth grew dry at the idea of speaking to the king.

"Whatever comes to you—not a planned speech. Honor Xerxes as a king, but speak to him as a man."

Esther smiled and nodded, and then she followed Hegai as he led the way to her king.

CHAPTER EIGHTEEN

Goose bumps rose on Esther's skin as she walked through the king's quarters toward his bedchamber. *Breathe, Esther. All is well.* She replayed the words in her mind, hoping they'd slow the pounding of her heart. Yet it did little good.

Carved furniture filled the rooms. Linen drapes hung from tall columns. Colorful mosaics displayed lions—a symbol of strength and power. They also were decorated with images from Persian mythology with abundant flowers and trees. *Symbols of fertility and life.*

The pounding of her heart continued. As they turned down one last hall, Esther fixed her gaze on the tall doors ahead. *Xerxes's bedchamber.*

Hegai walked by her side, pausing before two eunuchs who guarded either side of the door.

She stilled. Her eyebrows lifted in surprise when she recognized them as guards who sometimes guarded the King's Gate. *Bigthana and Teresh.* Yes, they'd sat and listened to her stories many times.

"Dido?" Bigthana whispered. Then he met eyes with Teresh, clearly as awed by Esther's transformation as she had been.

She gave him the slightest nod and held the rose tighter.

From the corner of her eye, Esther knew Hegai had turned in her direction. But she refused to look at him. Surely if she met his gaze, tears would come—just as when she'd left Mordecai.

"Ready?" Hegai asked.

"Yes." Esther smiled and took a deep breath. Since she was a child, she'd wondered about the man Yahweh would lead her to. *My husband.*

The doors opened before her, and she stepped inside. Then the doors closed behind her. She paused to allow her eyes to adjust to the dim candlelight. The king lounged on a long cushion. He motioned her forward without lifting from his elbows. He wore a simple tunic, so different from the uniform he'd worn as he rode in his chariot all those years ago. His dark hair was brushed back, and it curled behind his ears. His beard was trimmed shorter than the last time she'd seen him.

Esther felt the king's eyes above his grin, measuring her. A cold sweat broke out on her upper arms, and she again told herself to breathe. She knew the beautiful women who'd already passed through this room. She knew those who still waited. She remembered Vashti's elegance and beauty, and she couldn't compare. Instead, her goal was to honor the king, the one Yahweh placed on this throne.

Even if Xerxes did not choose her as queen, he would be her husband. Tonight she wouldn't think of any of the other women. She wouldn't even think of herself. Tonight she would think only of him.

"What is your name?" He tilted his head with his appraisal.

"Esther." She continued to him, and as she neared, she studied his face. His face was long, and his jaw was chiseled and strong like the rest of him. His brown eyes widened as if he were trying to keep emotion out of them.

"What do you think?" His hand swept toward the luxurious furnishing, statues, and tapestries. He sat patiently, waiting for her opinion.

He wants to know what I think about his furnishings? Did even a king protect his heart by erecting a wall around it, just as he constructed buildings and monuments? For some reason, that made her smile. She placed one hand on her hip and looked him directly in his eyes.

"Honestly, I didn't come to look at your couches and drapes." She wrinkled her nose slightly. "I planned to get to know you. I've been waiting twelve months to do so."

His mouth dropped open slightly, and the slightest laughter spilled out. "Please come join me."

Esther moved forward with soft steps as if the floor was made of glass. His eyes followed her. She paused and set the rose on the closest table. Then she reached up and removed her cape. The feathers fluttered softly as she placed it over a chair. Then she continued, Xerxes watching her every move.

She studied how he reclined, as he no doubt did most nights. Should she sit at his feet? Kneel at his side? She thought of her mother and father. Her favorite memories were of her mother reclining against her father's chest.

Before she could talk herself out of it, she sat on the cushion next to him so closely that she leaned against his arm. His brow lifted in surprise, and he readjusted to support her.

Without a word, his fingers curled under the strap of her gown. He gazed eagerly into her eyes. When she smiled again, his gaze softened.

"Are you not afraid?"

"I should be. This is the closest I've ever been to a man, let alone the king, but I know I will most likely not be chosen out of all the beautiful young women. I have decided this is my one chance to get to know you, and I will not lose that chance to fear."

"You have come to get to know me?"

"Who wouldn't want to know you? I've heard the stories. I've even *told* tales about you, but it's not as if you're a mythical creature. You're human." Esther shrugged. "I've always wanted to know the truth about who you are."

Xerxes released her dress strap. "What do you mean that you've told stories about me?" His breath was warm on her ear, sending a shiver down her spine.

"I'm a storyteller. Before coming to the palace, I'd often sit by the King's Gate, near the offices of the court officials. Maybe you've heard of me?"

Ignoring her question, he straightened his shoulders and his eyebrows lifted. "What stories did you tell about me?"

"Many stories of the uprisings you've put down and the battles you've won. Would you like to hear about how Egypt thought they'd revolt against your father, Darius, who died before he could deal with it? Thankfully, you rose to the throne at just the right time." She paused and tapped her chin with the tip of her finger. "Then again, since you lived it, perhaps you should tell me."

He laughed again and shook his head. "Can someone so beautiful be so knowledgeable too?"

Esther turned her face fully toward his. "You think I'm beautiful?" She had never thought of kissing a man before. Yet it would be easy to lean forward and touch her lips to his. Warmth spread through her stomach at the thought.

"Yes, I think you're beautiful." His voice was gentle now. "How can I not?" He reached up and pulled a jasmine flower from her hair, pressing it to his nose and breathing it in. "Your beauty is pure...." He stroked the flower's petals down her cheek, and her eyes fluttered closed for the briefest moment. Then they opened again.

"You came in here without silks and embroideries. Without jewels."

He smelled of cedar and citrus. Her lips parted slightly as she leaned her face closer. "You've seen jewels before, haven't you?"

"Yes, more jewels than you can imagine." His voice was husky.

"But you haven't seen me...." She waited for the kiss.

Xerxes adjusted and leaned forward. He kissed her cheek, her nose, and chin. He sighed, kissed just to the side of her lips, and then pulled back.

Her eyes opened in surprise.

"Esther, can you tell me a story?" He offered a crooked grin.

"You want a story?" she asked breathlessly.

"Yes." He wrapped an arm around her shoulder, stroking her arm with his fingers. She shivered at the sensation, and he laughed again.

Her heart pounded, and she was confident he could hear it—or at least feel it since their bodies were nestled so close.

Xerxes kissed her temple. "Go ahead," he teased.

Esther cleared her throat and chose one of her favorite Persian tales. "The first man to be king—to have a crown placed on his head and to sit upon a throne—was Kayumars." The words spilled out. She breathed in and then out, hoping to slow her words. "Kayumars lived in the mountains, and his people wore leopard skins for clothes. He taught men how to prepare food and sew clothing—because, you see, clothes were new to the world at that time."

He trailed his fingers down her arm and up again. Esther's breath caught, and she sighed.

Humor sparked in his eyes. "You like that touch?" He did it again.

"I haven't known a husband's touch before. It's nice." She reached up and squeezed the muscles in his arms. Heat rose to her cheek. She guessed they'd turned red because he laughed again.

"I remember when I first saw you on your chariot. Warmth grew in my stomach, and I had to look away." She wasn't sure why she'd confessed that.

"You looked away as the mighty king of the Medes and the Persians drove his chariot out to war?" His voice lowered slightly as if upset, but tenderness filled his gaze.

"I had to look away. I'd never felt such stirrings for any man, let alone the king."

"Speaking of a king. I need you to finish your story."

Xerxes reached up with his free hand and stroked her hair.

"As if I could put two words together with how my heart is pounding right now."

"Go ahead. I'm listening." He cocked one eyebrow and offered a crooked smile.

Esther nodded and attempted to focus. What had she been saying? "Yes, well, after Kayumars taught the men how to live, he settled himself on his throne, shining as splendid as the sun. Kayumars reigned for thirty years. His glory rose like the height of a cypress tree topped by a moon. Drawn to him, the animals of the world came and bowed down. And that king had a son, who had a son, who had a son, and so on until we come to the great King Xerxes—as strong as a bull in battle, yet as tender as a shepherd with a lamb—"

"And are you, Esther, my lamb?" He interrupted her words and kissed her gently, then deeper, firmer.

So full of lightness her body seemed to float, Esther wrapped a hand to the back of his neck, delighting in the feel of him.

Even though she knew this wasn't his first time with a woman, far from it, there was innocence in his touch. His arms moved around her gently as if afraid she would break.

When he pulled back from their kiss, questions filled his gaze. His eyes were hopeful and eager, as if he wanted to make her happy.

No matter what came of their relationship after this, Xerxes was her husband. She would always think of him as so.

As her eyes fluttered close, the scent of the rose wrapped around her, and she thought again of the vendor's words, *"She who wants a rose must respect the thorn."*

To see Xerxes as her husband, she had to offer her heart. A prick of pain jabbed her soul too.

His hand moved down her body, causing her to shiver. For many years, she wondered what it was like to be loved as a man loved his wife. She never imagined the one she'd give her whole self to would be the king himself—*my husband.*

***

Sometime in the night, two eunuchs entered Xerxes's bedchamber and woke her. Heat rose to Esther's cheeks for them to see her like this—in her husband's bed.

"Come. It is time to take you to your new place in the harem," one of the eunuchs whispered.

She wrapped a linen sheet around her and started to rise when Xerxes's hand grasped hers.

"No," his sleepy voice croaked. "Esther stays." Then he waved a hand dismissing the eunuchs.

Surprise widened the men's eyes, and they hurried away.

Esther lay in bed, unsure of what to say or do. Both of them were awake now, and from the view of the graying morning through the window, she guessed it would be only another hour before dawn.

As Esther curled against the warmth of Xerxes's body, she was thankful her husband had sent the eunuchs away. He tucked an arm under her, and she nestled against his chest and under his chin.

Her mind carried her back to the first time she saw Xerxes. She'd never thought she'd be here now. She'd believe it more likely that the desert sands turned to oceans than she'd be loved by the king—at least loved on this night.

All those years when he'd fought in Greece, she'd prayed that Yahweh would bring Xerxes back to Susa. She didn't know then that her prayers would mean he'd also return to her. What had he thought about during those battles? What had he experienced?

Minutes passed, and Xerxes brushed a strand of hair from her face. "Are you awake?" he whispered.

"Yes."

"What are you thinking about?"

"Honestly?"

"Yes."

"Greece."

The muscles in his arms stiffened. His breathing caught for a moment before it resumed again.

"Why are you thinking of Greece?" His voice was no longer as tender as it had been.

She considered changing the subject but guessed that would only make him angrier.

"I just want to ask you one question."

He pulled back slightly, bringing space between them. "You dare question me?"

His tone sounded more hurt than angry. Was he afraid to show any side of weakness? She guessed so. Yet something inside told her to press forward. To let Xerxes know that he could trust her with his losses and wounds as well as with his victories.

"Someone once told me the truth does not mind being questioned, yet a lie does not like being challenged." She turned her face and settled a kiss on his arm. "I only want to know the truth…what matters to you deep inside—not only what the scribes write in the annals of the king."

His heartbeat quickened slightly. Then he released a breath. "You may ask."

Esther considered her words, and then she leaned up on one elbow. She could barely make out his face in the flickering light of the one oil lamp that still burned. "I know your father wished to conquer Greece. But was that your heart's desire also?"

"I was born into this role and must play my part. Do you dare to question my goals?" His nostrils flared.

She sent up a quick prayer for the right words. "I do not dare, of course, but when I look at you, I see a warrior, but I see much more." She couldn't help but reach up to lay a gentle hand on his face.

"Do you, Esther?" He closed his eyes and touched her hand. "Amazingly, I think you do."

From the tone of his voice, she was sure that if she could see into his eyes, she'd see the pain reflected there. Longing too.

"Yes, I see *you*, Xerxes, and I cannot imagine it is easy to be king."

"Especially one who returns in defeat." There was no anger in his voice, and Esther knew he spoke his heart. She also guessed not a thousand young virgins could heal those parts of him. Yet maybe one compassionate bride could.

"I'm not an expert on such matters, Husband, but you are the King of the Persians and the Medes. That name alone declares victory. More than that, our deeds are not based upon the success or failure of one event."

"They're not?" He peered closer into her face. "Then what?"

Was Xerxes just humoring her, or did he care what she had to think?

"I believe success is made up of the story of our *days*. And from what I know, your story is one of victory. Your kingdom stretches from the Lapis Lazuli mountains to the edges of a salt desert, does it not? But more than that, the tender care you gave me last night shows me the greatness of your heart. I applauded you as a warrior, but there is so much more that I'm just beginning to see."

A heavy sigh, as if the release of a heavy burden, escaped from his lips. Then the warrior-man pulled Esther close once again.

As the first lights of dawn brightened the room, Esther met his dark gaze. A warmth filled her, moving into her limbs. As Xerxes leaned in for a kiss, her lips parted, and she sucked in a breath. "My lord." She could only whisper it as an unbelievable love for this man rushed through her.

CHAPTER NINETEEN

A knocking on the door hours later awakened Esther again. This time Xerxes allowed the eunuchs to take her away. He was a king with duties to tend to, after all.

She was led to a new wing of apartments where the king's harem lived. Thankfully, none of the other women were in the common areas, and she guessed they broke their fast and dressed in their private quarters.

Esther's seven maids waited for her in her new apartment, which was slightly bigger than the one she'd left. A tall, thin eunuch waited for her there.

"I am Shaashgaz, the king's eunuch in charge of the concubines," he said, introducing himself. "I will leave you to bathe, dress, and get settled. Food will arrive shortly, and I will come by and show you around the garden and explain your new life in the harem this afternoon."

Even though Esther could read questions in the eyes of her handmaidens, she wasn't ready to share about her night with the king. She doubted she'd ever be ready. She wanted to cherish her time with Xerxes.

Instead, there was only small talk as the maids unpacked her things. After eating, Esther excused herself to bed, asking her handmaidens to leave her alone.

Her mind spun with everything that had happened during her time with the king. She replayed each moment, and longing filled her to see Xerxes again. Yet she knew that wouldn't be so. Even now, she guessed one of the other young women was preparing to go to him. Though she'd promised herself not to dwell on that, Esther's heart felt bruised and tender. She snuggled deeper into her bed, pulling a pillow over her head to block the sun's light.

She must have fallen into a fitful sleep, because heavy footsteps on the polished floors of her apartment stirred her awake. Opening her eyes, she saw the sun straight overhead. Had she slept the morning away? She held her breath, wondering who approached. Then she remembered that Shaashgaz had said he'd be returning. Could she tell him she didn't care about the gardens or other luxuries he had to show her? None of that mattered.

Footsteps stopped outside her door, and she could hear voices. Shaashgaz talked with her maids just outside her bedroom door. Esther listened intently, but she couldn't make out the words. Then all was quiet again.

Her body grew tense in the silence. She sat up just as the door to her private bedchamber opened. Shaashgaz took a step inside.

She forced a smile. "I am sorry, but can we do it tomorrow—tour the gardens? I'm not—"

Shaashgaz held up a hand, halting her words. "Esther. We will not be going to the gardens today. You are requested again. The king asks for you."

"He asks for me?" She stood to her feet, and her mouth dropped open. The sun filling the room seemed to flood her heart too. Tears came quickly, and she wiped them away.

"I'm sorry. I don't know why I'm crying. This is wonderful news. How long do I have to prepare?"

Shaashgaz's lips hinted of a grin at her rambling. "Less than two hours."

She took a step forward, and her mind raced, thinking about all she had to do. Then again, she wanted to take advantage of the time with Xerxes.

Attempting to keep the tremor out of her voice, Esther asked, "Shaashgaz, would you help me prepare?"

"Yes, Esther, of course. Do you want help choosing a gown or considering a hairstyle?"

"All of it. Down to every last detail. Choose for me what you think is best."

Just yesterday, Hegai had guided Esther's maids. *Was it just yesterday?*

She hurried to the bathing area while Shaashgaz left to choose a gown. Her shoulders tightened as she remembered Anahita's choice of attire, and Esther hoped that Shaashgaz would not have her strutting around like a peacock.

Hegai had been her friend, someone she'd known and trusted. Hegai had valued her mind as well as her body. Now she was putting her trust in someone she didn't know and who didn't know her.

She trembled as she waited for Shaashgaz to bring the clothes.

When she'd finished bathing, Shaashgaz entered her dressing room with two new maids by his side. In his hands, he held an exquisite gown in royal purple. Esther stepped into it and lifted her arms. Long, trailing sleeves felt as light as air. Tiny beads decorated the waist. An intricate pattern of gold threads had been embroidered into the bodice.

Esther sat, and Shaashgaz slid dainty beaded slippers onto her feet. Then he instructed one of the maids to sweep her hair back from her face. A second maid swept a light powder on her face.

When they had finished, Esther turned to look at her reflection in the bronze. Her neck and shoulders were bare and appeared smooth as silk.

She touched her face and lifted her gaze to Shaashgaz. "Are you sure? It seems so simple." *Even simpler than last night.*

"Last night's attire was to capture the king's attention. But tonight is different, seeing that you already have his attention." Then Shaashgaz leaned close, whispering into her ear. "Esther, you are the first maiden he has requested for a second night. I've served the king for many years. I, more than anyone, know the king's taste."

"Thank you, Shaashgaz. I trust you." She rose and turned, feeling like a butterfly who'd just emerged from a cocoon. She lifted her arms and let her sleeves flutter down. Butterflies danced in her stomach too.

"There's one more thing." After leading her down the hall to a guarded door, Shaashgaz took her inside. Wooden chests lining the walls were open and filled with jewels.

She covered her mouth with her hand as she looked at the boxes that displayed hairpins, necklaces, arm cuffs, and more. Minutes ticked past as Shaashgaz studied the items. He finally chose one turquoise ring with gold flecks in the stone. He also chose a necklace with a miniature lion pendant. The image reminded Esther of one of the mosaics in Xerxes's apartment.

"Yes, perfect," she said as Shaashgaz helped to fasten it around her neck.

Then Shaashgaz led her out of the room and pointed down the hall. "We will have to pass through the inner courtyard," he said simply.

Esther nodded, understanding. She had to pass through the area where the harem now lounged.

"I'll be happy to see Xerxes." She didn't know what else to say. How could she tell Shaashgaz the other women weren't her primary concern?

Esther kept her gaze straight ahead as she walked by Shaashgaz's side. She didn't have to look into the women's faces to sense the tension in the room. As she passed through, Esther knew all eyes were on her.

I'm the only one he's requested twice. It was impossible not to smile. She didn't want to get her hopes up. She didn't want to be prideful and believe this was one step closer to being a queen. *But could it be?*

"So the king is expecting me now?" she asked as they walked.

Shaashgaz smiled. "Knowing Xerxes, I would guess that he already waits."

CHAPTER TWENTY

As the doors swung open, Esther entered the bedchamber to find Xerxes lounging on the cushions near the windows overlooking Susa. With the palace set upon a hill, the view was stunning. Yet Esther focused only on the man.

My husband.

"Esther, come." His voice was soft and gentle. He wore no shirt, and his skin glistened in the light of the afternoon sun.

Esther walked toward him with slow, sure steps. She paused before him and waited. Xerxes lifted a hand to her, and she placed her small hand in his. He gave the softest tug. With the release of a sigh, she lowered herself to her knees, allowing her body to sink into the cushions. Instinctively, she touched her husband's face, caressing his cheek. She couldn't help but smile.

"You sent for me." Emotion caught in her throat.

"How could I not, dear Esther? You are all I've been able to think about." He took her hand and pressed it to his lips. "My scribe had to start the same letter four times because I could not get my mind to think of the right words." He laughed and then turned her hand, exposing her wrist. Then he softly placed three kisses on the underside of her wrist, moving up her arm.

A shiver ran through her body. Goose bumps rose under his touch.

Xerxes laughed again. "So you like that, do you?" He placed another kiss.

"I like every moment with you." Heat rose to her cheeks, and she guessed he could see them growing pink. "I replayed last night over and over in my mind. All I could think about was you too."

"What did I ever do to deserve such a gift?" Xerxes whispered, pulling her even closer.

Esther allowed her body to relax and lie against her husband's chest, tucking her head under his chin. His hold engulfed her, the strength of his arms pulling her in.

They lay there in the quiet, and she dared to trace battle scars on his shoulder with her finger.

After a time, he pulled back slightly and kissed her forehead. "What are you thinking about, dear one? And, yes, the truth." He laughed.

She took a quick breath, embarrassed but also thankful he'd asked—that he wanted to know her thoughts. "I can hear your heartbeat as I press my ear against your chest. And when I do this"—she stroked down his shoulder to his arm and then back up again—"your heartbeat quickens."

Xerxes sighed. "So your gentle touch changes the heartbeat of a king, does it? I could have told you that. And how does that make you feel?"

"It feels wonderful to know that the king's heart beats for me tonight." Esther bit her lower lip. "Thank you."

With tenderness, Xerxes adjusted their bodies and placed her head onto a pillow. Next, he lowered his mouth for a long, involved kiss—his mouth teaching hers.

Gentle warrior. My gentle warrior. With all the things she expected her moments with Xerxes to be, she didn't expect this.

Xerxes didn't rush the moment. He pressed his mouth against hers and then lingered. Every few minutes, he drew away in small degrees, his gaze locking with hers.

"What are you looking at?" Esther whispered, daring to ask after his eyes met hers the third time.

"What am I looking at?" His voice was husky. "Your delight in being with me. Seeing the contentment and pleasure in your eyes gives me great joy." He kissed her chin and then smiled. "Knowing that you find satisfaction with any love I give makes me want to give you all of my heart."

"Then why don't you?" Esther lifted her head from the pillow, moving her lips to his. "I will gladly accept your heart, my husband, my king."

As the afternoon slipped into evening, two eunuchs brought dinner—far more than she and Xerxes could eat. Especially since food wasn't on either of their minds.

As they nibbled on grapes, cheese, figs, and bread, Xerxes's face grew pensive.

Esther picked up an almond and took a bite and then frowned. "What's wrong?"

He took a sip of wine and shrugged. "I was thinking about the morning."

She laughed. "We have hours before we have to think of that." She picked up a grape and tossed it, hitting his chest. But even that didn't make Xerxes smile. Instead, he stroked his beard, thoughtful.

Esther could tell that she shouldn't push him to talk. Xerxes would say to her what worried him when he was ready.

She ate more bread dipped in olive oil, and finally, he looked at her, focusing his eyes on hers. "I don't want you to go, and that is the problem."

"How can that be a problem?" Relief flooded her that he was already worried about her leaving. Then a wave of worry crashed over her when she noticed the distance in his eyes. He leaned back from the table, putting space between them. Was he building an invisible wall around his heart too?

Xerxes ran a hand through his hair. "I don't want you to leave in the morning. As we were eating, I was already making plans to send for you again too. But…"

"But…" Esther laid a hand on her pounding heart, finding it hard to breathe.

"Don't you see how it's easier to love many women than to love one?" He was silent for a time, looking away. "I did love Vasthi once, and I hurt her. My mind was gone from the wine. I would have never asked such a thing if I had been in my right mind."

Anguish distorted his face. She wanted to go to him, embrace him. But before she could, he stood and started to pace.

"I loved Vashti, and I hurt her." He said again, and he paused his pacing and glanced at Esther. "I do not mind disappointing many women I only see once. But because I care for you, I will be concerned for you. I will love you.

"A king must think of victory and conquest, not comfort. You, Esther, have become my comfort." He threw his hands up. "How can that be possible in only two days?"

Pushing her plate to the side, Esther couldn't hold back anymore. She walked to him, pausing before him. Her lower lip quivered, and she tried to hide it with a smile. "I would be foolish to ask for more than you can give, Xerxes. Know that I will come any time you send for me. I will love to spend time with you, whether another night or another hour. It does not matter."

With slow movements, Xerxes reached forward and placed his hands on her waist. "How did you ever find your way to me, dear Esther? What did I ever do to deserve you? I was told from the time I was a child that my life was for a purpose. For the first time, I glimpse what that purpose may be...in your eyes."

Then with one more kiss, the worry lines on his face faded. He gazed at her with a mischievous grin. Before Esther knew what was happening, Xerxes lifted her, slinging her over his shoulder like a bag of grain.

"Xerxes—" Her words cut short as he spun her once and then twice.

Laughter spilled out as he allowed her to slide back into his arms. "I'm sorry, dear, but I've just captured the most wonderful prize. Where were we before I let too many worries fill my mind? Oh yes, I was going to ask something of you."

Esther wobbled slightly on her feet as he set her down. She held up her hands, pausing him from approaching with another kiss. "Can you give me a minute to catch my breath?"

His eyebrows folded down into a frown. "Yes, of course."

Esther stepped back and then reached toward the chair closest to her. She grabbed a pillow from the chair and slammed it against him, surprising him.

"You were going to ask something from me? Was it a story?" Esther cocked one eyebrow. "Do you care for another story, my lord?" she teased, placing a hand on her hip.

"A story?" Xerxes laughed, grabbed the pillow she'd just tossed, and hugged it to his chest. He stepped forward, narrowing the distance before him.

For a moment, she thought she'd be hit by the pillow next, but then his smile softened. He tossed the pillow to the side and touched his finger to her chin, lifting her face, so her gaze met his.

Esther's knees trembled. "Yes, a story. Is that what you wanted to ask me about?" She reached up and placed a hand on his muscular arm, smiling at his reined-in strength.

"Not a story, at least not now. I have a different question, my queen." His head lowered for a kiss.

Esther lifted her face to accept his kiss but then paused as his words hit her.

"Queen?" Her word was no more than a whisper. "Xerxes?" Esther's throat tightened, and she didn't know whether to laugh with joy or cry with relief. So instead, she kissed him.

"Do you like the sound of that?" he whispered, his mouth inches from hers. "That's what I wanted to ask. If you agree, I will have it announced. Out of all the young women, I choose you, Esther."

"I love the sound of that." She flung her arms around his neck. "I'd love nothing more than to be your queen, Xerxes."

<hr>

The following day, the reality of what Xerxes had asked sank in. When morning came, Esther opened her eyes. Staring into the bright blue canopy overhead, she needed a moment to remember where she was. And that's when she remembered.

Xerxes wishes for me to be his queen.

She stretched out her hand across the bed, searching for her husband. His side of the bed was empty. The coolness of the sheets told her that he'd been gone a while.

For the second night in a row, she'd wakened off and on through the night as her body sought his. To feel him through the night—his body next to hers—made her truly feel like Xerxes's bride.

A year ago, when she'd been brought into the palace, her breathing would quicken and her stomach would churn at the thought of being led to the king's bed. But today, she truly felt like a bride.

Rising to one elbow, Esther noticed something resting on the pillow. A red rose and a piece of parchment. Lifting it, Esther saw a curved image sealed with the king's signet ring.

A heart. The king is giving me his heart.

Esther sat up straighter, a buzzing growing in her midsection. To be the queen was a great honor, but having Xerxes's heart meant even more.

An internal lightness and a sense of calm moved out from her chest, spreading to her limbs. Then cold reality hit her. What would the others in the harem think?

Esther shook her head, choosing not to focus on them. Today she would rejoice in her husband's love.

She lifted the rose from the pillow and drew it to her nose, breathing in its scent. Rising from the bed, she slipped into a colorful linen robe laid out for her and knotted it around her waist. In her chambers, she'd gotten used to her maids serving her and tending to her. Esther didn't know what to do.

Walking barefoot to the door, Esther opened it to find one of the king's eunuchs waiting there.

She let out a startled laugh. "I'm so sorry. I didn't expect you."

"I was told to wait and, after you'd wakened, tell you that the king would like you to dress."

Esther placed a hand over her heart. "Will he return here, back in his chambers?"

"No, the king wishes you to come to him in his council room where an audience awaits."

Tears rushed to Esther's eyes, and her hand covered her mouth. A sob escaped.

The eunuch took a surprised step back. "Are you all right? Do you feel ill?"

Esther managed to laugh as she looked up at him. "I'm sorry. What is your name?"

"Hathak."

"I am sorry, Hathak. These are happy tears." Esther squeezed her fist and placed it on her chest. "My soul soars with hope. Yes, these are the happiest tears."

CHAPTER TWENTY-ONE

With the help of her maids—and under the advice of Shaashgaz—Esther dressed in a colorful gown of blues and reds. Fringe decorated the sleeves and hem, swishing as Esther walked.

A drape of red, sheer fabric was placed over her shoulders, and a large gold pendant was set around her neck with additional beads.

Shaashgaz slid large golden decorated cuffs onto her wrists and up her arms. He directed her maid to style her hair in long curls to trail down her back.

Esther tapped her toes, eager to see her husband. Still, she smiled as her maid slid rings upon her fingers. Although she wanted to look her best, Esther wanted to see Xerxes more. She longed to look into his eyes to know if the glimmers of love she'd seen were just as accurate in the daylight.

Finally, after she'd stepped into fine blue slippers, Shaashgaz nodded his approval. "Come with me," he stated plainly, leading the way.

Today, as she was led to the council room, Esther didn't let her mind wander to the mosaics, tile frescos, statutes, or tapestries. She looked down the hall as she walked, and her heartbeat quickened.

Her slippers made no sound on the tiles as she entered the large room with high ceilings. Men lined either side of the room, and Xerxes sat on a raised throne. A thin band of gold circled his head, and he held a glinting scepter in his hand.

Xerxes was in deep conversation with a man. His shoulders were drawn forward, and he peered down the brim of his nose. Esther knew he wasn't pleased with the man's report.

The man pulled a scroll from a waist pack and started to open it.

Esther shifted her weight, wishing the man would finish his business quickly so that she could approach her husband and hear why he'd asked her to come.

Then, as if sensing her presence, Xerxes looked to the back of the room and saw her. A smile filled his face, and he stood. With a quick wave of his hand, Xerxes excused the man. Two eunuchs led the man away.

With his golden scepter, Xerxes motioned her forward.

Esther strolled toward the king. She gazed on his smile. While she still saw the warrior in his stance, she'd also come to know the man's heart.

Before Yahweh, this man was already her husband. And now her husband, her king, had chosen to declare her his queen.

As Esther approached, Xerxes reached for her hand, taking it in his.

"In my search for a queen, I have required my guards to be diligent. I requested they seek the four corners of my kingdom to find beautiful maidens to be considered for my future bride."

Esther saw that his scribe wrote down every word.

"My heart now fills with love for the one I choose. Although I have known many maidens, no one is as beautiful, kind, or thoughtful as Esther." Xerxes turned his face away from the crowd, and his eyes settled on her.

At that moment, she wanted to say something to declare her love for him—to thank him for choosing her. Instead, she pressed her lips together, waiting patiently, trusting that he'd let her know what to do or say.

"I, Xerxes, the king of the Persians and the Medes, declare that I have chosen Esther as my queen. From this day, she will be considered the fairest—the one I adore. Whoever chooses to break her heart will break mine and face my wrath."

Xerxes motioned to a eunuch, who walked toward a box sitting near the throne.

The eunuch opened the box, reached in, and pulled out the most dazzling crown Esther had ever seen. Bands of gold twisted upward, appearing like vines and flowers stretching into the heavens. Precious jewels were mounted on golden petals. Even though she'd seen many fine jewels recently, Esther had never seen anything as beautiful. The eunuch approached. With a smile, Xerxes took the crown from the man's hands.

As Xerxes lifted the crown over Esther's head, she tried to remain strong, attempting to keep her lower lip from quivering. But it was no use. Joyful tears slipped from the corners of her eyes as she looked into her husband's face.

Xerxes placed the crown upon her head, and its weight healed her heart like myrrh, oil, and honey. Her husband's kingdom stretched to the four corners of the earth, and deep in Esther's soul, she prayed that Yahweh would make her way clear as queen.

Esther opened her mouth to speak. Her husband's slight nod urged her to continue. "I have never known such great honor as being seen as worthy in your eyes, my great king. Forever, from this moment, I long to be your compassionate bride. I will give all of myself to the betterment of my king and his kingdom.

"I, Esther, desire not to make a name for myself but to be a helpmate to my husband. And as he has chosen me, I will forever choose him."

Seeing love radiating in Xerxes's eyes, Esther smiled.

"From the first day I stepped into the palace, I have desired to set my eyes on my king alone. Thank you for your trust, my dear King Xerxes. May your people know that their queen will strive to be worthy of their trust all her days."

Esther's words quieted, and a cheer rose around the room. Xerxes brushed a long, dark lock from her shoulder with a bright smile. Then he leaned down to whisper in her ear. "Look, my queen. The people celebrate you. And as they get to know you, they will love you just as I do."

Esther cast her eyes over the crowd with her heart pounding. Warmth seeped into every inch of her body. Beyond them, the king's highest officials sat on a raised platform. Nobles from every end of the kingdom clapped in celebration.

Yet as Esther's eyes moved back to her king, another face caught her attention. Haman sat just a few rows back from Xerxes's throne. His shoulders slumped as if his purple cape weighed as much as one of the pillars. Though Haman smiled and clapped, pure evil glared at her from behind his gaze.

Esther's stomach lurched, and she caught her breath quickly, turning her head away. Xerxes's hand moved around her back and tightened on her shoulder.

"Are you all right?"

Esther swallowed, pushing down her emotion. "I will be fine. It's just so much. It's so much to be thankful for." She quickly wiped away tears and looked at her husband's face.

"As much as I love the celebration," she said, only loud enough for him to hear, "I look forward to having a quiet moment with the king."

A smile broke out on Xerxes's face. "And that is why I have chosen you, my dear. Out of all the women I have ever known, I do not doubt that if you ever had to choose between me and this grand kingdom, you would choose me."

"Yes," Esther said as the laughter spilled from her lips. "Yes, my husband, my king, I would."

CHAPTER TWENTY-TWO

Esther fell asleep to the sound of music once again. This time the celebration was due to the announcement of a new queen. To celebrate the occasion, King Xerxes gave a great banquet in Esther's honor for all his nobles and officials. He even declared a public holiday for the provinces, giving generous gifts to everyone.

The night of the banquet, Esther stayed up as late as she could, laughing and feasting, but the music still played as she made her way back to her chambers.

As the weeks passed, Esther enjoyed time with Xerxes whenever they could be together. Some days they dined alone, enjoying private conversations. Other times, he invited her to dinners with nobles. At the end of each dinner, Xerxes urged her to tell a story.

Yet, as much as she enjoyed time with her husband, she always found an excuse not to attend any function that Haman planned to participate in. Deep down, Esther wondered if she should tell her husband about the story she'd told in the marketplace—and Haman's threats. But every time she thought of it, her throat clenched tight as if clamped with a vise.

For Xerxes to understand her conflict with Haman, she'd have to explain how her people had been enemies with

Haman's ancestors for generations. Although Esther was never ashamed about being a Jew, her cousin's urging to keep this fact to herself wouldn't leave her. *I will trust Mordecai.*

Not long after she'd been made queen, she and Xerxes lounged in the king's garden under the shade of a cypress tree. With the aroma of jasmine filling the air, Xerxes pulled her close, kissing her temple. "I was talking to one of my eunuchs, and it seems as if someone you know has been appointed to a palace office."

"Someone I know?" Esther attempted to turn, to look into his face, but Xerxes pulled her close.

"No use trying to escape," he teased.

Laughing, Esther melted into his arms. "I don't want to escape. There's nowhere I'd rather be, Xerxes." She rubbed his arm in long smooth strokes. "But you have to tell me who— someone I knew from the market?"

"Yes, and someone you knew from your home."

Esther squealed, and Xerxes released her, enabling Esther to turn to face him. She rose, her knees pressing into the cushions they lounged on, and she put her hands on his shoulders. "Are you saying that Mordecai is now a court official?"

"He is." Xerxes laughed.

Then placing her hands on the side of his face, Esther offered him a kiss. "Thank you," she whispered, returning to her spot by his side.

"You can thank me, but Mordecai earned his position." Xerxes twirled a strand of her long hair around his finger. "I found out because he wanted permission to meet with you." Xerxes's voice was solemn. "I was told the matter was urgent."

A sinking feeling fell in the pit of Esther's gut. "Did Mordecai say if something's wrong? Is he unwell?"

"I'm sorry. There was no specific information, but I asked my eunuch to set up a time for him to come to you tomorrow."

Esther leaned her head against him. Gratitude for her husband and worries for her cousin fought for a prominent place in her mind. "Thank you," she whispered. "Thank you."

As much as she wanted Mordecai to meet her husband, Esther needed to talk to him and discover this urgent matter first. She also needed to explain to her cousin that although she'd left his home in tears, she now truly loved the man Yahweh had put on the throne.

What would Mordecai say? Would he understand? She hoped it would ease some of his guilt about not traveling to Jerusalem or finding her a husband all those years ago.

The next morning, the warm wind ruffled her hair as Esther sat in her private garden. Today she would know what Mordecai's urgent message was about. Esther stood and paced, waiting for her cousin to arrive. At the sound of footsteps, she turned, and there he stood.

Immediately, her heart sank. Even though not two years had passed since she'd last seen him, Mordecai appeared to have aged twenty years. His previously dark hair was now mostly gray, and his cheeks were sunken. Only his bright eyes, as he approached her with open arms and a large smile, caused Esther's heart to leap.

Mordecai had barely made it onto the patio when Esther rushed into his arms for a hug. Yet his arms felt stiff. "I'm not sure what to do or say," he confessed.

Pulling back from his arms, Esther took Mordecai's hands and looked up into his face. "Dear cousin, you don't have to do or say anything differently than you did throughout my life."

Mordecai's eyebrows lifted. "Easy for you to say. You left as a young woman and now stand before me a queen." He cocked his head as he took in the light blue gown and the beaded necklaces she wore. "You look beautiful, as you should."

Yet even as he smiled, she noted fear in his gaze. After dismissing the eunuchs, Esther motioned for Mordecai to sit on the carved bench. Then she sat next to him.

Taking his hand in hers, she leaned in close. "Please tell me what bothers you. I fear your urgent visit is not because you want to share good news."

Mordecai ran a hand through his hair and looked around. "Are we alone?"

She glanced around her, nodding. "Yes, this is my private patio."

"Esther, there is a problem. There are men in this palace who wish to kill your husband. You must go to Xerxes, tell him. There isn't a minute to wait."

Esther had never been more thankful to receive word that Xerxes had requested her presence in his chamber that night.

But Xerxes wasn't in his chambers when she'd arrived. She paced as she waited, twisting the silk sash of her robe in her hands. *Yahweh, today may I have Your favor. Help me to relay the message correctly. Help my husband trust my warnings.*

When Xerxes arrived, he must have seen the worry on her face. "Esther, what is it? Surely the news from Mordecai hasn't crushed your heart."

She motioned to a sofa. Xerxes sat, and she sat beside him.

"I spoke to my cousin, and you know I trust him, right?"

"What is it, Esther? You look troubled." He placed a hand on her knee.

"My cousin, Mordecai, was on duty at the King's Gate, and he overheard two of your guards."

"What do you mean?"

She leaned close, speaking in a whisper. "Two of your eunuchs, Bigthana and Teresh—who guard the doors of this bedchamber—are angry with you. They are so angry that they are plotting to assassinate you." The words didn't sound natural, even as she said them. "Your life is in danger, Xerxes."

Xerxes sucked in a breath, the color draining from his face. He rose to his feet and turned away, placing his hands on his hips. "Why didn't your cousin tell me himself?"

"He is a low-level court official. He does not have access to you." Esther rose and placed her hands on his back. "He wanted you to know, to act."

"And so he got the message to you." Xerxes blew out a quick breath.

"Mordecai raised me from a child. He knows I will trust him." She wrapped her arms around her husband, pressing her cheek to his back. "And he knows I will warn you."

Esther felt the pounding of Xerxes's heart. She held her breath, praying he'd believe her.

"Should I trust him?" Xerxes whispered. Then he turned to face her, searching her eyes.

"Do you trust me?" Esther grasped his hands.

"Yes." He squeezed her hands. "I do. Which means I've been betrayed."

With one quick movement, Xerxes pulled his hands from hers. Anger flashed in his eyes, and he squared his shoulders. "I have dealt with a revolt in Egypt and another in Babylon," he said, keeping his voice low. "I have gone to war and have the scars to prove I did not leave my men to fight alone. Yet now, I must face this in my bedchamber?"

Esther stepped back. Her body trembled seeing the warrior rise up within him. With slow movements, she sat back on a chair as Xerxes raised a fist into the air.

"I was afraid that was going to happen. Murmurs have erupted all over the kingdom that I have unfairly raised taxes." He stuck out his chin. "Men do not like to part with the coins in their pockets. Yet they enjoy traveling over my roads, having food on their tables and fine roofs over their heads." He moved to the door. "I will get to the bottom of this."

The quaver in his voice was unmistakable. Although he'd ridden out with thousands of men, this was his home. Those men protected his door.

Esther thought back to just last week when she slept by his side. Her husband had cried out, having a nightmare. She'd always thought that his nightmares were filled with things he'd seen or lived through—the fighting, blood, and death. It was more than enough to haunt one's dreams. But what if her husband also had nightmares of what was to be? Of the evil that lurked around him at every corner? Of the betrayal of those closest to him?

Xerxes did not return to his chamber that night, and when she exited in the morning, two guards she'd never seen before guarded the door.

She returned to her chambers and changed, dressed, and waited all day for news from her husband. *Why hasn't he sent for me? What's happening?*

Could the eunuchs have acted on their threats? Were other servants involved? Was Xerxes safe? She didn't want to think otherwise. Couldn't think otherwise.

It was only after dinner, when Esther planned to undress and prepare for bed, that a messenger arrived.

"The king requests you join him in his bedchamber, my queen."

"Yes. Take me now."

Esther walked with quickened steps, barely pausing for the guards to open his door for her. Xerxes sat on a chair, perched on the edge. His hair was disheveled, and he wore the same clothes he'd had on last evening. She rushed to him, kneeling before him. Tears filled her eyes as she grasped his hands. "You're all right. Oh, Husband, I'm so glad."

With weary, jerky movements, he lifted his hand and stroked his hair. "I haven't slept. How could I when I didn't know who to trust?" His voice sounded hollow and empty. "There has been an investigation. And what you said was true. Bigthana and Teresh's quarters were searched, and their plot was confirmed."

"Was it them alone?" she asked.

Xerxes nodded, and relief flooded over her.

"And what will happen to them?"

"Do you mean what *happened*? It's already done. They were impaled on sharpened poles." His hands trembled. "As soon as it was done, I sent for you."

He lifted his face, and red-rimmed eyes met hers. "Thank you, Esther. You have my love. And moreover now my trust."

She took his hands in hers and kissed them. "I am so thankful. So thankful." Then she sat straighter. "It was my cousin, Mordecai, who warned me, remember? He told me to tell you."

Weariness caused Xerxes's eyes to grow heavy, and he nodded. "Yes, of course."

Then Xerxes took her hand. He rose and helped her to her feet, and then led her to his bed. "Would you stay with me?" His voice sounded lost and afraid.

Xerxes climbed into bed, not bothering to change. He pulled a blanket over him.

"Yes, of course."

Esther curled by his side, also fully dressed. She lifted her hand to his hair, stroking it. It was only a matter of minutes before his snores told her that he slept.

By his side, Esther prayed for him. She also prayed that Yahweh would protect her husband from anyone who wished to hurt him. Prayed that every enemy among them would be found.

CHAPTER TWENTY-THREE

Esther stayed by her husband's side as long as he needed her. One week passed and then two, and Xerxes regained his confidence.

The first day when her husband did not send for her, Esther was sad not to see him. Yet she was also thankful that his confidence had returned. Every day, nobles arrived, seeking the king's audience. Xerxes's wisdom wasn't just needed in Susa but in all four corners of his domain.

When months passed and things had seemed to settle, Esther called for Mordecai to meet her in the queen's garden.

She smiled as her cousin entered, offering him a chair. "Yahweh used you greatly," she confessed. "I don't want to think—"

Mordecai held up his hands, pausing her words. "I am so thankful that you went to the king. I am even more thankful that he trusted your word—my word."

Esther straightened in her seat and tilted her head. She looked closer at Mordecai. Something was still wrong. Dark circles rimmed his eyes. New worry lines creased his face. "Maybe there is something Xerxes can do for you? To honor you?" *Surely there's not another threat that burdens him so.*

"I don't need to be rewarded, Esther." Mordecai smiled, but the smile did not reach his eyes. "I only did what was right.

Still, I know many people who are angry at Xerxes." Mordecai sighed. "The building projects are increasing, straining the coffers. The war on Greece was expensive. Taxes and tributes are on the rise.

"The people mumble because most days they only have enough coins to buy bread and lentils, yet their king finds it necessary to expand his palace." Mordecai cleared his throat. "I hope you don't mind me being so forthcoming."

"Of course not. It's me." She pressed her lips together, rose, and sighed.

Esther wished she could defend her husband, but Mordecai was right. Xerxes often was more focused on what he could build or obtain than on the people in his city, this kingdom.

She hadn't minded either. As long as Xerxes was immersed in an extensive building project, he didn't have time for visits from his concubines. More than that, he enjoyed talking to her about the designs that would go into the new buildings. She cherished that time together.

Maybe she needed to talk to her husband about the needs of their people. If there was one plot against his life, there might be more. Esther refused to dwell on that now, but she knew the worries would come soon enough. Losing him had been closer than she had imagined.

"I'm telling you this because people will only be unhappy for so long before they do something." Mordecai sighed.

"I don't want to think of what could happen. I don't want to lose my husband." Esther bit her lip. "It's selfish, I know, but what would become of me if that happened?" She placed a hand over her heart. "You're the only one I can admit that to, of course."

Mordecai stroked his beard, and Esther knew he worried about the same thing, even if he didn't voice it. "Yahweh cares for you, my cousin. You are the queen for a reason. Out of all the young women…" Even as Mordecai spoke, it sounded as if he was trying to convince himself as much as her.

Neither of them spoke for a while. Yet even in the midst of a garden full of birdsong, flowers, and trees, there was no peace. And when Mordecai cleared his throat, she braced herself.

Esther focused her attention on Mordecai. "What is it? Bad news has been bubbling up inside you since the moment you've arrived. I can see it, and I need to know."

Finally, Mordecai folded his hands in front of him. "Your husband, the king, has honored Haman, son of Hammedatha. He has elevated Haman and given him a seat of honor higher than all the nobles."

Coldness moved through Esther's veins as if the sun had just been plucked from the sky. "No, please do not tell me it is so. When did you hear this?"

"Just today. And I have no doubt that very soon you'll receive an invitation to the celebration of Haman's great honor."

Almost on cue, from off in the distance, music drifted from the king's banquet hall.

"No." Emotion caught in her throat. "If it's Haman, it will not be the type of event my husband invites me to." She thought of Vasthi, and the anguish to her soul propelled her to her feet. Esther turned and moved to the stone wall overlooking the hillside. The desire to run, to leave the palace while the music played, overwhelmed her. "At least let's hope he doesn't."

The music reminded Esther of her first night in the palace. Xerxes had invited all the men of Susa to a banquet, knowing they were preparing to leave for war. What her husband didn't know was that danger lurked again. Placing power in the hands of Haman could bring no good. At least when Xerxes marched to Greece, he knew who his enemy was.

How could her husband not see the truth about Haman? Even as Haman flattered Xerxes, his true desire was to rise in power, and no one would stand in his way.

"What does this honor mean for you?" Esther asked over her shoulder. She held her breath, waiting for the answer.

"For me?" Mordecai released a groan with his words. "All the royal officials at the King's Gate must now kneel and pay tribute to Haman, for the king has commanded this concerning him."

Esther spun around. "All the officials?"

"Yes, from the least to the greatest."

A sinking feeling came over Esther. Even now Mordecai's gaze narrowed and his nostrils flared.

In all the years he had worked at the King's Gate, Mordecai had no problem honoring those who deserved honor, such as the king. But her cousin would never pay homage to a man like Haman. To bow to him would be to give honor to the dark forces that guided Haman. It would be the same as worshiping the false gods Haman had embroidered on his vests, turbans, and cloaks. It would be like bowing to the idolatrous medallions that Haman hung around his neck. For Mordecai to glorify a man like that? Never!

Yet to refuse?

Esther closed her eyes, picturing Mordecai at his office at the gate, just as she'd seen him a thousand times. She felt her body slump, remembering how Haman had ripped off her headscarf. Esther clenched her teeth at the thought of it.

Haman had also come to their home and had ordered the soldiers to take her to the palace, to be part of Xerxes's harem. Haman had no love for her or her cousin. She knew their enemy would do anything to put Mordecai in his place.

Esther sucked in a breath. "So what are you going to do?"

Disgust flashed in Mordecai's eyes. "I, bow before that proud and haughty man—an ancestor of Agag? I, bow before a man who works in the dark arts and who ripped my cousin from my home? Shall I kneel before him? No!"

CHAPTER TWENTY-FOUR

Esther stood by the tall window as the first rays of morning light streamed in. She'd not been able to sleep. Dark dreams awakened her. Even though the images had faded from her mind with the dawn, the heavy presence on her chest pressed down. *Yahweh, please, I need to know. What is wrong?*

Through the night, she had prayed for an answer, and part of her had wondered if it had something to do with her husband. Even though they had spent a lot of time together in the four years after she'd been crowned queen, things had been different as of late.

With building projects in Susa finished, Xerxes had turned his attention to his palace in Persepolis. She had spent many days sitting by his side as he showed her his plans to build the Gate of All Nations. The structure had come to him in a dream and consisted of one large room, its roof supported by four stone columns with bell-shaped bases.

"Instead of the glory of my kingdom only seen within the palace walls, the outside walls will be adorned with riches, for all people," Xerxes had told her.

"It sounds lovely, Xerxes," Esther had declared, listening to her husband discuss every detail. Then, she'd been disappointed when Xerxes hadn't asked her to go to Persepolis with him.

Now word had come that weeks ago Xerxes had returned home. And still, he had not sent for her. Even though Esther had dressed and waited each day, her efforts only led to her disappointment as she undressed at night.

Esther searched her mind for what she had done to offend the king. Tawana and her other maidens hadn't shared any palace gossip, and Esther hadn't asked. Was Xerxes spending time with another? Perhaps it was better she didn't know.

Through the long, waiting days, Aafreen and others attempted to keep Esther's mind occupied.

"My queen, can you tell us a story?" Aafreen asked, sitting at Esther's feet again this morning.

Esther attempted to ignore the pang of loneliness that struck her heart. She forced a smile, even though it felt like a wagonload of bricks sat on her shoulders. She struggled for breath, and her mind raced, trying to choose which story she could tell without having to give it too much thought.

"Let's see, what is this month?" Esther asked mindlessly. "Nisan," she said, answering her own question. "This is the month when long ago a group of slaves were saved from an Egyptian ruler, Pharaoh. The Hebrew people call the time of salvation the Passover. It was then Yahweh smote the Egyptians with a terrible visitation.

"Because the pharaoh did not agree to free the Hebrews from slavery, Yahweh cast ten plagues on them. He even slayed the firstborn of every Egyptian. The Hebrew slaves survived this destruction by sprinkling the doorposts with the blood of lambs."

"The Hebrew God is powerful indeed," Aafreen said.

The words were barely out of Aarfeen's mouth when her apartment door opened without a knock. Esther turned to see Tawana there.

"What is it?" Esther gasped as she noticed tears streaking Tawana's cheeks. A sinking feeling came over Esther. She wrapped her robe tighter around her. *Death.* From their pained expressions, she was sure of it.

"Majesty, it is your cousin." Tears glided down Tawana's dark face. "Something is wrong, to be certain. He's torn his clothes and put on sackcloth and ashes."

Another one of Esther's handmaidens rushed in. "It was reported that he walks the city, wailing loudly and bitterly."

Esther's trembling fingers touched her lips. "Can you bring my cousin to the gardens so we can speak?"

"No, Your Majesty, no one who wears sackcloth is allowed to enter the gate, to come into the palace."

Yes, of course, she knew that. But she needed to know what grieved his soul.

"Tawana, please take Mordecai a set of clothes to put on instead of his sackcloth."

When noon came, Esther couldn't stop pacing. Finally, Tawana and her attendants returned. "I'm sorry, Your Majesty. Mordecai would not accept these clothes." Tawana's face pinched, and her words rose and fell with emotion.

Was there something more Tawana knew but hadn't told her? Esther didn't blame the young woman.

"Please go get Hathak." Esther needed to talk to the head eunuch. She trusted him to discover the problem.

"Yes, my queen," Tawana said with relief as she hurried away.

Esther closed her eyes. Images of last night's dream came into focus—a figure in black, like a great death angel hovering at the doorway to Mordecai's home. A shiver ran down her spine.

Ten minutes later, Hathak entered with quickened steps. "My queen, what is wrong?"

"It is my cousin. Please find out what is troubling him."

It didn't take long for Hathak to return. "I found Mordecai in the open square of the city in front of the King's Gate." Hathak held a piece of parchment in his hand. He walked heavy-footed toward Esther, pausing before her. Red rimmed his eyes. "Your cousin told me to give you this. He insisted I explain everything to you."

Esther stood, taking the parchment from Hathak. But before she opened and read it, she scanned the room and those gathered there. "My heart is broken." Esther blinked. "And to have you carry my load means more than you know." Her eyelids felt heavy and sticky from trying to hold back her tears.

Each one nodded their agreement.

Esther read the words—an edict from the king—and knots tightened in her stomach. *An edict for our annihilation.* A decree had been drawn up, permitting the people to slay the Jews on the 13th day of Adar. Esther's body grew weak, and she hurried to a chair to sit. Why would Xerxes create such a brutal and senseless decree?

"And this has gone out?" Esther's voice caught.

Hathak nodded. "A copy of the text of the edict was to be issued as law in every province and made known to the people of every nationality so they would be ready for that day. Furthermore, spurred by the king's command, the couriers went out. To Susa first."

Esther readjusted herself on her couch, wringing her hands.

His face ashen, Hathak stepped forward. "My queen, Mordecai explained to me how this decree came to be. And every word he told me is true."

"And how do you know it is true?"

"I don't know if harm will come to me for telling you this, my queen." Hathak's voice trembled. "But it does not matter. Not too many days ago, I was attending Haman." The eunuch looked to his feet, his shoulders slumped. His fear was palpable.

"Hathak, I give you my word that I will do my best to assure your safety." Esther shuddered, remembering Haman's warm breath on her at the marketplace and the heaviness that weighed on her chest at his closeness. "As soon as possible, I will ask my husband that you are transferred to work in the women's wing. There will be no need to set foot near Haman again."

Relief softened the eunuch's features, yet still he studied his feet as if determining how much to say. Finally, Hathak lifted his gaze to her. "I knew this edict was coming, my queen. It's from the hand of Haman, not the king. The powers of darkness are on Haman's side."

The man shivered, and Esther knew it wasn't from the cold.

Tension tightened in Esther's neck, and her back stiffened as if she physically needed to prepare for whatever news was to come next. "What do you mean power of darkness?"

"Haman is a man, but his power is not man-made. Even as Haman made his plans, he used the dark arts to do so." Hathak shivered, struggling to say the words. "Haman had two lots cast, looking for a lucky day. A lot was cast for the month and then for the day." Hathak's eyes widened and he gripped his chest, as if the memory of that moment brought physical pain.

"And the day chosen—it is the one on the decree?" Esther dared to ask.

"Yes, the thirteenth day of the twelfth month, the month of Adar."

A shiver ran down Esther's spine. "And the purpose of this day—as in the edict?"

Hathak's lower lip trembled and fresh tears filled his eyes. "Yes, to have the Jews destroyed, killed, and annihilated, and all their goods to be plundered. As Haman planned, it is now so."

The words hit Esther like a punch to the stomach. She pressed her hands to her face trying to dam her tears.

Haman is behind it. The one her husband had made the most powerful official in the empire. Haman had waited patiently to play his hand. Like the Amalekites—and like King Agag himself—it was now Haman's turn to attempt to snuff out Yahweh's chosen people. But why now?

Even as the question filled her mind, Esther remembered her last conversation with Mordecai. *"I will not bow down to that man,"* her cousin had seethed.

Esther clasped her hands before her. "Can you tell me, Hathak, what brought this about? Why did Haman convince the king to issue such a verdict?"

"It was because Mordecai the Jew disobeyed the king's command and refused to comply with the order to show Haman respect and bow to him whenever Haman passed by."

"Of course."

"When Haman saw that Mordecai would not bow down or show him respect, he was filled with rage. He had learned of Mordecai's nationality, so he decided it was not enough to lay hands on Mordecai alone. Instead, he looked for a way to destroy all the Jews throughout the entire empires of Xerxes."

"And how did he convince my husband?"

Hathak's eyes met hers. "I only tell you this because you promised my protection." The eunuch sat on the nearest bench, as if his legs could no longer hold him up. "Haman told Xerxes, 'There is a certain race of people scattered through all the provinces of your empire who keep themselves separate from everyone else. Their laws are different from those of any other people, and they refuse to obey the laws of the king. So it is not in the king's interest to let them live. If it pleases the king, issue a decree that they be destroyed." Hathak paused. "Haman even promised to give ten thousand sacks of silver to the government administrators to be deposited in the royal treasury."

"And Xerxes went along with it." Esther pulled her arms tight against her. *Of course he did.* Her husband's heart still stung from the betrayal of his two closest bodyguards. He trusted Haman, especially when his loyal adviser told him there was a certain race of people in his kingdom who refused to obey the king's laws.

Hathak glanced away, and she knew he hadn't told her everything. Not yet.

"What is it, Hathak?" she asked.

"The king took off his signet ring from his finger and gave it to Haman, and he said…" Hathak paused.

"What did he say?"

Hathak released a moan before he offered the words. "The king said to Haman, 'Keep the money, and do with the people as you please.'"

CHAPTER TWENTY-FIVE

A cry escaped Esther's lips, and fresh hatred for Haman rose up within her. The wicked man not only wanted to destroy her cousin—and all her people—but he'd manipulated her husband to do it.

She glanced around at the eunuchs and handmaidens gathered round her. She scanned their faces—they sat around her with red eyes, puffy faces, and quaking shoulders. They mourned because she mourned. They mourned because they realized why this mattered so much to her. Since Mordecai the Jew was her cousin, the king's edict was against their queen too.

"I know the response for Mordecai. But what of the city?" she asked.

"They are bewildered, my queen."

"And how about Haman and King Xerxes—" Her voice caught as she said her husband's name.

Hathak lowered his head. "As soon as the decree was sent out, they sat down to drink."

"And?" Esther's voice trembled.

"They are drinking now."

She dabbed a tear at the corner of her eye. And perhaps her husband had already been drinking before the edict was written. Hadn't he learned? Xerxes himself said when he'd made that edict concerning Vasthi that his mind had been gone from wine.

"Mordecai gives you this instruction," Hathak continued. "You must go into the king's presence to beg for mercy and plead with him for your people."

Esther took a deep breath, trying to comprehend what Mordecai asked.

If this request had come months ago, she wouldn't have had such apprehension. After becoming queen, she had seen Xerxes nearly every day, and they had talked about everything. But now? How many days had it been since she'd been with her husband? Too many. More than that, how many days had Xerxes been drinking?

Hathak waited patiently for Esther's response. Finally, she approached him, placing a hand on his arm. "Please. I have a message for Mordecai. All the king's officials and the people of the royal provinces know that for any man or woman who approaches the king in the inner court without being summoned, the king has but one law: that they are put to death unless the king extends the gold scepter to them and spares their lives. But thirty days have passed since I was called to go to the king."

"Is that all you want me to say?"

"Yes." With that, Hathak left her.

Drunk on wine? Even if he'd ever loved her, there were no guaran-tees when Xerxes lost his mind to drink.

Esther paced as she waited for Mordecai's response. Frustration built within her, in the waiting. She wished

Mordecai would cast off his sackcloth and ashes and come so that she could talk to him face-to-face.

Finally, as darkness fell, and Esther wasn't certain she could keep her eyes open, Hathak returned.

"These are Mordecai's words," he stated simply. "'Do not think that because you are in the king's house, you alone of all the Jews will escape.'" Hathak lifted his chin and fixed his eyes on Esther's. "'For if you remain silent at this time, relief and deliverance for the Jews will arise from another place, but you and your father's family will perish. And who knows but that you have come to your royal position for such a time as this?'"

Esther pressed her fingertips to her forehead. Would she join her people in their time of need? Or was she going to hide behind the palace doors—or at least try? "Yahweh is with us, and He will provide."

Not just Mordecai's God. My God too.

"Is there anything else?" Esther asked.

"Mordecai simply urged that you must go to Xerxes. You must plead for your people. If you don't, the Jews are without hope."

Esther studied Hathak's eyes. She'd never seen so much fear in the eunuch's gaze, and it wasn't even his life on the line. "I know what I have to do, but Xerxes has not sent for me in a while." Emotion caught in her throat.

"But you are the queen. Surely he will accept you," Tawana insisted.

"We both know what happened to the queen before me, don't we?" Esther answered bluntly. She wiped her brow, hoping that Hathak and the others could not see the beads of sweat forming there. She attempted to swallow, but it was no use. She closed her eyes and lifted her chin to the sky, seeking strength.

And in the moment her own anger burned toward *him*. Though strong, Xerxes had proven to be careless with life. Haman must have spun quite a tale as to why the destruction of the Jews was necessary. *Perhaps he is a greater storyteller than even I.*

The room spun around her, and Esther's lungs longed for fresh air. She hurried to the balcony. Questions swirled through her mind as she studied the pale golden sky through the lens of the shade trees. *What have I done to displease him? Why has he not sent for me? Is he in love with another?*

Before she'd been with Xerxes, she had not known the love of a husband could be so beautiful. Day by day she'd waited for him to send for her only to go to bed at night alone. As deep as the love she felt, even deeper now was the ache of rejection.

"I cannot do this. How can I do this?" Esther cried into the night air. Yet even as the words spat from her mouth, she paused and looked around. She, a Jewish orphan, lived in the palace of Xerxes, the King of the Medes and the Persians. More than that, the ruler of 127 provinces had made her his queen.

There was no reason why she should be here. She hadn't even wanted to come. Her path had been led by Yahweh, just as certain as Yahweh had guided Abram's steps to the promised land.

Footsteps approached, and she knew Hathak needed his answer.

She pressed her hands to her hips. "You don't know what this means." Esther turned and lowered her head, wiping away the infuriating tears. Then she looked up to meet his gaze.

Hathak moved closer and spread his arms wide. "What if I do? What if I've always known? Mordecai the Jew is your cousin. I understand how this affects you."

Esther looked down at her hands and saw their quivering. "My heart is shaking even more inside, but I don't have a choice, do I?" Esther lifted her face to the sky, now dark. Yet she didn't focus on the darkness. Instead, she allowed her eyes to dance over the pins of light. *Abraham's children need me now.*

She lowered her head and locked her eyes with Hathak's. "Please, send this reply to Mordecai: 'Go, gather together all the Jews in Susa, and fast for me. Do not eat or drink for three days, night or day. My attendants and I will fast as you do. I will go to the king when this is done, even though it is against the law. And if I perish, I perish.'"

Hathak nodded once. "I will deliver your message, my queen." Sadness filled his gaze. "A true queen shines brightest in the darkness. In my eyes tonight you are stronger than an Immortal."

"Thank you for saying that, Hathak. Any strength I have comes from the true Immortal One."

CHAPTER TWENTY-SIX

After Hathak left, Esther gathered her maids together in her inner chambers.

"Esther, how can we help?" Aafreen asked, walking in step with Esther.

Esther sat upon her bed platform, and she motioned for her handmaidens to gather around.

"What must we do, our queen?" Aafreen asked. "I know you are a queen, but you're more like a sister to me. Not a day passes when I do not feel gratitude that, out of all the people in the palace of Xerxes, it's you I serve."

"I told my cousin that we will join him and not eat or drink for three days as a petition to the Hebrew God. I sent word to my eunuchs that we will be abstaining from all food for that space of time."

"But what is the purpose of this fast?"

Esther brushed a strand of hair back from her face. "As we fast, we will pray." She reached out and grasped the hands of the two maids sitting closest to her. "We will intercede for the Hebrew people. And after three days, I will go before the king."

"Why must we withhold food? How does this please Yahweh?" a maid asked.

"Fasting is in token of humiliation for our sins and a sense of our unworthiness of God's mercies. It is a reminder to us that all we have that brings us life comes from the Lord. I have chosen you—my closest friends—to join me, because I have seen each of you reverently serving me and living pious lives. And as we fast, I will tell you stories of Yahweh, true stories and not made-up legends. Forgive me, sisters, that I have not done so already. From the time I was a child my cousin asked me not to disclose my true identity, but those times are no more.

"The threat of death has caused me to consider my life and be willing to share the truth I know. Will you join me in these holy duties of fasting and prayer? In interceding for my people?"

"Even if you have not spoken of your god, my queen, we have seen his hand upon you." The words spilled out of Aafreen's mouth. "Your pure heart is evident to all. We've discussed this in our bedchamber, and we understand why you were chosen above all women. You are beautiful, yes, but even more beautiful in heart. You became a storyteller because you are interested in people, in vices and virtues."

A knock at her door caused Esther to jump. "Enter," she called.

Hathak approached once again. "There is a final message for you tonight, my queen. Mordecai told us that he would do as you requested. He will carry out all your instructions."

"Thank you, Hathak."

As the moon rose as an orb in the sky, Esther smiled as she looked at her maids. "I have told you many stories." She sighed. "Most are just that...stories."

Love swelled in Esther's heart for the young women around her, and she now knew she could speak the complete truth about Yahweh to them.

"While legend has it that Perseus is the progenitor of the Persians and later became the father of Archaemenes, there is only one true God, the maker of heaven and earth."

Questions still filled Aafreen's eyes. "With so many legends and stories, how do you know this god we will pray to is the right one?"

Esther placed a soft hand on her heart. "I know because when I cried over the loss of my parents, I felt Yahweh's closeness and tenderness, as if He wept with me. When I prayed for wisdom, truth came. I felt Yahweh's breath upon me when I prayed for strength. I have seen Yahweh through the care of my cousin and, before that, my mother's song and my father's hope."

"My queen. You tell us many stories, yet with each one, there are new gods." Tawana's brow was furrowed, and it was clear she wasn't yet convinced. "So are you saying that there is only one true God out of all the tales you speak of?"

"That is what I'm saying, Tawana." Esther grasped her hand. "Most of those stories are just that—tales. But I have been taught as a child about the one true God. He is a seen God. He is not made of gold to be melted down. Yahweh is the Creator of heaven and earth. He created the world in seven days. He formed man and woman, and when they multiplied and the world was filled with sin, He made way for the earth to be renewed. He asked one man and his sons to form a vessel. A remnant was saved then, just as one was saved after the destruction of Jerusalem. I am part of that remnant."

Aafreen nodded. "I have heard of the power of the Hebrew God. My grandmother served in Belshazzar's palace as a young woman. She told me about the mighty deeds done to protect Yahweh's servant, whom the Hebrews call Daniel."

"So, is this the god we must pray to?" one of the young maids asked.

"Yes, and we must pray that Yahweh, who protected Daniel from the hungry lions, will protect us now too."

They gathered and prayed until sleep overcame them. The next day, Esther and her maids rose and did the same.

Throughout the day, reports came to the queen. "In every province to which the edict and order of the king came, there is great mourning among the Jews, with fasting, weeping, and wailing. Many lie in sackcloth and ashes."

On the second night, Esther climbed under her blankets. She was tired and hungry but strong too. She'd found peace knowing that at this moment, in the home where she had spent most of her life, Mordecai was still praying—as were Jews around the city.

"Yahweh, as my cousin has taught me, You are my inheritance," she whispered, even as she heard the soft snores of the maids who slept around her. "I used to believe it was Jerusalem that drew my heart, but now I know it's You."

CHAPTER TWENTY-SEVEN

The morning of the third day, Esther rose, knowing what they were to do. She gathered the young women around her. "I know what Yahweh asks of me. Today His strength fills me, and I will go before my husband."

Esther turned to Aafreen. "Choose two others to help me dress."

Then she turned to Tawana. "And you and the rest, with the help of our eunuchs, must prepare a banquet." Esther grasped her hands before her. "I will ask my king to come. And I'll request he bring Haman too."

A gasp rose from the young women. "Why Haman?" one of the maids asked. "Why here?"

Esther stretched out her arms. "Can't you feel Yahweh's presence in this place? He has heard our tears, and He has come down."

"And what will happen when you bring the king and Haman to this banquet?" Tawana's eyes clouded with concern.

"I will confess who I am." Esther swallowed her emotion as she pressed a hand to her brow. "I will plead for my people."

Hope danced in Aafreen's eyes. "This is a good plan, my queen. Since we pray to Yahweh, the One true God, it seems that perhaps your role will save many lives."

Moving to Aafreen, Esther sighed. "While I hope that is the case, we must trust in Yahweh no matter what happens."

Aafreen's eyes widened. "Surely, my queen—"

Esther held up a hand, pausing Afreen's words. "Perhaps in my storytelling, it had become easy to think of Yahweh as simply a character. But now..." Esther placed a hand over her heart. "I used to know Yahweh with my mind, but now I know Him with my whole being. He will be my strength as I approach my king. He will be my hope, knowing the outcome is in His hands. Fear grips me, but it will not leave me immobile."

"Even as you go, we will pray," Aafreen said, lifting a purple gown and holding it up to the light of the window. "It will be our service to you. We can see that your heart is pure and not filled with pride. Maybe that's what the king will see too. Perhaps he will see that and choose you again today."

The young woman's words fell over Esther like a soft misty rain, but an even more powerful emotion stirred in her heart. "While I hope my people are saved and that the power of the One true God will change things, I will tell you today that I am changed. And if the king does not accept me, and I am disposed of just like Vashti, what I have discovered deep in my soul will make it all worth it. Remember that, sisters."

After she had dressed, and while the banquet was still being laid out. Esther's handmaidens gathered around her. Maybe they believed this would be the last time they would see her. If so, Esther knew what she must leave them with. With a sigh, she lifted her hands in prayer.

"Yahweh, the Creator of this world and all-powerful One. We seek You today. We do not seek You for Your power. Instead, we come to You because we see You alone as worthy." Esther's words spilled out. "From every story I've heard and retold, I have discovered that no God is as great as You. Even when the Jews have failed You as Your chosen people, You have not failed us. Even if the king does not accept me, this burning in my heart reveals to me that I will never be rejected by You, my One true God, Yahweh, the King of Kings...

"O Yahweh, my King, spare Your people so that we may live. So that we may lift our voices to You in praise. Your great name we lift on high. Yahweh, You promised our patriarchs Abraham, Isaac, and Jacob that You would make their descendants as numerous as the stars in the sky and the sand on the seashore. And it is for the sake of the descendants that I come to You now.

"Yahweh, if Your people are destroyed, who will be left to read Your law and call upon You? Have compassion on Your people who are about to be destroyed. Yahweh, help me to be strong. I have no helper but You."

After the prayer, Esther allowed Aafreen to place upon her her royal robes. With strength Esther didn't know she possessed, she walked alone through the three central courtyards that created a grand walkway through the palace to the king's throne room. With sure steps, she approached the king's throne. Many heads turned her direction, but Esther looked neither to the right or the left.

Esther entered the inner court of the palace, just across from the king's hall. Her breath caught, and she paused.

The king was sitting on his royal throne, facing the entrance. His face lifted. The pounding in her chest overwhelmed Esther, yet still she stood.

"Please, my king," she whispered under her breath.

Xerxes leaned forward. Then, with a flourish, he reached out his hand, grasped his golden scepter, and held it out to her.

Esther's knees trembled as she approached.

Xerxes smiled at her. "What do you want, Queen Esther? What is your request? I will give it to you, even if it is half of my kingdom!"

"If it please the king, let the king and Haman come today to a banquet I have prepared for the king."

Xerxes turned to his attendants. "Tell Haman to come quickly to a banquet, as Esther has requested." Then he turned to the court. "The rest of you may go." And when all had filed out, Esther stood alone.

With tenderness in his gaze, Xerxes approached. "I heard Haman's footsteps...." He leaned down and brushed a kiss across her forehead. "I almost wished I were going alone."

She smiled up at him. "I hear there is a reason to celebrate… with Haman's new role." Esther grasped her husband's hand, feeling its warmth. "But it is good to see you, Xerxes, my king."

Haman approached, and Esther refused to meet his gaze. Instead, Esther held her husband's hand as they walked—a prayer going up with each step.

They made their way to the queen's chambers, and as they entered, Esther's eyes widened with delight. Couches had been laid out, and a table full of food stretched across her main room. Esther's stomach growled as she led her king to a cushion and sat by her side. Haman sat on the other side of Xerxes, and though she forced a smile as she looked at her husband, Esther didn't have the strength to look at Haman.

Food was served and with it wine. Esther placed a fig to her mouth and bit into its sweetness, as her husband lifted his glass to be filled.

After taking a sip, Xerxes turned to her. "Now tell me what you really want. What is your request?" He winked. "I will give it to you, even if it is half of the kingdom!"

Wait. Tomorrow.

The words echoed through her mind. Esther frowned.

Xerxes placed his glass down and leaned forward. Touched a hand to her cheek. "Esther, is something wrong?" Concern filled his gaze, and Esther's heart leaped seeing the man she knew. Yes, he was there. Her husband, not just her king.

"I've missed you." Her words were real. She offered a half smile. "If I have found favor with the king, and if it pleases the king to grant my request and do what I ask, please come with Haman tomorrow to the banquet I will prepare for you. Then I will explain what this is all about."

Laughter spilled from Xerxes's lips. "You do miss me, don't you?" he offered with the softest of kisses. And then the king turned to the man beside him.

Esther dared to follow her husband's gaze. She held her breath, preparing to see evil in the man's eyes. Instead, Haman's eyes were large and round. Happiness filled them. His voice rose in laughter.

Was this the same Haman?

"I'd love to come back!" Haman glanced around. "To be honored by even the queen." Haman reached over and patted Xerxes's back. "How could we say no?"

"Wonderful." Esther smiled as she reclined against the king, yet deep in her soul a question stirred. *Why wait? What did Yahweh desire?* Esther didn't know, but at least they had another day to pray.

CHAPTER TWENTY-EIGHT

There was a new lightness in Esther's step as she woke early to dress and prepare the banquet. Yahweh's request had been so clear. She did not know why, but seeing the love in her husband's eyes had made it easier to face whatever the day held.

Esther had just finished dressing when a knock sounded at the door. Her breath caught as Hathak entered. The eunuch didn't seem surprised to see her dressed in her royal robes, and he approached her with quick steps.

"Is something going on?" Esther's palm grew sweaty. "Is something wrong? Is the king still coming?"

Hathak stroked his chin. "The king still comes, but you must come with me first. There is something you must see."

Esther glanced around. She pointed to the table behind her. "Are you asking me to leave?" She shook her head. "I can't do that. Xerxes and Haman will be here in an hour's time."

"An hour's time, really?" Humor lit Hathak's eyes.

Esther took a step toward him. "What is it? You have to tell me what's going on."

"Esther, last night the king could not sleep. He tossed and turned, so he ordered the book of the chronicles, the record of his reign, to be brought in and read to him."

Esther waited, knowing there was a reason for Hathak's visit—more than just the fact that Xerxes couldn't sleep.

"It was found recorded there that Mordecai had exposed Bigthana and Teresh, two of the king's officers who guarded the doorway, who had conspired to assassinate King Xerxes," Hathak continued.

"Yes, I remember."

"The king asked what honor and recognition Mordecai received for this. 'Nothing has been done for him,' his attendants answered."

Esther sighed. "That is true."

Hathak opened his hands, continuing, as if he were the storyteller. "One of the king's officials was there early. So Xerxes asked the official, 'What should be done for the man the king delights to honor?'

"The official had a good suggestion. 'For the man the king delights to honor, have them bring a royal robe the king has worn and a horse the king has ridden, one with a royal crest placed on his head. Then let the robe and the horse be entrusted to one of the king's most noble princes. Let them robe the man the king delights to honor, and lead him on the horse through the city streets, proclaiming before him, This is what is done for the man the king delights to honor!'"

Esther gasped. A sunbeam of light pierced through her heart that had been heavy with grief for days.

Surely this is the start of an answer to our prayers.

"Did the king take the official's advice?"

"Yes." Hathak's face brightened. "More than that, the king asked the official to be the one leading Mordecai on the horse."

A soft gasp released from Esther's lips. "What official?"

"I thought you would like to see. Will you come with me to the outer courtyard?"

Esther glanced at her handmaidens and saw excitement in their gazes. "Yes, of course."

She walked in step with Hathak through the palace. An ache filled her. First, that she'd soon be seeing her cousin. Second, because he would finally be honored.

They hurried to the outer courtyard, and Esther paused her steps as she peered down to the King's Gate. There Haman led Mordecai on the king's horse. Goose bumps rose on Esther's arms, and she didn't know whether to laugh or cry.

Esther's stomach quivered. Heat rose up her neck. Even from this distance, she could see how stunned and humiliated Haman was to honor his enemy.

Part of her wanted to gloat in the fact that this descendant of Agag was forced to honor a Jew. When pain like a dagger pierced her heart, Esther knew it was no time to gloat. She remembered the evil in Haman's eyes. She would never forget the smug smile on Haman's lips as he ordered the guards to take her away to the palace.

Haman had her dragged away to cause heartache and pain for both her and Mordecai. By sending her away to be part of King Xerxes's harem, Haman knew Esther would never be able to marry and have a home and children of her own. He also knew the pain of separation from Mordecai—for both of them. Haman never could have guessed that it would be Esther who King Xerxes would choose as queen.

Haman's first humiliation was the crown placed upon Esther's head. And now the second—to honor his enemy, when Haman believed he was someone who deserved the honor.

Then Esther saw something else off in the distance. Something that hadn't been there before. She pointed. "Hathak, do you know what that pole is for?"

Hathak looked at the large pole, and then he turned to her, face pale. "That is Haman's house. He must have plans—"

"No. Do not say it." She cut off his words. "*I have plans too.*" Hathak, can you please send attendants to fetch Haman and the king for today's banquet?"

In just over an hour's time, Xerxes and Haman lounged beside her. Haman's face was bright, but this time Esther saw past his smile. *Is that fear I see in your eyes?* she wanted to ask.

As Xerxes enjoyed the wine, Haman's attention turned to her.

"Dear Queen Esther"—his voice was smooth—"to know that you invited me out of everyone—I am honored. I am thankful that you now see that I knew, deep down, bringing you to the palace would only lead to your good. And what plans did your cousin have for you? Jerusalem—a city of rubble filled with jackals."

"I've settled my heart that this is my home now," she stated simply. "I know now that I have a purpose here, as queen. But more than that as a wife."

Esther glanced at her husband, seeing the delight in his eyes at her words. While she continued to press on a smile, Esther was sure her heart would pound out of her chest.

She leaned toward the table laden with food. "Please allow my servants to serve you. I have chosen more of your favorites today, my husband. Lamb with herbs, apricots. And your favorite stews."

Xerxes took another drink and then smiled. "Are you attempting to try my patience, dear wife? Yesterday we feasted, and I have to admit as the evening passed I found myself wondering what your request could be. What could be so great that you couldn't tell me yesterday?" Xerxes scooted closer and settled beside her. He lifted her hand and kissed her fingers. "That is why you asked us back today, Esther, for fear I would not be happy with your request?"

Xerxes squeezed her hand and then pressed it to his cheek. "Tell me what you want, Queen Esther. What is your request? I will give it to you, even if it is half of the kingdom!"

Esther straightened, feeling the power of Yahweh within. "If I have found favor with the king, and if it pleases the king to grant my request, I ask that my life and the lives of my people be spared. For my people and I have been sold to those who would kill, slaughter, and annihilate us. If we had merely been sold as slaves, I could remain quiet, for that would be too trivial a matter to warrant disturbing the king."

"Who would do such a thing?" King Xerxes demanded. "Who would be so presumptuous as to touch you?"

"This wicked Haman is our adversary and our enemy." Esther turned her gaze to the man. Color drained from Haman's face.

Xerxes jumped to his feet. His eyes widened. His arms shook as he planted his feet. A guttural roar poured out from the depths of him.

A pounding thrummed in Esther's ears as she watched Xerxes rush to the garden. She had known her husband as a king and as a lover, but she saw the warrior in him too.

Haman rose to stand on trembling legs. Esther expected him to run. Instead, Haman rushed in her direction. Throwing himself across Esther's lap, Haman gripped the fabric of her gown so tightly his knuckles turned white.

"Please, Esther. Save me," Haman's shrill voice assaulted her. "Ask the king, your husband, to spare my life." Haman's chin trembled. His eyes blinked rapidly. His breaths came quickly, and though she tried to push him away, he clung to her.

"Get off of me. Get off! Help!" The words scratched her throat as she tried to breathe under the pressure of his body.

Footsteps sounded. Xerxes's hand reached out, grabbing Haman by the collar of his gown. Haman's eyes bulged, and his body jerked back as Xerxes threw the man off Esther.

Esther released another cry as relief flooded through her. Standing over Haman, Xerxes's nostrils flared, and the veins and muscles in his neck bulged.

"Will he even assault the queen right here in the palace, before my very eyes?"

Xerxes grappled Haman by the neck. Haman wriggled, like a fish on a hook. Two of the king's eunuchs rushed up. In one swooping motion, the taller servant covered Haman's face with a black cloth.

The sign of Haman's doom. Death.

The servants jerked Haman from Xerxes's grasp, ignoring Haman's screeching cries.

Esther covered her mouth with a trembling hand. She closed her eyes and shook her head, rocking back and forth.

She tried to compose herself. Xerxes rushed to her side, sitting next to her. He wrapped his arms around her, sure and strong.

"It will be all right, my darling. The enemy of you and your people will hurt you no more."

Esther dared to open her eyes. Harbona—one of the king's eunuchs—approached. "Haman has set up a sharpened pole that stands seventy-five feet tall in his courtyard. It can be seen from the outer courtyard, as you look into the city. Haman intended to use it to impale the faithful Mordecai, the man who saved the king from assassination."

"Seventy-five feet high?" Esther gasped.

Harbona nodded. "A pole high enough for Haman to observe Mordecai's corpse while he dined here at the palace, my queen."

"Then impale Haman on it!" Xerxes ordered. "And since it can be seen from the palace, I will be able to look at it while I dine," Xerxes seethed. And then he left.

CHAPTER TWENTY-NINE

After the banquet had been cleared away, Esther sat at the window, her eyes looking to the hills beyond the city. It seemed as if all the tears she'd been holding back flowed forth, refusing to be restrained any longer.

With each breath, it felt as if her lungs were made of stone. Word had come that the wicked Haman was dead, but the edict remained. *We are not yet saved.*

Though the day was warm, Esther's hands felt cold, and she rubbed them together.

A knock sounded at the door.

"Enter."

Hathak walked through the door. He strode over to her with soft steps, pausing before her.

"I called for you because I need to go before the king," she stated simply.

Hathak shook his head. "He's in his royal office, and…"

"And?" Esther took a step forward. "And what matters could be more urgent than my need to save the lives of my people?"

"You don't understand." Hathak wrung his hands. "Anger fuels him. Xerxes's hatred toward Haman makes his blood boil. Even Haman's death isn't enough to appease him."

"You cannot discourage me from this."

"My queen, you have not seen him in this state. I wouldn't advise it."

"You cannot stop me. If you don't take me, I will go alone again."

Hathak released a heavy sigh. His eyes fluttered closed, and he nodded. "Please take time to prepare yourself, and I will take you to him."

Esther touched her face. "I'm sure my eyes are swollen, and my face is blotchy." A small burst of laughter bubbled out with more tears. "I'm not certain anything can help me look presentable to see the king, but I'll see what my maids can do."

Esther felt more confident after her face had been washed and her hair had been rebraided, yet Hathak's words still rang in her mind. *"You have not seen him in this state…."*

The eunuch's warning gave her pause. Twenty minutes later, Esther still sat at the dressing table. Only when the ache got too immense did she stand.

Hathak entered, but instead of his face pinched in worry, he smiled. "The king just sent for you. We can go now."

Esther entered his large office chamber then approached and lowered herself on one knee before her husband. As she bowed, she lifted her hand to him. Xerxes kissed the back of her hand and then pulled her to him. His arms wrapped around her tightly as she pressed into his chest.

"I do not know how I deserve your love and all that you have given me, but, Xerxes, I want you to know more of my story. The truth—all of the truth. And it includes a man named Mordecai."

"Yes, I know of Mordecai. He is the one who saved me from assassination—the man I recently honored with royal clothes and my own horse." Xerxes's brow furrowed. "What do you have to tell me?"

"My king, Mordecai is my cousin—the one who raised me." Not able to hold herself up any longer, Esther fell at her husband's feet. "Please, my king, my husband, my love. Please, can you put a stop to the evil plan of Haman the Agagite? He has devised this plan against all the Jews. If you ever loved me…"

She felt his hand upon her head.

"Esther."

She sucked in a breath, trying to hold in her weeping.

"Esther, my love. Esther, if you love me, if you have ever loved me, lift up your head."

Esther took a deep breath and lifted her face to Xerxes. She studied his face and looked deeply in his eyes. Even though she knew her husband was a mighty warrior, from the narrowed gaze she saw there, she knew that his fight wasn't against her.

"Esther, I will not send you away. I will not bring any harm to you. Please tell me what you need. Tell me, my wife, my queen." His words caught in his throat. "Tell me what you desire." Then he pulled her to her feet.

"If it pleases the king," she said, "and if he regards me with favor and thinks it the right thing to do, and if he is pleased with me, let an order be written overruling the dispatches that Haman son of Hammedatha, the Agagite, devised and wrote to destroy the Jews in all the king's provinces. For how can I bear to see disaster fall on my people? How can I bear to see the destruction of my family?"

Xerxes looked to Esther and then motioned behind her, as if urging someone forward.

She turned and gasped as she saw the man standing at the end of the hall. "Mordecai?"

"When I sent for you, I sent for Mordecai too, because I wanted him to know this." Xerxes smiled. "Because Haman attacked the Jews, I have now given Haman's estate to Esther," the king explained. "Also, I have heard from my guards that Haman is dead. They have impaled him on the pole he set up. From what I hear, it was what Haman had designed for you, Mordecai."

"Yes, I have heard that as well." Mordecai's face was solemn.

Xerxes glanced at Mordecai. "I talked to the men you work with. They had nothing but the best to say about you. The same was said of you by the men at the gate. They say you are a trustworthy man. They claimed that not once did you ever try to deceive or to steal." Xerxes cleared his throat. "Or to give yourself more honor than is due."

Mordecai cast down his eyes. "That is not the way of our people. We are taught to know the Lord's laws and His ways."

Xerxes looked over at Esther. "I would like to hear about these laws."

She wiped a tear from her cheek. "Yes, well, I would love to tell you sometime."

"I also heard that you have skill with a pen," Xerxes continued, turning back to Mordecai. "Now write another decree in my name on behalf of the Jews as seems best to you, and seal it with my signet ring—for no document written in the king's name and sealed with his ring can be revoked."

Xerxes's face showed little emotion as he extended his hand. Mordecai's jaw dropped and his eyes widened as he quickly recovered and extended his hand. And into Mordecai's palm, Xerxes set his signet ring.

Joy flooded Esther's heart, and she grasped her cousin's hand. "And I have a job for you too. Haman's property is now mine. Please, Cousin, will you be in charge of it?"

"Yes, Cousin, of course." Mordecai laughed. "Who am I but a simple man? But now I work for the king and the queen!"

Two months later, Esther was called to Xerxes again. Even though her husband had been busy, he'd made time for her. And as she approached him, she hoped it was the good news she'd been waiting for.

As Esther approached Xerxes's throne, he smiled down upon her.

"Esther, I want you to know that my edict granted all the Jews in every city the right to unite to defend their lives. They are allowed to kill, destroy, and annihilate the armed men of any nationality or any province who might attack them and their women and children.

"More than that, my decree also states that they may plunder their enemies."

Esther's mouth dropped open. "You did all that for me?"

"Yes, my love. I did all that for you." His eyes twinkled. "I did it because it is right."

"And the day?" she asked.

"The thirteenth day of the twelfth month. The day you and your people were to be slaughtered is the day I have proclaimed that your people have the right to fight against their enemies.

"I want you to know that as of this morning a copy of the text of the edict was to be issued in every province and made known to the people of every nationality." Xerxes winked. "I saw them go out, my queen. The couriers rode on horses, spurred by my command."

Esther's knees grew weak. She looked to the bench behind her, preparing to sit. But then she remembered the strength of her husband's arms. Esther took two steps toward him.

In that moment, she allowed herself to be weak. She had prayed and fasted with her maids, and with the Jews from throughout the kingdom, so that she might have strength. But as her husband wrapped his arms around her and pulled her close, Esther also knew that her ability to be weak was an answer to prayer too.

She needed him, just as much as he needed her. And the king did need her. Xerxes needed a wife who would pray for him. As much as she was able, Esther would.

Esther pulled back and looked into her husband's face. His features softened, and his eyebrows drew together. Worry filled his gaze. This man, who she first saw as a mighty warrior, was willing to split open his heart and tarnish his pride for her.

Xerxes touched her face tenderly, wiping her tears with a thumb. He took her hands and kissed them. "Forgive me. Forgive me."

"You did not know—"

"I did not ask." He released her hands and raked a hand through his hair. "I should not have trusted Haman. My father told me to watch for those who offer flattering comments with a crooked tongue."

He dropped his forehead to hers, and Esther closed her eyes. "I love you, Husband," Esther whispered. "And I forgive you."

On the day chosen for the destruction of the Jews, Esther stood in the garden overlooking the city. She frowned as she looked down past the King's Gate to where Mordecai's house stood. The sounds of war clattered. She saw movement on the streets, including in front of her cousin's door. Esther's body quivered, and she wished she could have convinced Mordecai to find refuge in the palace, but he had refused.

"Esther, come inside." It was her husband's voice. She turned to see Xerxes approach.

He opened his arms to her, and she stepped into his embrace. "My beautiful Esther."

Hours later, darkness had fallen over the city. Not knowing what else to do, Esther gathered her attendants in her chambers to wait, to pray.

A knock at the door startled her, and even more distressing was the request for Esther to join the king in his chambers—saying that it was urgent. The cries of her maids, as she hurried after the eunuch, reflected the cries of her heart. Why would the king beckon her at this hour unless he had news—bad news?

Xerxes was still dressed, and his apartment was filled with officials when she arrived.

"I have a report," he told her. "The number of those killed in the citadel of Susa was reported to me." Xerxes stared at her for five heartbeats, and she tried to read the expression on his face. Finally, he cleared his throat.

"The Jews have killed and destroyed five hundred men and the ten sons of Haman in the citadel of Susa." He smirked. "What have they done in the rest of the king's provinces?" He shrugged. "We will see. Now, what is your petition, Esther? It will be given to you. What is your request? It will also be granted."

Esther sucked in a breath, overpowered by the tenderness in his voice. She closed her eyes and remembered the declaration of the prophet Samuel to Saul. Angry heat rose with her, and the truth of why she was here radiated in her heart. Yahweh put her in this palace for such a time as this—not only to save her people but also to destroy the enemies of the Jews.

She opened her eyes and looked into her husband's face. "If it pleases the king," Esther answered, "give the Jews in Susa permission to carry out this day's edict tomorrow also, and let Haman's ten sons be impaled on poles."

Xerxes nodded. "So, I see my queen has a warrior's heart too."

Esther tipped up her face, and Xerxes kissed her lips. Then she closed her eyes and swallowed, allowing the king to take her hand.

Xerxes turned to his scribe. "I command this to be done. Issue an edict tonight. By my order, the Jews at Susa may rise up against their enemies tomorrow. More than that. The bodies of Haman's ten sons are to be impaled."

The next night, as Esther again waited in her chamber with her maids in prayer, she was once again summoned to the king.

"Your people have overcome, my queen," he announced to her. "They put three hundred men to death in Susa, but unlike my warriors, they did not lay their hands on the plunder."

"I understand why. My people's only wish has been for our preservation. We don't need the wealth of this world when we have Yahweh, who knows our needs."

Over the upcoming days, more news trickled in. The remainder of the Jews who were in the king's provinces also assembled to protect themselves and get relief from their enemies. It was reported to the king that the Jews killed seventy-five thousand of their enemies but did not lay their hands on the plunder.

Finally, the sound of music stirred Esther from her sleep. She opened her eyes and remembered the days when she'd lived with Mordecai near the King's Gate. At the time, she listened to the music coming down the hill.

Esther stretched. Today she was in the palace, and she knew the music wasn't from this complex.

Esther sat up, and Tawana rushed to her, robe in hand. Esther stood and slid her arms into the fine linen. Then she waited as Tawana tied the belt.

"Where does the music come from?" Aafreen asked. She hurried to the windows overlooking the city, hoping to get a glance.

"Couldn't you guess? It is the Jews." Laughter shook Tawana's shoulders. "Word has already come from the marketplace that the queen's people are proclaiming this, the fourteenth day of the month of Adar, as a day of resting from the struggles with their enemies, and also and a day of feasting and joy."

Laughter spilled from Esther's mouth, and she lifted up her arms in praise. "A lot was cast by Haman, yet he didn't know it was for the destruction of the enemies of the Jews." The words poured from her mouth like water from a cup. "This whole time, Yahweh knew us, and He cared. That fact is clearly seen now. He transformed captives into princes. He gives the best to those who trust Him—those who allow Yahweh to guide their paths."

Later that day, Esther heard Mordecai's singing as she neared the vizier's office in the administration wing. Her cousin must have heard her footsteps, because Mordecai stopped his singing, and he looked to Esther with a smile.

Pausing in the doorway, Esther crossed her arms over her chest. "You don't have to stop because of me, Cousin."

"I stopped because I wanted to talk to you."

"To me? Whatever about?"

"I am writing a letter to be copied by the palace scribes. It is to be sent to all the Jews throughout the provinces of King Xerxes, near and far."

"It sounds important. What is this letter about?"

Mordecai rubbed his brow. "I have been thinking. Our people have just received so great a salvation, and we need to remember this. It must be a story that fathers will tell to their children. An event that women will celebrate with their sisters, mothers, and friends.

"We will have an annual celebration on the fourteenth and fifteenth days of the month of Adar. This will be a remembrance of the time when the Jews got relief from their enemies. Rejoicing in the month when their sorrow was turned into joy and their mourning into a day of celebration. Can you help me?"

A smile broader than any she'd ever smiled filled Esther's face. "Yes, of course."

So Queen Esther wrote with full authority to confirm this second letter concerning Purim—which is what they decided to call their special day—named after the lots which Haman cast.

And Mordecai sent letters to all the Jews in the 127 provinces of Xerxes's kingdom—words of goodwill and assurance—to establish these days of Purim at their designated times, as Mordecai the Jew and Queen Esther had decreed for them, and as they had established for themselves and their descendants in regard to their times of fasting and lamentation. Esther's decree confirmed these regulations about Purim, and it was written down in her husband's records.

Thank You, Yahweh. Thank You.

Esther strode confidently into the king's chamber, for the first time truly believing that her husband looked at her through eyes of love. Their marriage would never be what she'd dreamed of as a girl. No young Jewess ever dreamed of marrying a Persian king. But if her husband had been willing to extend his scepter to her when she was at her lowest and weakest, Esther had hoped he'd extend his scepter to her today.

She approached and paused at the door. Seated at a long table, Xerxes welcomed her in. "Come, my queen, and see these new building plans. I'd like to hear your thoughts."

Laughter punctuated each of her steps. "My husband and my king, why am I not surprised? You look at lines scribbled on tablets and, in your mind, see stone and cedar rising from the sand. It's truly a gift. I've always admired that about you."

Esther sat on the carved bench, scooting close to her husband's side.

Xerxes smiled and then leaned close. He brushed loose hair back from her shoulder and kissed just above her ear. "If only the nobles in my provinces would admire me so. They grumble about the taxes and tributes instead."

Esther breathed in the scents of him. Xerxes smelled like the sun and the cedars of Lebanon that he loved to import. "They do not know you as I do, and for that I am glad."

Xerxes pushed out of his chair and nearly leaped onto his feet with enthusiasm. "There is something else for you to be glad about. I have sent an inquiry, wishing to know the state of Jerusalem. For so long, it was simply one of the provinces I inherited from my father, but now it means so much more." He stroked his beard. "Years ago, when I began my reign, I received a letter of accusation against the people of Judah and Jerusalem. But now I will reexamine the matter. I did not realize at the time how many were enemies of Judah."

"Your care for me and my people… I never expected such a thing."

Crinkling his dark brown eyes in a smile, Xerxes placed his hand on hers. "From the first day I saw you, my queen, I felt you could be trusted. That is not common for a king."

"I hope you will forever see me as such, and I will strive to be your compassionate bride." Esther smiled to herself, considering her words.

I will always be your Esther. More than that, your Hadassah. What Yahweh brought together may He use for the good of His people. For now and all time.

A eunuch approached, bowing low. "Great King, your vizier is here."

Xerxes nodded. "Send him in. I'm thankful that the gods have provided me with a wise adviser, who is vested in his own interests and mine and those of my kingdom."

Lightness danced in Esther's chest as Mordecai walked in. His face had filled out, and his features softened. The fruits and vegetables he ate in plenty at the palace renewed his youth and reminded Esther of how he'd looked when she was a child, when he didn't have to fret about Greek wars, finding a husband for Esther, or hiding his heritage.

Mordecai approached Xerxes with a bow. "I've prepared a chart of expected tributes, my lord. The cost of war with Greece was great, but since I've worked with imports since I was a young man, I am aware of which regions can provide more to the king. There are also new tributes we can ask for." Mordecai's eyes sparkled. "Cypress is producing important sculptures that I believe would please the king. From my own coffers I recently commissioned a sculpture of Sipehsalar's daughter for the queen."

"Sipehsalar's daughter? From the ancient tale?" Esther grasped her hands together before her chest. "My cousin remembers."

Delight danced in Mordecai's eyes. "How can I forget? You were such a small child."

Xerxes leaned back and stroked his beard. "Now this is a story I want to hear."

Esther smiled as she rose and spread her arms before the king. "It was just after my father died, and I was crying in the night. Mordecai had a visiting guest who offered to tell me a Persian legend. I still remember the story of the vizier's daughter, who the king thought was the most beautiful lady in all the land. The king loved her, so he brought her to his palace to make her his queen."

Esther glanced at Mordecai and smiled at the amused look about him.

Laughter spilled from Xerxes's mouth, a deep laugh that bubbled from deep within. "You're making this up. It isn't true, is it?" His eyebrows furrowed. "I know this story," her husband said. "Although it doesn't have a very happy ending. Sipehsalar was angry at the king and plotted revenge, did he not?"

Clapping her hands together, Esther couldn't hold in her own laughter. "It is the truth, I promise. And that is the part that my cousin teases me about. I was just a child. The rhythmic words of the old storyteller soothed me back to sleep. All I heard of the story was the beauty of the daughter, the king's delight, and the message of their wedding being sent to all the lands." She laughed again, touching her cheeks that ached from her grinning. "It was that night I decided I wanted to tell such stories, and it wasn't until much, much later that I heard the rest about Sipehsalar's revenge."

Mordecai nodded. "I still remember the horror on Esther's face when she discovered the vizier waged war on King Azadbakht because he'd snatched her from the road like a brigand and rode back to the palace with her like a piece of loot."

Xerxes's smile faded then, and he returned to sit by Esther's side. "Please forgive me, my queen, if you ever felt that way."

Esther drew in a heavy breath and released it, peering into the king's eyes. "While there was a time I dreamed of traveling to Jerusalem, I do not regret that by Yahweh's hand I became your wife and your queen. I know now that even though we may not know the whole story until the end, there is a grander purpose than we'll ever fully understand."

Esther reached and placed her hand over her husband's heart. "My respect for you as a king is great, but my love for my husband even greater. By Yahweh's hand, my people who were destined for slaughter can now rest without worry about their enemies."

Tears clouded her vision, but Esther continued on. "And now the greatest empire in the world—the empire of the Medes and the Persians—will benefit from the same care that I received." She glanced at her cousin. "Care that made me the woman that I am. For such a time as this…

"For such a people, such a king, and such a God has my heart been broken, only to find its true home."

Letter from
THE AUTHOR

Dear Reader,

We all know the story of Queen Esther, don't we? As I researched this time in Persian history, I was also praying that I could bring Esther's story to life. I am so thankful that the whisper of inspiration that I received was to make Esther a storyteller. Persia was an empire comprised of many provinces, and I grew excited as this world was brought to life through the tales told by the people at that time.

While I thought I'd known Esther's story before, I was amazed how this biblical tale was also found in the historical records of other nations, like those from ancient Greece. Lining up world history and biblical history was exciting. Daily, I shared what I was learning with my husband and a good friend. What joy it is for me for this history to come alive for YOU within the pages of this novel.

My favorite part of working on this novel was to see Scripture in a new light. Before writing this novel, I didn't understand how the enemy of the Israelites in the desert—and the Israelites at the time of King Saul—were tied to the enemy of the Jews during Esther's reign. As I read about the Amalekites throughout Scripture, I better understood how God used an ordinary orphan to bring victory over the enemies of the Jews. Yes, Esther dared to trust God, and even more thrilling to my heart is that God chose to trust Esther. My prayer is that each of us will see that we can accomplish God's purposes for our lives too. *For such a time as this…for us.*

Signed,
Tricia Goyer

BOOK GROUP QUESTIONS

1. What did you learn about the time and setting of the book of Esther?
2. What did Esther's story teach you about prayer and about gathering others to pray?
3. In Esther 4:16, she says, "If I perish, I perish." What did you learn about Esther's faith through her dedication?
4. What character traits of Esther stood out most to you?
5. How does Esther's faith inspire your own?
6. How did the revelation that Haman was a descendant of the Amalekites make other parts of Scripture more understandable to you?
7. How did this novel help you better understand God's hand in history?

A SCHOLAR'S VIEW OF ESTHER

The primary purpose of the Book of Esther was to establish the origin of the Jewish Festival of Purim. At the same time, even though the name of God is never mentioned in the book and the story happens completely outside Israel, divine sovereignty and faithfulness are demonstrated through Esther's trials and survival. As Esther's story unfolds, the hidden working of God is revealed through the choices and actions of Esther and Mordecai.

Esther is one of only two books in the Bible named for a woman. Ruth is the other one. In addition, the absence of the name of God occurs in only one other book. The Song of Solomon, or the Song of Songs, doesn't mention the name of the heavenly Father. Should this bother us?

Obviously, the ancients who compiled the books of the Old Testament did not think so. Rather, they found that the underlying themes of the two books demonstrated the Divine Presence. Esther's story stands as a reminder that the circumstances and situations in our lives may seem perilous, but our heavenly Father still stands in the unseen. In their darkest hour, the Jews were not forgotten by God.

The irony of this story is that the method by which Haman intended to destroy the Jews became the means of his own destruction. In an unexpected way, the book of Esther fore-shadowed what happened to the Jewish people in our era. Like Haman, Adolph Hitler intended to eradicate the Jewish race. The death camps became the means by which he would kill six million Jews. Yet even out of these heinous execution chambers Jews still emerged at the end of the war. They suffered unimaginable loss, but nonetheless survived as a people.

An example for anyone faced with death, Esther maintained a humble and godly spirit. Because she found favor with everyone around her, Jews were saved. While the story doesn't mention the name of God, Esther's character demonstrated the qualities that are pleasing to Him.

From Esther 3:6-7 we discover the origin of the name Purim. Meaning "lot" as in casting lots, the Hebrew word *puru* became the name of the festival. Today, thousands of years later, millions of people remember and celebrate Purim. Far from forgotten, Esther's story remains contemporary.

Jews gather in synagogues for the *Megilah* (the Book of Esther), that is read aloud in the original Hebrew. When the name of Haman is mentioned, the congregation boos, hisses, and swings noisemakers. In contrast, Mordecai's name brings cheers and clapping. Everyone wears costumes that range from looking like Queen Esther to television characters. Children have the time of their lives with their capes and cowboy hats flying around the room. While the children play, the adults exchange gifts, treats, and food prepared at home. Finally, a wonderful, exciting meal is served. Prayers are said, and the banquet begins.

While the frivolity settles, a small ensemble plays Jewish folk music. In a traditional service, men begin dancing with men and women with women. The dance steps are the same as Jews have practiced for centuries. Esther's example and message of endurance in the face of evil is remembered in celebration. Haman has been put down again!

Jewish festivals have been an important part of ensuring the endurance of the Jewish people through the centuries. Like celebrating the Fourth of July, the past lives again. Even in the darkest times, the light of celebration has not gone out. Because these festivals are linked to historic events, the meaning of the past continues to be remembered.

For example, fifty days after Passover, the Festival of *Shavuot,* or Weeks, kept the memory of endurance during trial alive. After escaping enslavement, the Hebrews wandered in the desert until they came to Mt. Sinai. An unruly lot, undoubtedly their ethical values had been warped by slavery. The need for a concrete sense of direction was answered as fire and lightning clashed on top of the mountain. Moses came down with the Ten Commandments.

The Exodus story became not only a moral code, but the Path of Judaism. The way to the future had been revealed to them.

During Shavuot, the Book of Ruth is always read. Although a Moabite, Ruth embraced the ways of Naomi and her religion and embraced the Torah. Ruth became a Jew and stood as part of the lineage of David. Shavuot embodies the importance of the Torah, recognizing that it has unfathomable depths. Jews are reminded how important it is to receive, study, and be devoted to the Word of God. No matter where they live, Jews are reminded to be "People of the Book."

Sukkot, or the Festival of Booths, is a literal physical reminder of the wandering in the wilderness after escaping slavery in Egypt. Over 3,000 years old, Sukkot probably predates *Yom Kippur* and *Rosh Hashanah.* Because the Jews slept in tents while crossing the desert, structures are erected in the backyard. If possible, the shelters are made from the stalks of reeds or cane. During observance, people sleep outdoors. The entire family enjoys the beauty of the night and is reminded not to become too attached to the comforts of modern society.

While the nightly remembrance may seem strange, the experience takes celebrants out of their daily routines and creates a vibrant memory of what years of struggle crossing the desert must have been like. We are hurled back into the Exodus as well as Esther's time.

Tish B' Av, literally meaning the ninth day in the month of *Av* (August), commemorates the day that both the first and second Temples fell. The Jews were driven out of Spain on this same day. Some scholars maintain that the Nazi crematoriums began to burn on this day. It is a day of mourning indeed!

Of course, the primary Festival is Passover. This event is Israel's "Declaration of Independence." As was true for Esther, Passover was salvation for the Jews as Egypt's firstborn died in the plagues. The Hebrew word for this festival is *Pesach,* which literally means "skipping over" or "passing over," as the death angel did with the Hebrews.

Today the festival is almost synonymous with spring house cleaning. Every particle of leaven must be found and removed as Jews prepare for eating unleavened bread. Cleaning is often done with a candle and a feather. In addition, *tzedakah,* or charity, must be practiced. All of which is to raise the question, "Why are we doing this?" The answer reminds children and adults about the importance of remembering to stay faithful to the ways of God.

Fiction Author
TRICIA GOYER

Tricia Goyer is the award-winning, bestselling author of more than eighty books, writing both fiction and nonfiction related to family and parenting. She is a frequent speaker at events and conferences, as well as a podcaster. Tricia loves teaching others how to write and get published.

A homeschooling mom of ten, including seven by adoption, Tricia is also a grandmother to many and wife to John. With a busy life, she understands the importance of making every word count.

Nonfiction Author
ROBERT L. WISE, Ph.D.

The Rev. Robert L. Wise, Ph.D., is the author of thirty-five books and numerous articles published in English, Spanish, Dutch, Chinese, Japanese, and German. On the internet he weekly publishes *Miracles Never Cease* and monthly presents live interviews on YouTube with people who have experienced divine interventions.

Read on for a sneak peek of another exciting story in the
Extraordinary Women of the Bible series!

A HEART RESTORED: MICHAL'S STORY

BY BETH ADAMS

Michal heard about the arrival of the harp player long before she saw him herself. It was Chava who mentioned him first, when she came to help Michal and Merab dress their hair one cool spring morning. Merab had been out of bed for some time, working at her loom, while Michal was still lolling under the thick wool blankets.

"Good morning." Chava threw open the heavy cloths that covered the small window openings. From her position in the bed, Michal could see blue sky. "It is a beautiful day."

"It is too cold to get up," Michal said. "I will just stay here today."

"Get up," Merab, Michal's older sister, called from the corner. "Abba is expecting us. Today we will play him the song we've been preparing."

Michal wrapped the blanket tighter around her. "Abba does not want his ears to bleed. He will not mind if we do not play him this song."

"It is only your pipe that is out of tune," Merab said as she fed a saffron-colored thread through the loom. "If you would have practiced like you were supposed to, we would not sound like—"

"Would you like me to start with your hair, Miss Merab?" Chava asked. Chava had attended to the sisters and their mother since their father had built this palace. She was a small woman, mousy and quiet, with an eye that made it always seem as though she was looking two directions at once, but she had a calming presence and was able to steer the sisters toward peace most days.

"Fine." Merab finished lining up the thread, pressed on the frame, bringing up the alternating threads, and then set down her shuttle and leaned back so Chava could brush out her long dark hair. Michal pushed herself up in bed, still clutching the blanket around her. Even high-strung Merab seemed to enjoy when Chava pulled a brush through her hair until it gleamed. Her shoulders relaxed, and the scowl that seemed her favorite expression settled into a neutral countenance. Merab's hair was smooth and silky, falling to her waist in thick waves, while Michal's was wildly curly and difficult to tame.

"There is a new boy in the palace," Chava said. "A shepherd. He is said to play the harp beautifully."

"See?" Michal said. "Abba does not need our song. He has his new harp player."

"I believe your father is very much looking forward to hearing your song," Chava said. This, they all knew, was a lie. Abba did not even know Merab had written a new song to celebrate his victory over the Amalekites, and he rarely sat still long enough to listen to music anyway. But Michal appreciated that Chava was trying to coax Merab out of her sour mood.

"Why does he need a harp player at the palace?" Merab asked.

Merab, Michal knew, would be thinking about the cost. She would have their father save every coin to include in her dowry. Merab had visions of marrying a wealthy prince from the East and settling in a palace much finer than this drafty place.

"I can't say," Chava said, as she set down the brush and began to braid a section of Merab's hair. "But it is said that when David plays his harp, your father becomes much more calm and relaxed."

"Then it is worth every coin he must spend," Michal said. Since he had come back from the battle against the Amalekites, Abba was even more on edge than usual.

"I cannot see why he must hear the harp to be calm," Merab said. "Abba is the king chosen by Yahweh. He has nothing to fear. He does not need to be so concerned with losing his kingdom."

Michal did not pay much attention to the intricacies of her father's role, but even she could see that things were not as simple as Merab would have them be. The prophet Samuel might have anointed their father to be the king the Israelites wanted, but that did not mean their enemies would simply give up the land God had given to their people. Their father was working hard to establish Yahweh's people in their homeland and to rule a disparate group of people whose desires changed by the day.

"Be that as it may, it is said that the music from this boy's harp can calm your father's moods like nothing else can." Chava finished the braids and twisted them into a knot at the back of Merab's head.

"If that is true, he will be most welcome in the palace," Michal said.

"If he can calm Abba's moods, he will be celebrated from east to west," Merab added.

"Many of the servant girls are saying he is quite nice to look at as well," Chava added, raising an eyebrow.

"Then I truly cannot wait to meet him," Michal said. They did not get much excitement around here. The last time Michal had found something amusing around this palace was when she and Jonathan had given secret names to all of her father's closest advisors, and that was only fun until a guard overhead them referring to Abner, the head of their father's military command, as a squirrel, for his tendency to stuff far too much food into his mouth. Their game ended quickly after that, with a stern lecture from their father. Michal had not minded—their father rarely showed her any attention at all, and even a lecture was better than being ignored—but Jonathan, the king's eldest son, had been chastened. "A good-looking musician will at least give us something nice to see around the palace."

Merab shook her head at Michal but mercifully did not say anything in response.

"If you want to see him, you must first get out of bed." Chava secured the twist at the back of Merab's head with a polished piece of bone, and then she turned toward Michal. Michal threw back the blanket and pushed herself off the pallet. The stone floor was cold under her bare feet. Chava held out a tunic made of fine-knit wool and helped Michal secure it with a sash dyed the color of jasmine leaves. "Now then. How shall we do your hair?"

"Whatever is the quickest." Michal did not care much for the elaborate styles Merab chose. As long as it did not get in her way, Michal did not mind how it was styled. No one was looking at her hair anyway, not with Merab and her perfect glossy hair and her neat and tasteful dress always catching eyes first. Most of the time, Michal missed the days before their father had been anointed king, when she had been free to run around with the other children and to hunt and build fires with the women. Now, they must act in ways befitting daughters of the king, Imma said. Something one of the king's daughters had more interest in than the other.

"A nice braid will be just the thing." Chava was already brushing the tangles out of Michal's hair, and it wasn't long before she had plaited the thick mane into a long, loose cord that fell down her back.

"Now then," Chava said, clapping her hands together. "You have just enough time to eat something before you are expected in the Great Hall."

Chava had a breakfast of yogurt, honey, and fresh bread brought in to their room, and it wasn't long before Efrem knocked and told them the king was ready for them. Michal picked up her pipe, while Merab carried her lyre, and they walked down the hallway, out of their family quarters, past the rooms where the king ate and entertained, and into the Great Hall, the grandest room in the palace—in all of Gibeah. The floor was rough-cut stone, like elsewhere in the palace, but it had been polished to a high sheen, and the walls were decorated with murals of colored stone, depicting some of the most important moments in the history of the Israelites—the crossing of the Red Sea, Moses meeting with Yahweh on Mount Sinai, the capture of Jericho. At the far end of the room stood their father's throne, a tall wooden chair covered with an embroidered purple and gold tapestry on a raised dais. Abba sat on the throne, a vacant look in his eye. He was surrounded by various guards and advisors, as well as Merab's brothers. Jonathan, their oldest brother, winked at Michal as the sisters crossed the long room, but their father showed no sign of recognizing them.

"Good morning, Abba," Merab said, stopping only a few feet from the edge of the raised platform. King Saul waited a moment before nodding to acknowledge them. "We have written a song to celebrate your recent victory over the Amalekites. My sister and I will perform it in your honor now."

Michal watched Merab and, on her signal, began to play the notes as Merab had instructed on the pipe. Merab strummed the lyre and sang the words she had written, and though Merab sang beautifully, there was no pleasure in their father's face. His lips were pressed taut, and his fingers were curled around the arms of his chair. Michal could see that his knuckles were turning white. As Merab sang, Abba almost acted as though he couldn't hear the words she had written so carefully.

When the song was over, their father's advisors clapped politely, and Jonathan let out a whistle, earning him a glare from Ishvi, who was four years younger. Malki-Shua, who was younger than Merab but older than Michal, appeared bored. Ish-Bosheth was but a year younger than Jonathan but seemed to the youngest of all. He was rocking back and forth on his feet and muttering to himself. After a moment, Abba joined in the cheering, clapping his hands together, but there was no joy in his eyes.

"Thank you." Abner stepped forward from the group gathered at the side of the throne. "That was a beautiful tribute. Your father is so grateful."

Michal waited for their father to add some words of acknowledgment, but none came.

Merab was waiting, her eyes fixed on her father. It almost hurt to see how much she desired her father to respond with kind words, but he did not say anything.

"You may go," Abner added.

Michal did not understand how Abner, their father's uncle and commander of his armies, had come to hold such a position of power within their father's household. He was among their father's closest advisors, though his expertise lay in fields of battle and not governance.

Michal turned to go, and after the briefest pause, Merab turned and began to walk down the long room beside her.

"You sang beautifully," Michal said quietly, but Merab did not seem to hear.

As the sisters neared the door at the far end of the room, she heard Abner address their father.

"David is here to play his harp for you, as requested," Abner said.

Before them, the door at the end of the Great Hall opened, and a young man stepped in, a lyre tucked under his arm. Michal tried to keep her eyes down, out of respect, as she and Merab walked back toward the door through which he had just entered but found she could not. She was too curious. The man who was walking toward them was tall, with wavy dark hair that touched his shoulders and a sturdy frame. He was strong, Michal could see that, but there was also something gangly in his movements, as though he hadn't grown into his body yet. His robe was woven of rough thread, and the cut was not of the latest fashion, but the way he wore it, with his head high and his shoulders back, drew the eye. And his face—it was not handsome. Not exactly. His forehead was too wide, his chin too pronounced to be considered handsome. But there was something in it that was arresting nonetheless. Michal found she did not want to look away. David continued toward the king, but as Merab and Michal approached, he looked up at the sisters. His eyes—intelligent, hungry, knowing—glanced at one and then the other, and then his mouth curled up into a hint of a smile before he cast his glance back down, walked past them, and continued on toward the king.

Michal did not want to turn back, not when she knew Merab was in a hurry to get out of the room, but she could not help it. She turned and watched as David stopped before the throne and grasped his harp. Her brothers and the other advisors stood still, watching, waiting.

"David," King Saul said, "this morning has been a trial. Play something nice, and help me forget."

"My king." The harp player nodded and raised his instrument. "This is a song I wrote myself," David said. "It's a prayer to Yahweh."

His voice was deep, yet somehow soft.

Saul nodded, and David began to play. As the soft notes of the song filled the room, Abba closed his eyes and leaned back in his chair. A smile spread across his face.

"Come on." Merab was pulling on her arm. "Let us go."

Michal turned and followed her sister, but just before they got to the door, Michal turned her head and stole one last look back at the harp player. There was something about him that made her want to find out more. Something that made her want to capture his gaze. She knew he was just a lowly court musician, one of her father's many servants, but she could not help but think there was something special about David.

A Note from
THE EDITORS

W̶e hope you enjoyed another exciting volume in the Extraordinary Women of the Bible series, published by Guideposts. For over seventy-five years, Guideposts, a nonprofit organization, has been driven by a vision of a world filled with hope. We aspire to be the voice of a trusted friend, a friend who makes you feel more hopeful and connected.

By making a purchase from Guideposts, you join our community in touching millions of lives, inspiring them to believe that all things are possible through faith, hope, and prayer. Your continued support allows us to provide uplifting resources to those in need. Whether through our communities, websites, apps, or publications, we inspire our audiences, bring them together, and comfort, uplift, entertain, and guide them. Visit us at guideposts.org to learn more.

We would love to hear from you. Write us at Guideposts, P.O. Box 5815, Harlan, Iowa 51593 or call us at (800) 932-2145. Did you love *Jewel of Persia: Esther's Story*? Leave a review for this product on guideposts.org/shop. Your feedback helps others in our community find relevant products.

Find inspiration, find faith, find Guideposts.

Shop our best sellers and favorites at
guideposts.org/shop

Or scan the QR code to go directly
to our Shop

Find more inspiring stories in these best-loved Guideposts fiction series!

Mysteries of Lancaster County

Follow the Classen sisters as they unravel clues and uncover hidden secrets in Mysteries of Lancaster County. As you get to know these women and their friends, you'll see how God brings each of them together for a fresh start in life.

Secrets of Wayfarers Inn

Retired schoolteachers find themselves owners of an old warehouse-turned-inn that is filled with hidden passages, buried secrets, and stunning surprises that will set them on a course to puzzling mysteries from the Underground Railroad.

Tearoom Mysteries Series

Mix one stately Victorian home, a charming lakeside town in Maine, and two adventurous cousins with a passion for tea and hospitality. Add a large scoop of intriguing mystery, and sprinkle generously with faith, family, and friends, and you have the recipe for *Tearoom Mysteries*.

Ordinary Women of the Bible

Richly imagined stories—based on facts from the Bible—have all the plot twists and suspense of a great mystery, while bringing you fascinating insights on what it was like to be a woman living in the ancient world.

**To learn more about these books,
visit Guideposts.org/Shop**

Printed in the United States
by Baker & Taylor Publisher Services